THE REMINDERS

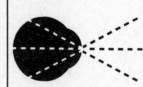

This Large Print Book carries the
Seal of Approval of N.A.V.H.

THE REMINDERS

VAL EMMICH

THORNDIKE PRESS
A part of Gale, a Cengage Company

GALE
A Cengage Company

Farmington Hills, Mich • San Francisco • New York • Waterville, Maine
Meriden, Conn • Mason, Ohio • Chicago

A Cengage Company

**LIBRARY OF CONGRESS CIP DATA ON FILE.
CATALOGUING IN PUBLICATION FOR THIS BOOK
IS AVAILABLE FROM THE LIBRARY OF CONGRESS**

ISBN-13: 978-1-4328-4217-8 (hardcover)
ISBN-10: 1-4328-4217-X (hardcover)

Published in 2017 by arrangement with Little, Brown and Company, a division of Hachette Book Group, Inc.

Printed in the United States of America
1 2 3 4 5 6 7 21 20 19 18 17

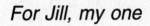
For Jill, my one

It takes strength to remember, it takes another kind of strength to forget, it takes a hero to do both.

— James Baldwin

I'd give you anything I've got for a little peace of mind.

— John Lennon

Most Remembered In History

(# of years remembered)

— Jesus (1,980)
— Joan of Arc (582)
— John F. Kennedy (50)
— John Lennon (33)

＊ All start with the letter J!

COME TOGETHER

1

Dad forgot me.

I'm waiting with my guitar on the hard steps and there's an ant by my sneaker. She's just a tiny thing, but I'd rather be that, a tiny thing that no one notices, than a real girl who everyone sees but isn't worth remembering.

Miss Caroline is waiting with me. The man in the car is ready to take her home, but she can't leave until I do. "I'll try your father again."

She only has to press her phone once because she's already called Dad and left him a message. After a quiet minute she pulls the phone away from her ear and makes her voice extra-sweet. "Don't worry, Joan. I'm sure he'll be here soon."

She's acting so nice, which only embarrasses me more. The one good part about this whole thing is that today was my last Young Performers class and as soon as Dad

13

picks me up, I'll never have to face Miss Caroline again.

"What time is it?" I say.

"Almost five," Miss Caroline says.

Class ended at 4:30. Dad and I are usually in the car by 4:40. "I'm sorry."

"Forget about it, Joan."

But I can't forget about it. That's the whole problem. I can't forget anything.

This isn't just about Dad not coming to pick me up today. It's about Dad and me seeing a red bird in a tree in 2011 and then me asking him if he remembers the other red bird we saw two years before that on Wednesday, April 29, 2009. He has to think about it for a while and then he says, "Yes," but the way he says it, I know he doesn't remember the other red bird at all and I don't feel as close to him as I want to feel.

And it's about Mom saying, "It never fails," and me doing a quick count of all the times she's said "It never fails" in the past six months (twenty-seven). Then I ask Mom to guess what the number is and I give her a hint that the number is less than fifty but more than ten, but instead of playing my game, Mom says, "What do you want from me, Joan?" and walks away.

And it's about people telling stories about things that have happened to all of us and

14

them making faces when I mention how they got a certain part of the story wrong. Then Dad has to explain to me that for most people, memories are like fairy tales, which means they're simpler and funnier and happier and more exciting than how life really is. I don't understand how people can pretend something happened differently than it actually did, but Dad says they don't even realize they're pretending.

Miss Caroline walks down the steps to speak to the man in the car. They talk quietly and then the man turns off his engine, which is good for the environment, and leans his seat all the way back like Grandpa does when it's nap time.

Miss Caroline comes up the steps and says, "What are you drawing?"

I shut my journal. "Nothing." I don't mind if my future husband shows everyone my drawings after I die, like Yoko did for John, but right now my drawings are private.

John Lennon is Dad's favorite musician and mine too. Dad wanted my first name to be Lennon but Mom vetoed that, which is something a wife can do, says Mom. So Dad put Lennon in the middle and that makes me Joan Lennon Sully. The middle is a good spot for important names. John Lennon's middle name was Winston, after Winston

Churchill, who is a person that everyone remembers.

People have all kinds of reasons for why they don't remember. They blame it on their batteries dying, or their ears not hearing right, or just being too busy, or too old, or too tired. But really it's because they don't have enough room inside their boxes.

When I was turning five, Mom bought me a box for all my art. She was fed up with me leaving my drawings and projects around the house. She told me to choose which pieces were most important because there wasn't enough room in the box to keep everything. That's how it is with people's brains. There's only enough room for the most important memories and the rest gets thrown away. When I'm the thing that gets thrown away, because I'm not important enough, it's hard not to get the blues like John Lennon on *The White Album* when he sings, *I'm lonely and I wanna die.* Especially when I would never throw anyone else away, because my brain never runs out of room. I just want it to be fair.

I wish I could always be important and never forgotten like John Lennon and Winston Churchill, but I know I can't. I learned a few years ago that I'm not safe in anyone's box, not even my own grandmother's.

Saturday, February 13, 2010: Grandma's new home.

"Grandma, it's me, Joan."

She looks confused. "I'm Joan."

"I know, Grandma. I'm Joan too. I got my name from you."

Dad pulls me aside. "She's just tired, honey."

"She doesn't remember me."

"Yes, she does. Of course she does. She just . . ."

"Grandma. It's me."

She tries. She really tries. But I'm not there.

Grandma Joan had to throw me out of her brainbox so she could have enough room for the lyrics to all her favorite songs. She remembered those until the day she died (Saturday, October 8, 2011).

I've tried to help people remember by leaving them notes and giving them hints. I even paid attention to the news when it said blueberries make brains stronger and I asked Mom to buy a huge carton and I made my family eat them all, but it was just a waste of time. If Grandma Joan was able to forget me, that means anyone can. Even Dad.

"What time is it now?" I ask, strumming my guitar.

"Five after five."

A car is coming fast, but it passes by. I play a minor chord because I'm not in the mood for a happy sound.

Miss Caroline looks up at the clouds in the sunny sky and says, "It's been so long since we've had rain."

"Actually, it rained on June twentieth, which was a Thursday, and that was less than three weeks ago."

"Is that right?"

"Yes, it is."

She seems impressed. "Did you always have such an amazing memory?"

"No," I say. "I got it when I fell on my head in Home Depot."

Miss Caroline laughs, but I'm telling the truth. My friend Wyatt knows all about comic books and the Internet and he told me that falling on my head in Home Depot is what gave me my highly superior autobiographical memory and falling on my head *again* in Home Depot would make me lose it. That's why I haven't gone back to that store after all these years.

I was only two when it happened (I'm ten now). Dad stood me up in the back of the orange shopping cart and he wasn't watching me and I leaned over the edge and fell. My head slammed onto the concrete and Dad yelled out, not like he yells at other drivers but like he yells when he doesn't use an oven mitt and his hand touches the top of the toaster. He lifted me off the concrete and rushed me out of the store.

But I don't tell any of this to Miss Caroline because she's too busy looking at her clipboard. Her finger is sliding down the page to where it says *emergency contact.*

"Who's Jack Sully?" she says.

"My grandpa."

She pushes her lips out like she's being forced to kiss an ugly man.

"I can walk home," I say. "I don't live far away."

"I can't let you do that, Joan."

She calls Grandpa and leaves him a message. She's already called Mom. "Has this ever happened before, where you can't get in touch with anyone?" Miss Caroline asks.

"No," I say and it's true. Sometimes people can't believe that I can go through all my memories so quickly, but it's not like trying to find the one pen that works in Mom's junk drawer. It's more like turning on a light, and the switch is always right under my finger.

"Here's what we'll do," Miss Caroline says. "At five twenty, we'll call everyone one more time. If we still can't get in touch with them, we'll see if we can get some help."

"What kind of help?"

"Maybe someone can drop by your house."

"Who? Your friend?"

"No," Miss Caroline says. "But let's not jump the gun just yet."

I wonder who she's talking about and why she wants to keep the person a secret and then I think about the words *emergency* and *help* and *gun* and I know who Miss Caroline wants to call. I keep my eyes on the street because I'm worried that if I look over at Miss Caroline a tear might accidentally slip out.

I can probably make a run for it because I pretty much know my way around Jersey City, but even if I did make it home I don't have house keys. I look around for that tiny ant but she's gone. I hope she made it back to her family.

I hear a rumble like light thunder and I look up to the sky, but the sun is still shining. The rumble gets louder and closer and it's coming from an engine. The engine is inside a big white van that appears up the street. It honks its horn and stops right in front of us. *Sully & Sons* is written on its side and I'm expecting Grandpa to step out of it, but it's Dad. He tells us there was an accident on the turnpike and his phone died. "I'm really sorry," Dad says. "Thank you so much for staying with her."

"It's totally fine," Miss Caroline says, but it's not even a little bit fine. What was Dad doing on the turnpike anyway? He was supposed to be home, working in his studio.

Dad helps me into the passenger seat and belts me up. There are no seats in the back of the van, which is why Dad is letting me sit up front. It makes me think of when I sat in the front of Dad's old van four summers ago and watched him fill it up with all his drum equipment. I asked him if I could go with him to Boston and he said, "Maybe when you're older." I'm older now but he sold his van last year and he doesn't really play shows anymore.

"Why are you driving Grandpa's van?"

"I was helping him out today." The way Dad says it, it's like he isn't too sure about the words he wants to use. Songwriters like Dad and me are very careful with our words.

The back of the van is full of tools, which makes me think of Home Depot, which makes me think of the one way I can lose my gift or condition or disease or whatever you want to call it. If I can't get other people to remember better, maybe I can force myself to remember worse.

"I don't want to go home," I say.

"Okay," Dad says, trying to be cheery. "Where would you like to go?"

Maybe it's finally time to go back to Home Depot. I could climb to a high spot and dive down so my head would hit the concrete. It would hurt a lot, but only for a little while. Afterward I'd finally know what everyone means when they say *I don't recall* and I'd always have an excuse for why I didn't do something I said I was going to do, like pick my daughter up on time from Young Performers class.

But I don't really want to go to Home Depot. I just want to feel better. Maybe I'd be okay if it were just small forgetting, like when people miss my half-birthday or they don't remember to put suntan lotion on the tops of my ears or they forget that my least favorite saying is *Forget about it.* But it hurts too bad when the thing people keep forgetting is me.

We're at a red light and Dad is trying to get my attention by waving his hand in front of my face. Instead of looking at him, I grab the newspaper that's lying on the floor of the van and pretend to read it.

"I saved that for you," Dad says.

The newspaper is folded back to show a certain page. "What's my name, Dad?"

"What are you talking about?"

"My name. What is it?"

He answers very slowly. "Your name is Joan."

"Sure, you say that today. But who knows about tomorrow."

Dad breathes out like he's really tired. "Joan, I'm sorry I was late. I don't know what else you want me to say."

I look down in my lap and spot something in the newspaper that Dad saved for me. There are tons of little boxes on the page and inside one of the boxes are five words in big capital letters:

THE NEXT GREAT SONGWRITER CONTEST

I read all the information in the box and I start to get a brand-new idea.

"Tell me where I'm going, Joan. I need an answer."

Grandma forgot a lot of things at the end, including me, but not music. Just like Dad will sometimes forget to buy almond milk at the store even when it's on his shopping list, but he will always hum along to every single note of the guitar solo in Michael Jackson's "Beat It," even if he hasn't heard the song in years. The best part about music is that it keeps playing. When Dad forgets about someone like Michael Jackson for a while, he'll hear one of his songs and all of a sudden he'll remember how much he likes him. That's because songs are like reminders.

"I can't drive around in circles, Joan."

"Go home, Dad."

"I thought you didn't want to."

"I changed my mind."

Dad mumbles something as he spins the wheel and the big white van spins with it. My head is spinning too, like the top of a helicopter, and I'm lifting over all the bad feelings, because I might have just found a way to make sure that Dad and Mom and Grandpa and Miss Caroline and everyone else in the world never forget me.

2

There's this idea of the phantom limb. A man who's lost his arm still feels the arm and behaves as if the arm is intact. What I have, then, is a phantom love.

We lived together for four years. Two years in Sydney's West Hollywood apartment and two years here, in our house in Los Feliz. He died one month ago and ever since, I've lived alone. But I don't feel alone. Everywhere I turn are reminders, some three-dimensional, others invisible, all of them speaking and taking up space.

For instance, this chair I'm in now has plenty to say. We found it at the Rose Bowl. It's a nineteenth-century antique, English, with lion's-paw feet and a floral design. Syd had an eye for this type of stuff, could discern the prize from the junk.

I remember when we first brought it home. I can hear myself now, complaining about how uncomfortable the chair is. I hear

Sydney laughing, explaining that it's not supposed to be comfortable. *It's a visual piece,* he's telling me. *Please, Mr. Winters, if you must sit, sit on the couch.* And yet he himself would sit in the chair. He loved this chair.

But I can't say I love it, not anymore. Not when the voice I hear isn't even Sydney's but some distant and muted approximation of the way he sounded.

I stand up and drag the heavy chair through the house, through the kitchen, and into the backyard. I lay the chair on its side, raise my boot over the top leg, and stomp down. The broken limb dangles from chewy fibers, the amputation not complete until I've twisted a dozen times and yanked the thing off. I detach the other three legs in the same fashion.

I uncover the fire pit and form a tepee with the legs. The rusted lighter near the grill still has juice, but its blue flame won't stick to the antique logs. I could quit now. Or I could go get some kindling.

In the straw box under our bed, I find notes, photos, envelopes. We really were sentimental saps, the pair of us. We kept everything: the crude portraits we drew of each other while giddy on molly; my shoe-lace headband from our first hike in Griffith

Park (my hair was long when we started dating); the paper airplane I made with *Swissair* on one wing, *Take Me with You* on the other; and, from one of our marathon dinners in the canyon, a matchbook.

While I'm here, I strip the bed. His scent lingers, real or phantom, I don't know. I toss the linens on top of the memory box and carry the whole lot through the bends of our bungalow.

I dump it all in the pit and wave the lighter again. A crackle as the flame takes and spreads. I watch the mass heat up and grow, feeling a sense of accomplishment.

It takes many trips, but I rid the house of all reminders:

The rug where I found his body.

His phone.

Forest painting from nobody artist.

Linen curtains, chosen by Syd, hung by me.

Wireless speakers from one of his clients.

New Age guides to success and enlightenment.

Issues of *Food & Wine, Forbes, Esquire* that had been neatly stacked on Danish modern coffee table.

Danish modern coffee table.

Earbuds, mine, but we shared them once in the theater before previews began; we each took an ear and enjoyed half-stereo Passion Pit.

Pictures in frames, both laptops, clothes, favorite tea mug, ski poles, Ping-Pong balls, unused parenting books, mail, postcards, birthday cards, business cards, sympathy cards, it's-the-holiday-look-at-our-children cards.

All these items lie scattered on the overgrown grass, waiting their turn in the fire. There won't be room until the pile melts down. At the moment, nothing much is happening.

I grab Sydney's tennis racket, jab at the heap. I poke and prod, breaking up the cluster, letting air squeeze into the gaps. Something sizzles, and the rubble finally ignites.

Even this, staring into the fire, is a memory. We were out here with our cocktails, resting our feet on the low brick wall. We had just bought the house and out of this new feeling of adulthood came a list of plans: more traveling, rings, even talk of a baby.

A spark leaps from the pit into the cuff of my pants. Syd bought them for me during one of our last shopping runs. I untie my boots, slide the chinos down, and sail them across the western sky. They land atop the summit like a fallen flag.

In the kitchen, I fix myself a cocktail. Gin, Campari, sweet red vermouth: a Negroni, Syd's drink of the moment. The fridge is empty, so I do without the orange rind. Reaching into the freezer for ice, I notice the bracelet on my wrist. It's an ugly thing made of cheap leather. We purchased two of them — one for each of us — while on vacation in Mexico. Only this one remains.

I reach for the metal clasp, start to undo the circle, but stop myself. Nose pressed to the leather, eyes shut, I inhale, and there it is, the past, awakened. A flash of us in Mexico, Sydney's gringo tan. I don't visualize it as much as experience it a second time, the sensation of it, just for a few seconds. But it's long enough. I decide to spare the bracelet for now.

I rinse a dirty fork and plunge it into the cherry-red mixture. While I'm stirring, I see it through the back window, what I've done. It's glorious and way out of hand. Illuminating the night, a zigzagging fury spitting orange danger everywhere.

I run outside, giggling. Maybe terror or elation or madness, all of the above, but I'm laughing. I raise my glass in front of the blaze.

"Good-bye," I say.

"I love you," I say.

And then: "I'm sorry."

Around me, the night buzzes. Voices through the fence, a figure in a neighbor's window. Hot wind blows against my neck. I turn back to the fire, now spilling from the pit and climbing the post that supports the porch awning. I step away, finish the last of my drink, and watch all our memories rise in smoke and vanish in the night.

3

The deadline for the Next Great Songwriter Contest is two weeks away and it's perfect because school is over and now I can spend all my time writing. The winning song will stream on a very popular website that people from all over the world visit. That's what the ad in the newspaper says.

To win the contest I'll need a song that can make people want to dance or cry. Those are the two strongest feelings music can give you. When people dance they forget and when they cry they remember. I don't know which is better for votes, dancing or crying, forgetting or remembering, so I'm starting with the dance song.

I'm down in Dad's studio right now, wiggling my pick over my G chord like I'm shaking up a carton of OJ. I'm using a special guitar pick that has my name on it, which was a gift from my mom's friend Sydney (Sunday, September 9, 2012).

I tap Dad's shoulder and he slides his headphones off one ear.

"How does this sound?" I say, playing him my dance idea.

He doesn't look excited. "I'm pretty sure that's 'I Want You to Want Me' by Cheap Trick."

The contest song has to be an *original,* which means I can't send them something that was already written by another person. I don't understand how Dad can remember the name of every single artist there ever was and which songs they sang but can't remember which password he uses for which website.

Dad makes music for commercials and TV shows and movies, which is probably one of the best jobs anyone could ever have, especially because he gets to do it at home. We live in a building made for two families but instead of having two families, we have our family on the top half and Dad has his recording studio on the bottom half.

Dad's studio is crowded with stuff, but not in a way that makes you crazy; in a way that makes you excited. Everywhere you turn there's something to look at (posters, books, souvenirs) and ask about ("What does CBGB OMFUG mean?"). It's packed with odd-looking instruments, like a Stylophone, which is a tiny synthesizer that you play with a pen, and a theremin, which makes a spooky ghost sound when you wave your hands over the top of it. Dad's studio is a factory where songs get made and also a museum full of strange objects and also a secret hideout where no one bothers you and also a place where you can dream about what might happen with your life when you grow up.

I'd much rather be down here than upstairs in our own house, not just because the furniture is newer and the couch is more comfortable, but because I get to be with Dad. He teaches me about old music and lets me bang on the drums and trusts me to refill his coffee mug.

Also, he lets me play his guitars. Dad has a dozen guitars down here, but the one I'm playing right now is my favorite. It's the Gibson J-160E, the same one John Lennon liked to use.

Everyone remembers John Lennon because his songs play in supermarkets and elevators and arenas and also in commercials and movies and on the radio and across the Internet. He's remembered in England and in both Americas, and Dad says he's even huge in Japan. Dad has his music on MP3 and CD and vinyl and cas-

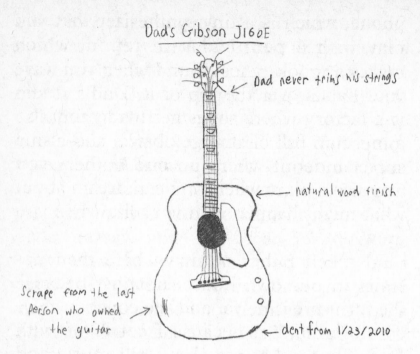

Dad's Gibson J160E

Dad never trims his strings

natural wood finish

Scrape from the last person who owned the guitar

dent from 1/23/2010

sette. All I have to do is write just one song as good as John Lennon did, a song that can keep playing forever and ever, always reminding people.

But I can't do it alone. "Are you going to help me, Dad?"

"I can't right now."

He's already got his headphones back on and his eyes are pointed at the computer. It looks like he's mixing a song, which means he's setting each instrument to the perfect level.

I'm flipping through my journal, looking at all the songs I've written over the past few months, and I'm wondering if there's something in here I can use. My journal is like having a second copy of all my memories, just like Dad makes a backup of all the music he records. We do this so that if something bad happens we won't lose our important stuff, which is what happened to Grandma Joan when she got sick.

She was a musician too. One of the last songs I ever heard her sing was an Elvis song (*Don't be cruel to a heart that's true*) and I was really wishing she'd do a better job of paying attention to the lyrics. When she forgot me, it felt like she was taking the end of a giant pencil and erasing me right as I stood there. It must be the best feeling in the world to be able to stop worrying about how much you mean to people. Once I win the Next Great Songwriter Contest, I'll finally know how that feels.

I tap Dad again. "What if we record ten songs and we choose whichever one comes out the best? Because sometimes a song will sound good when you write it, but then it sounds totally different after you record it. What do you think? Maybe we can record one song every day and then after ten days we'll still have extra time at the end to make one song absolutely perfect. Also, we need to find a great singer, like maybe Christina.

Do you think she'd do it?"

I'm done speaking but maybe Dad doesn't know it because he's not looking at my mouth, he's looking down at his lap and taking a long time to answer. "I'm not going to be here tomorrow."

"That's okay. We can start the next day."

"Joan."

I love hearing my name but sometimes it means trouble. "Yes?"

"Put down the guitar, please."

Now I'm really nervous. Dad and me always like to play our instruments while we talk to each other, even though it annoys other people when we do it.

He leans over with his elbows on his knees and he faces the carpet and pulls at his hair. "I've been meaning to tell you." He looks up and his eyes are soupy and his hair shoots into the air like a porcupine that's lost his points on all sides but one. "I told you I was helping out Grandpa today. Well, I'm going to be helping him out every day from now on. I'll be working with him full-time."

"What about working here in your studio?"

He takes a deep breath, which is always bad news, and he says, "We're closing the studio."

Friday, April 1, 2011: Dad drops me at school and he hands me my lunch and he says, "We ran out of hummus, so I made you a mustard sandwich instead," and my face gets hot, but then Dad smiles and says, "April Fool's."

But it's not April. It's July.

"I don't understand."

"I love being a musician," Dad says. "You know that. Ever since I was your age, it's all I've ever wanted to be. But making a business work is another thing. This new job will allow us to do a lot more. We can fix up the house upstairs and we can sign you up for more classes and before you know it, it'll be time to send you off to college. Your mother won't have to work so hard over the summers; she can relax. And guess what — she's already planning a family vacation. When's the last time we all got on a plane together?"

Dad gets on a plane every year when he goes to the South by Southwest festival in Texas, and last summer Mom took me to see a doctor in Arizona, but Dad couldn't come because he was finishing up an important project, and just last month Mom and Dad flew alone to Los Angeles for Sydney's funeral. But all three of us have never been on a plane together, not even once.

We were supposed to take a vacation last year, but that didn't happen for some reason. I wasn't upset about it like Mom was. Planes sound cool but they're actually pretty boring once you're in them. Not like a recording studio.

"What about my song?" I say. "You said you'd record it for me."

"Of course. The plan is to rent out the space, but that's not going to happen until September, earliest. I won't start moving out until August. I've still got a few projects I'm working on. I'll finish those up on nights and weekends. After that, I'm all yours."

This studio used to be an empty apartment before Dad moved his equipment in and before he set up his red phone, the one he answers by saying, "You've reached Monkey Finger Productions. This is Ollie." I look around at Dad's amazing stuff and I wonder where it's all going to go and I also wonder where *I'm* going to go when I want to write my songs or just hang out with Dad while he's working.

"Hey," he says, trying to stop my tears before they start. "Remember how you felt when you left Concordia and started at PS Eight? You thought you were going to hate it, but now you love it? It'll be hard at first, but it's for the best. I really think so. I really do."

He pulls me in. I always like to hug Dad but tonight he's crunching my bones and it's giving me a scary feeling in my chest.

"Ollie!"

It's Mom shouting through the speaker on the wall. Dad lets go of me and shows a smile, but it's not a true one, I can tell.

"Ollie! Come quick!"

That's when we realize that Mom isn't calling just because she can't figure out how to work the DVR.

Dad and I run up the stairs to our apartment, and Mom is in the living room, standing in front of the television with her arms crossed tight over her bedtime shirt. She clicks the remote and the volume gets louder. It looks like the news and I hate the news because there's always a sad story about people crashing their cars or getting diseases or breaking their backs while skiing and the next day it's some new story and you never hear about the first people ever again. I'm the only one who wonders what happened to those twins who were stuck together when they were born and got pulled apart. Are they okay now? And what about that rich guy who invented his own spaceship? Did he ever make it into space?

I usually try to walk out of the room if the news is on but the other night I was very interested because they were talking about a man who broke into SeaWorld in Orlando and he stole a walrus. He let the walrus swim into the ocean and then he tried to go back to get more animals but the police arrested him. Of course, the lady giving the news never mentioned the walrus again after that first night but I found a website where you can see where the walrus is swimming because SeaWorld stuck a sensor in his blubber.

Now the news lady is saying, "Gavin Winters plays Officer Beau Kendricks on the crime drama *The Long Arm,* whose second season, coincidentally, premieres tomorrow night." Dad looks at Mom, and Mom looks at Dad, and I look at the television screen.

I've never met Gavin Winters, but I know him. I know him as my parents' friend from college and also Dad's old bandmate and also an actor on TV and also the boyfriend of Sydney, who used to come over to our house. But the way I'm seeing him right now doesn't fit with any of those things. Tonight, on television, he looks like a man in his underwear standing very still in front of a giant fire.

4

A bird sings a lilting melody, serene and eternal. With my eyes closed, half asleep, I'm briefly fooled as to where I am. Maybe everything is okay. Maybe it was all a dream.

I awake, officially, and realize I'm face-down on a naked mattress in my ransacked bedroom, the sun bursting in. Waking up is harsh on most days. Today it's especially cruel.

I take a moment to recalibrate. The bird outside my window is still singing. Sydney is still gone. I'm still here. Our house is in a shambles and that's my fault. My head is in a shambles and that's also my fault; the firemen quelled the fire but had no dominion over my thirst for cocktails.

It's more bad news in the living room. The room is a shock and so is what's happening outside my front window. There are three vans parked at the end of my driveway. On the sidewalk a half dozen people train long lenses directly at me. They wouldn't have such a clear view into my home if the curtains were drawn. Unfortunately, the curtains can't be drawn. I torched them.

I grab some towels to drape over the glass and take a seat on the couch, the only place left to sit in the living room, not counting the floor. The change in décor is drastic, to say the least. But somehow it feels appropriate; Syd always wanted us to declutter.

At some point my phone rings. I can't say how long I've been sitting here pondering the mess; long enough to be startled by the sudden interruption of sound.

It's a friend calling and I'm not sure I should answer. I pull the towel aside and take another peek at the media stakeout along my property line. Feeling outnumbered, I answer the phone: "Paige."

"You're alive," she says.

"Unfortunately."

The line goes silent. Maybe my joke was too macabre. My sense of funny has gone to shit.

"Listen," Paige says, "you know I love seeing you on TV, but I prefer that it not be on the nightly news."

She tells me my neighbor captured my impromptu bonfire from his window. Apparently he was more committed to getting the shot than saving me from peril. I'd like to say this behavior is strictly an L.A. thing, but the filmmaking bug is now a pandemic.

The footage may exist, but the night still feels unreal. Ditto the night before and the one before that. The days since I lost Syd have been less of an adjustment. I've always had stretches without work or auditions, times where I'm still in pajamas until late afternoon. But at night and on weekends, Syd and I were together. Now those are the parts of the week I dread most.

"Are you okay?" she asks.

It's the single most popular question posed to me in the past few weeks. "Yes, I'm fine."

"Are you sure? What about the house?"

"It smells like an ashtray, but it's still standing."

Turns out Ping-Pong balls are highly flammable. Who knew? Only the porch roof took a hit. The trucks arrived before the fire had a chance to spread inside.

"What happened?" Paige says.

"I don't know."

"It looked like you were burning furniture."

"Just a few items."

"Gavin . . ."

She doesn't say more. What can she say?

What can I say? Whatever revelry or relief I felt last night was stamped out long before the flames were. By the time I heard the sirens, I had regained enough clarity to search frantically for the fire extinguisher I assumed we had but couldn't recall ever seeing. I was already asking myself over and over: *What have I done? What the* fuck *have I done?*

Whatever I did, I accomplished nothing. I dragged everything outside but still couldn't empty the place. My phantom love lives on.

"Where are you right now?" Paige asks.

"Home."

"I don't think you should stay there."

"Where would I go?"

"Can't you crash with someone for a while?"

There's nowhere to run. I realize, now, that this phantom love of mine isn't a separate entity. He's more like a limb after all. He's part of me.

"You could come here," Paige says.

"New Jersey?"

"Yeah, New Jersey. What's wrong with that? When's the last time you visited?"

I was born there, raised there, spent two-thirds of my life there. But since leaving, I've been back only once and that was many years ago.

"Maybe you just need to get out of L.A. for a while. You're done filming, right? You should take a trip."

"Maybe I'll climb Everest."

"I'm serious. We have a whole separate apartment downstairs. You can come and go as you please."

"Thanks, Paige. I appreciate it."

"Don't blow me off."

"I'm not."

"We miss you, Ollie and I both. We should've checked in on you sooner."

She and her husband flew out for the funeral last month. Before that, I hadn't seen my old college friends in years.

"Don't worry about it," I say. "I appreciate you calling."

I hear voices through the window. I had already forgotten they were out there, the paparazzi or whoever they are. Some are dressed in plain clothes, some appear camera-ready. All of them confirm the fact that the fire was real and not a figment of my imagination.

"Will you think about it?" Paige says.

"Yes."

"Promise?"

I'm not sure I believe in promises anymore, but I promise anyway and we say our good-byes.

I almost didn't answer Paige's call, but I'm glad I did. It's so easy to forget that not everyone I see and hear is a phantom. Though at times it feels like I'm experiencing an extended hallucination, this is indeed real life and there are still real people out there with whom I have actual ties.

Paige and Ollie are the ones who set me up with Syd. Paige was Sydney's childhood friend. I was Ollie's college roommate. That rarely works, the wife's friend dating the husband's friend. But this time it made sense. Syd and I met out here in California as New Jersey transplants. We saw each other as new but also familiar.

But enough about that.

It's time to see the backyard and assess the damage. I'm about to walk outside barefoot but I realize it's too treacherous. After putting on my boots, I step over the downed porch roof and onto the patio. A ring of black-gray char surrounds the perimeter of the pit. Overall, though, it's good news: three-quarters of what I hauled outside never reached the fire. Most of it remains intact, laid out on the grass and patio like for-sale items at a flea market.

It's a surreal thing, greeting my interior life outdoors. Even more strange to see it all under a bright sun. The night had obscured the intimacy of what I was trying to burn. Now, in open daylight, it's impossible to ignore my ties to these objects.

On the grass I find Syd's duffel bag. I retrieved it last night from the back of our bedroom closet. When Syd passed, I stuffed a bunch of his belongings into the bag, just to get everything out of sight, and I haven't opened it since. Until now. I kneel down and open it.

Most of the things, besides the framed photograph of his mother, which he kept on his nightstand, are toiletries and small personal items. There's an electric toothbrush, a tube of Kiehl's moisturizer, hair paste, his black horn-rimmed reading glasses, his wallet (still full of cash), and a few bottles of medications. There's also his navy hoodie, the white strings bitten up and hardened. But it's the item that's sunk to the bottom of the bag that has my full attention. His electric shaver.

I open the soft black travel case and hold the razor in my hands, gripping the cold metal. The razor clicks on, its vibrations shooting up my arm. I turn it off and a rain of debris falls on my fingers. Tiny dark hairs.

I run my thumb over the serrated edge. A blackish residue clings to my skin. Like ash, something formerly human, formerly alive.

47

I close my eyes and try to picture his chin, cheeks, face, that exact portion of him. I shouldn't be doing it. It's stupid and masochistic and indulgent. But what makes the act truly regrettable is that I can't actually see his face, not entirely, not as clearly as I'm expecting. My imagination, not my memory, is doing most of the work.

But I wanted to forget, didn't I? Last night, yes, I wanted to forget. Today, I'm not so sure. My memories of Sydney are finite. He and I will never build a new one. To burn what little remains in a burst of self-pity or despair or frustration feels now like a terrible mistake.

I'm not sure what to do next. There's so much to clean up. It seems insurmountable.

I start with a simple task: Put the razor back in its case, the case back in the bag, zip the bag up. I wipe my hand on the grass and then on my shorts. The faint blackness remains. Some spit and a vigorous rub won't remove it either. The stain keeps. Already, I'm exhausted.

Instead of rising to my feet, I stay in the overgrown grass, staring at the rear of the house. I picture myself walking back inside, having to exist within those walls, trapped there with my phantom love. Even worse, with all those eyes peering in, all the unwanted attention I've created.

Paige is right. I can't stay here any longer.

5

I use a fork to break apart an English muffin and throw one half of the muffin into the toaster. Mom is on her cell phone and she's walking around the kitchen, holding a little pad.

The house phone rings and I lift it out of the holder, but Mom pulls it out of my hand. She looks at the number and makes the ringer go quiet.

I sit at the table and wait for the toaster to ding or for Mom to tell me why she's so excited. Mom makes the first sound.

"Okay," she says, ending her call. She plops her pad on the table and her butt on the seat. "That was my friend Melissa. She's been everywhere. She thinks we should look into Costa Rica. It's a short flight and they've got rain forests and beaches and zip-lining *and* a volcano. Doesn't that sound like fun?"

"I can't go to Costa Rica. I have to write

my song."

"No, cuckoo. This is for next spring. It's perfect. You and I have the same week off in March and the wet season doesn't start until April. I'll start looking at flights right away. Maybe we can get a deal since we're still far out."

The toaster dings and Mom grabs my muffin for me. She takes out the butter and a knife and she spreads the butter on the muffin and brings it to me on a plate. Mom always tells me that she's not my waitress but this morning it seems like she's changed her mind.

"So this is really happening? Dad is closing the studio?"

"I know you're upset. It's upsetting for all of us."

I've never seen Mom look so happy.

Actually, that's not true. She looked this happy when she was trying to plan our vacation last year, and when our vacation didn't happen she looked extremely unhappy. But it's very true that this whole thing is upsetting me and Dad.

"He loves his studio," I say. "Why would he close it?"

She opens her mouth to answer but the words don't come out for a few seconds. "Because we can't afford it anymore."

Mom likes to make graphs on the computer and she likes to keep every receipt. She'll get rid of the TV channels we don't watch and she'll tell the person on the phone that she's going to cancel our service unless she gets a lower price. She always knows which toilet paper is the better deal, the package of eighteen regular rolls for $11.69 or the package of twelve double rolls at $9.39. So if Mom says we can't afford the studio, I guess I have to believe her. But I don't understand how we can't afford the studio but we *can* afford a trip to Costa Rica, wherever that is.

"You make all that extra money tutoring," I say. "Why can't *you* just pay for the studio?"

"Because I don't want to anymore."

"What?"

"Forget it."

"I can't."

"If you want to pay for the studio," Mom says, "be my guest." She points the butter knife at me but not in a mean way, in a teacher way, which is what she is. Even though it's the summer she still teaches kids almost every day because she says her normal paycheck amounts to pennies and there are only so many books she can read on the couch before she starts to get antsy.

I'm pretty sure Mom would keep herself busy even if she were rich because she hates to sit around. She calls Dad a homebody, which I guess makes her an out-of-homebody, which is probably why she's so excited to buy us all plane tickets.

"Try not to make a mess today," Mom says. "We have company coming."

"Who's coming?"

"Our friend Gavin will be staying with us for a little while."

"The same Gavin who was on the news the other night?"

"Yes. That Gavin."

After we saw Gavin Winters on the TV, Mom told me to go to my bedroom and put my pajamas on, which meant that she and Dad needed to talk. When Mom came to my room later it looked like she had been crying. It was probably because she was thinking about her friend Sydney. She cried a lot right after he died, but she's been pretty good lately, unless something reminds her.

"Why is Gavin coming here?"

"Because I invited him."

"But why?"

"He's going through a really rough time right now," Mom says. "I thought it might be good for him to take a little trip."

53

"You're obsessed with trips."

She drops the knife into the dishwasher. "Dad's picking him up from the airport tonight after work."

When Mom says *work,* I'm imagining Dad recording music downstairs, but by *work,* she means "doing construction with Grandpa." I'm not ready to start changing what words mean in our house because the studio isn't closed yet and it can't close until I finish my song. Actually, maybe it's not such a bad thing that Dad is doing his new kind of work because that means the studio for once is all mine.

I hurry up and eat my muffin because I want to write as much as I can before our guest arrives. Now it makes sense why the house smells like lemon and the kitchen tiles are shiny and all the things on the coffee table are lined up straight.

As I'm leaving my dirty plate on the table, I suddenly have a very important thought. "Is Gavin famous?"

Dad is always talking about the difference between being famous and being remembered, how the first is easy but it lasts only fifteen minutes and the second is hard but it lasts much longer. But before you get the second, you have to get the first, which means people have to *know* my name before they can remember it. If I can win the Next Great Songwriter Contest, people will finally know my name (the famous part) and then my song will keep reminding them never to forget it (the remembering part).

Mom is busy on the computer in the living room, probably trying to find the best deal on hotels in Costa Rica. "I don't know if I'd call him famous," she says. "He's on TV. I guess he's a little famous."

A little famous is still a pretty good amount of famous. "What time will he be here?"

When the door to the studio opens and Dad and Gavin walk in, I'm sitting with my legs crossed and my boots on and my hair falling over my eyes. Even though my leg is asleep from sitting this way and my feet are sweaty from the heavy boots and I can't see a thing through my hair, I don't mind because I'll bet you any amount of money I look amazing.

"Oh, hey, honey," Dad says. "I didn't see you there."

I stand up and brush my hair to the side because I've already made a good impression and now I want to be able to see.

"Joan," Dad says, getting me ready, "*this* is Gavin." The reason Dad says it like that, stretching out *this* like it's a longer word than it really is, is that Dad knows that it's a little strange that I'm only meeting Gavin now for the first time when I've heard about him for so many years and I've already seen his face in pictures and on television.

Tuesday, March 18, 2008: Mom and I are watching American Idol *and the commercials are starting, so I go to the kitchen for more veggie straws. Mom screams and I'm worried that there's a spider, but then she says, "It's Gavin!" I look at the TV and I see Gavin wearing a suit and driving around in a nice car in some commercial.*

Dad is giving me a look with his eyebrows raised like those bridges that let the boats through. He knows that I'm always in two places at once: where my mind is and where my body is.

The real Gavin, the one in front of my body right now and not the one who was just in my mind, is wearing skinny pants, pointy shoes, a striped T-shirt, and a navy suit jacket. His hair is curled over like a big wave and he looks tired. He has a big pack on his back and he's tall enough to reach the ceiling and his eyes are blue and bright. He looks like he could do something special.

He stares at me like he's a camera. I never know what face to make when someone takes my picture so I just stand there and look dumb.

And then he bows like I'm a princess or something and he says, "Hello, Joan."

He knows my name.

He looks around at the rack of guitars and the control desk and the upright piano and Dad's drum set. He checks out all the colorful things on the walls and peeks through the square window into another small room where people can sing into a silver microphone (Dad says it's an isolation booth, but I call it the Quiet Room).

"Beautiful," Gavin says. "I guess this is the Coke side of life." Gavin winks at Dad, but Dad gives him only a small smile back. The line that Gavin just said is from a Coca-Cola commercial that used Dad's music, but I don't want to think about all the cool commercials that used Dad's music right now because it only reminds me about what's going to happen to his studio.

Gavin is looking down at me from his great height. "I hear you're quite a musician yourself."

I'm wondering if I'm already known around the world and I just didn't realize it.

Dad leads Gavin down the hall. "Towels are in here," Dad says, pointing to the narrow closet. "Bathroom is over here." And now we're at the end of the hall and Dad switches on the light in the guest bedroom.

Gavin walks over to the framed poster on the wall that says *Awake Asleep*. It's the name of Dad and Gavin's college band. Dad was the drummer and Gavin was the singer.

Dad and I are waiting for Gavin to say something or do something but he isn't moving an inch. He'd be great at freeze tag.

"Is this where Sydney used to stay?" Gavin says.

"A few times," Dad says.

"Four times," I say, because why say *a few* when *four* is the right answer? "I can tell you the exact dates."

Dad tries to push me out of the room. "I'll meet you upstairs, honey."

"You remember all the days he stayed here?" Gavin says.

"Yes," I say.

Dad lets go of my shoulder. Gavin looks down at the floor and then at me. "What else do you remember?"

"Everything."

Gavin makes a face like he doesn't believe me. Dad tries to push me out of the room again but I make my body stiff. I don't like the idea of Gavin thinking I'm a liar. "On September tenth, 2012, which was a Monday," I say, "Sydney was wearing a gray suit with no tie and the suit had light gray stripes on it."

Dad loses his patience and says, "Okay, Joan."

As I'm walking out the door I hear Gavin say, "From Ted Baker."

"What?"

"That was his Ted Baker suit," Gavin says.

"Oh."

I'm frozen. We all are.

Then Gavin smiles and says, "Good night, Joan."

And I smile and say, "Good night, Gavin."

6

Ollie shoos his daughter out of the room, shuts the door behind her. "Sorry about that."

"She's fine," I say.

"She's a handful, but we keep her around anyway."

I had heard about the girl's unusual memory, but to see it in action is another thing. Sort of startling, actually. Even more startling is coming all this way to put distance between me and my phantom love only to confront him almost immediately. Not that I'm blaming Joan. Of course she has memories of him.

Sydney made an effort to drop in on Paige and the family whenever he was in New York. His job as a marketing exec brought him out east quite a bit over the last few years. He'd even, on occasion, forgo the swanky hotel in Manhattan and slum it over here in Jersey City, in this very room, just to spend extra time with his dear friend Paige.

So, yes, all this should come as no surprise. But I hadn't considered Joan. I was more focused on what I was escaping *from* than what I was fleeing *to.*

And now, judging by the look on Ollie's face, it would appear I've wandered too deeply into my own head.

"You all right?" he asks.

"Yeah. It's just weird to be back."

I turn once again to our old band poster on the wall. To be fair, I had been forced to reckon with the past well before Joan appeared. I felt its presence acutely on the ride over here; as Ollie drove us away from Newark Airport and the rank stench of industry seeped through the AC unit; seeing the highway signs announcing towns I hadn't considered in ages (West Orange, Union, Hackensack); watching Ollie have to take the jug handle on the right to make a left turn; sitting in the car while the gas attendant conveniently filled the tank for us; passing the Dunkin' Donuts and the WaWa and the C-Town; and, finally, turning onto Ollie's street and beholding that iconic skyline in the near distance, as vivid and bright as if it were generated by CGI and then projected onto an enormous screen.

And now, again, coming upon this ancient band poster on Ollie's wall. There were still parts of me that Sydney hadn't experienced.

"Do you still have copies of our album?" I ask.

Ollie walks to the mirrored closet. He slides it open, revealing rows of CDs and vinyl records. Dozens of copies of everything he's ever worked on. "Take as many as you want," he says.

But I have no use for it now. Actually, I can't stomach most music these days, all the songs of longing. On the ride over, Ollie was playing something folky and harmony-laden, and I so badly wanted to turn it off. If I had, though, I'd only be reinforcing the idea that he should be worried about me.

"In the mood for a drink?" Ollie asks.

"Yes." I turn and notice Paige leaning against the door frame, as if she's been watching us this whole time. She abandons her post, throws her arms around me. People seem to want to hug me extra-hard now.

She lets go of me, makes a full-body assessment. "You look really skinny."

"It's called camera-thin."

"I'm jealous."

"There are moms in Beverly Hills who pay large sums to have a body like yours."

"Don't call me a mom."

She's kidding, I realize, but the fact that I have to think about it for a second underscores how long it's been since we've spent quality time together.

I take a good look at Ollie and Paige, the two of them together. I hardly remember them at the funeral, almost a month ago. I hardly remember being there myself. But I see them now. They were one of those meant-to-be couples back in college and still very much in love all these years later. Ollie remains gaunt and disheveled and striking; Paige with that wariness in her eyes even when she's smiling. We look older — I can see it, but I don't *feel* it. I'd believe it if you told me we were back in our freshman dorm right now.

"Thanks for having me," I say.

"We're so happy you came," Paige says.

Ollie reaches into his pocket for a set of keys. "The door to our apartment is always open. But if you go out through the front door, just make sure you lock the dead bolt. It's the ground level."

"He's paranoid about the equipment," Paige says.

"I bet," I say. "It's like a little musical heaven down here. I think I had one of those old Casios as a kid."

"Yeah, they've become pretty sought-after," Ollie says.

"I'd love to hear what you've been working on."

"Definitely."

Instrumental music, which is what Ollie does, I can handle. I'm half expecting him to crank up the speakers now. Usually he can't wait to share. But tonight he's subdued, perhaps on my account. Little does he know I'd much rather hear about his life than have to talk about mine.

"I'll pour us that drink," Ollie says, leaving Paige and me in the bedroom.

"He showed you where everything is?" Paige asks.

"Yeah. I'm all set."

Alone now, Paige and I have trouble meeting eyes. Maybe it's just me who's finding it difficult. The more I study her — the unfading smile, the frequent deep breaths, the way she's hugging herself despite the room being plenty warm — the more I'm reminded of my own feeble attempts to hide the underlying angst.

"I really didn't expect you to come," Paige says.

"I can go back."

She tilts her head, studying me from a new angle, and then she closes in for another hug. "Ollie will be gone in the morning. I have a few students coming for tutoring sessions, but I'll be around."

"You're not going to join us now?"

"Another night. I'll let you two catch up." She's already in her pajamas: a pair of sweatpants and a worn-in tee. "Oh, and I don't know if Ollie told you, but when you use the shower you have to turn the faucet all the way up to get it hot. Something's wrong with the boiler."

She backpedals to the door and regards the space with bemusement, as if she's seeing it only now after living here so long. "It's really weird," she says.

"What is?"

"Sydney was here when the studio first opened, and now you're here when it's closing."

"Closing?"

Paige nods, eyes low. "Ollie's going to be working for his father."

That explains why he was wearing that shirt, a baby-blue button-down with *Sully & Sons* over the heart. I assumed he was sporting his own surname in an ironic gesture. Maybe that's why he wasn't keen on sharing his newest creations. Maybe there aren't any.

Paige bids me good night and now I'm alone.

But not really. Sydney slept in this same bed. He stared up at this same poster. I flew more than three thousand miles and I'm still in his shadow.

I look away from the poster, open my bag, and start unpacking. With no idea how long a trip this would be, or where it would lead, I figured a week's worth of clothes would suffice. I slide my blazer off, hang it up in the closet. It's not unlike the Ted Baker suit jacket that Joan mentioned Syd wearing on one of his visits.

I remember when Syd first modeled the suit for me in our bedroom. *Distinguished* was the word, the way it complemented his salt-and-pepper beard and silver temples.

I can specifically recall his Ted Baker suit only because Syd had such a limited wardrobe. His closet was as barren as a SoHo boutique. I envied his restraint. I also loathed it. It only highlighted my clutter.

I try to recall more about that particular day. Try to visualize Sydney posing in front of our floor mirror, but the picture's too blurry. That one day doesn't stand out from the others. Nothing abnormal or extraordinary happened. It was just a regular day and those are the easiest to forget.

66

And now I'm doing it again, allowing myself to be sucked into the past. For what purpose? It's true there's a brief thrill that comes with digging up what's been lost, like the strange joy one feels when poking a tender wound. But when the thrill passes, the wound still remains.

7

The next morning, after I've written down twenty good song titles, like "Time Traveling" and "A Song to Dance To," and after I've filed down my crooked pointer nail so that my chords sound smoother, and after I've hopped onto the computer to check where the walrus is swimming (Hilton Head, South Carolina), I walk into the kitchen and see Mom and Gavin sitting at the table.

I slap my journal down so everybody knows I'm here and I open the cabinet because I'm thinking it's another English muffin day.

"Gavin bought bagels," Mom says.

Gavin reaches into a paper bag and pulls out a fat bagel. "Your mom said you only like plain."

I can't lie, it feels pretty exciting that Gavin knows which kind of bagel I eat. I give him a thank-you nod and pop one bagel half in the toaster oven. I notice Mom touching my journal and I grab it off the table.

"Relax," Mom says. "I was just looking at it."

I take the journal with me to the bath-room. As I'm leaving the room, I hear them talking about me.

"Ever since Arizona she's been keeping a diary," Mom says. "She goes through a new notebook every month. Apparently it's pretty common for people with her condi-tion."

The doctor I saw in Arizona, Dr. M, says I'm the only kid he's ever heard of who has highly superior autobiographical memory, or HSAM. The rest are grown-ups, about thirty of them, and Dr. M thinks that makes me pretty special. Most of the time I don't feel special, just lonely. I'd rather everyone in the world have HSAM, especially my parents and my friends, so we could all see the same memories.

When I'm finished in the bathroom, I stop in the hallway because they're still talking about me. "I remember Syd saying you were reluctant to have her see someone," Gavin says.

"It's true," Mom says. "But I'm glad we did it. It's just now we have to deal with all the phone calls."

"Phone calls?"

"I made a mistake."

"What do you mean?"

"When we got back from Arizona after Joan was diagnosed, I posted something about it on Facebook. It was an innocent thing. I was just relieved to finally have a name for what she had. But then the study she took part in was published and HSAM started getting attention in the news, and even though they never released her name, I guess someone found my post online. Suddenly strangers were trying to friend me and I was getting random phone calls from universities, pharmaceutical companies, you name it. It's still out of control."

It's true our phone rings a lot, but I never knew those calls were about me. Mom said it was people trying to sell us stuff we don't need.

"I wish I'd handled it better," Mom says. "Ollie and I just want her to have a normal life."

"Don't worry about it," Gavin says. "She'll be fine. There's no such thing as normal anyway."

It gets quiet for a minute so I come back into the kitchen and rush over to the toaster before my bagel burns. I take a seat at the table next to Gavin and I realize I've never once sat next to a person who's been on TV.

Gavin looks at me. "I like your outfit."

Mom thinks I dress like a gypsy. I hate wearing the same thing twice because it reminds me of another day when I wore the same thing and then I get stuck thinking about that day instead of living the day I'm in. Since Mom doesn't want to keep buying me new clothes, I have to come up with different versions of the stuff I already have. Today I'm wearing a T-shirt that I've worn before (June 11, a Tuesday, when I smeared almond butter on it at lunch), but I've never worn it with this black vest (April 26, movie Friday) and these jean shorts (June 24 *and* June 25). But it's okay because Dad says the guitarist for the Rolling Stones looks like a gypsy, and he's a rock god.

I notice that Gavin is wearing the same bracelet Sydney used to wear. Now he's looking down at my plate. "No butter or cream cheese?"

"I hate cream cheese."

I want to tell him why I hate it — because it smells like shit — but I'm not sure how Gavin feels about cursing. Dad's rule about cursing is this: If it's been in a song, it's okay, as long as the song is good. Bob Dylan

71

and Pink Floyd say *shit* in good songs, and Johnny Cash says *son of a bitch* in a good song, and John Lennon says the worst curse in a great song called "Working Class Hero."

Mom slurps the rest of her coffee, which she has in a travel mug even though she's not traveling anywhere. She picks up Gavin's regular mug and says, "More coffee?"

Gavin is busy with his phone. "Sorry, I have to take this."

He stands up and he's wearing shorts and the hair on his legs doesn't have a color, which is spooky. He opens the front door and walks down to the studio.

The bagel on Gavin's plate has only one small bite in it and Mom takes it away so she can make room on the table for her big textbooks, which means she's got students coming today. You would think she loved kids because she spends so much time with them, but actually she gets very annoyed when we're out somewhere like a restaurant and there are kids around. She's always talking about needing more *adult time.*

What I need today is *writing time,* so I stand up and grab my journal.

"Excuse me," Mom says. "You left your plate."

I guess she was pretending to be my

waitress only for yesterday and now she's ready for everything to go back to normal, which is okay by me if it means Dad will keep the studio and we won't be going on any vacations. But the way she's smiling I don't think she's ever going to shut up about Costa Rica until we're on the plane and the lady tells us to put away our iPods for takeoff.

"Where are you going?" Mom says.

"Downstairs."

"Just stay out of his hair, okay?"

That's what she tells me when Dad is busy with something, so I'm wondering what type of something is keeping Gavin so busy.

Gavin's bedroom door is closed and I'm down the hall strumming the Gibson on the studio couch. I'm putting my chords in a new order and the sound makes me feel heavy and that's when I know I'm writing a crying song.

Normally when I'm strumming a few chords I can turn to Dad and ask him how they sound. Without him here, I decide to turn to the next best person: John Lennon.

John Lennon's Ten Rules of Songwriting is a set of rules I came up with after listening closely to John's forty best songs. I'm not sure yet what I want my song to be about but it should probably follow rule no. 4, which is Use First Person Unless You're Writing "Nowhere Man." That means the lyrics to my song should use *I* instead of *he* or *she* or *Bungalow Bill.*

I grab my iPod and record myself playing my new chord pattern and humming a quick melody that comes into my head without me having to do anything. I put on a pair of Dad's big headphones and walk around the studio listening to the recording over and over. I'm thinking about Arizona because Mom mentioned it at breakfast.

It was last year, on the third Sunday in July, that I met Dr. M at the college in Tucson. He knew all about my certain kind of memory, how it isn't "photographic," which means I can't fit *everything* in my brainbox, just memories. When it comes to remembering facts and trivia like the name of the eleventh president or how many sides there are on a trapezoid, I have to study like everyone else. And if Mom says, "Shut the light when you leave the room," I'll remember she said it, but sometimes not at the exact time I'm leaving the room, so I'll "forget" to shut the light. But that kind of small forgetting doesn't bother me. It's the other kind, the big kind, when people forget what happened in their lives, that gives me the blues.

I asked Dr. M, "Does HSAM hurt?" He asked me, "Are you in any sort of pain?" I didn't know what to say and that's when he told me, "Many HSAMers find it helpful to keep a journal. They find it provides some relief. A way to unload."

Thinking about Arizona and Dr. M gives me an idea. I open my journal and write down a few lyrics.

I went to Arizona
To meet a smart man
He told me not to worry
He could understand

There are lots of songs about California by artists like the Beach Boys, Red Hot Chili Peppers, and Katy Perry. But I can think of only one song that talks about Arizona and that's "Get Back" by the Beatles. That makes me feel like I'm on the right track with my song.

I wonder if Gavin has ever been to Arizona because I know it's pretty close to California, which is where all the actors live. When he comes out of his room, I'll ask him. I also want to know why he was standing still in front of that giant fire instead of running away, which is what I would have done, unless that fire was just special effects and Gavin was only acting. An actor seems like a fun thing to be, but more people listen to old music than watch old TV shows, which means music is remembered more. Also, Dad is a songwriter, so that's what I want to be.

I think of the hundreds of songs Dad wrote and recorded down here in his studio. I can hear the songs in my head and I can also see the things that took place here, like the string quartet that Dad hired, and the picture that fell off the wall when Dad was playing his drums too hard, and the blackout that erased one of his songs and made him have to go back and record each instrument a second time.

It's hard to think about what's going to happen to the studio next. I see it every school year when we change classrooms or when a restaurant closes down at the shopping center and a new one opens up in the same spot. Soon Dad will clear out his things and this apartment will look empty and the new people will want to fill it up with all their stuff. But this place will never look empty to me, it'll always be full, because everywhere I turn, all around me, I see what no one else sees: the memories.

8

"So, wait, you're in New Jersey?" my sister asks.

"Yeah."

"Does Mom know you're there?"

"Not yet."

I pull the phone away from my ear. I can hear someone strumming faintly through the wall. I count only two musicians in the house and one of them left before the sun came up. It must be Joan.

"You could've come here, you know," Veronica says.

She says it in her nonchalant way, but I worry I've broken some sacred law in the sibling handbook. She's right, I could've flown down to Florida. Veronica moved to Key West from Miami about a year ago and I've yet to visit her new place. But then I would've had to hang with her boyfriend too, and that would've required more energy than I can muster right now.

"I'm sorry," I say.

"Don't be sorry."

Such a simple request and yet most thoughts of my sister begin with an apology. She was just a baby when our father died and ever since I've felt an obligation to her, never met, that goes far beyond the normal duties of an older brother.

"I'll come visit you next," I say.

"Only if you want to."

"Of course I do. How are you? How's island life?"

"I see what you did there," Veronica says. "Don't think I'm letting you get off the phone without telling me what happened."

Veronica never seems to experience anxiety about her own life, but she isn't immune to worrying about mine. "I told you I would've stayed after the funeral," she says.

"I'm sorry I made you worry. I'm good now. I'm with friends here and I'm taking it one day at a time."

"One day at a time? Did you really just say that to me? Now I definitely don't believe you."

She's right. It sounded scripted, a go-to phrase for mourners. It's just so damn taxing thinking up fresh ways of assuring people that I'm all right. Besides, it happens to be true. I am very much taking it moment by moment, ignoring what will and won't happen tomorrow.

"I know how you are, Gavin."

I don't like where this is going.

"You don't know how to shake anything off," she says.

It's unsettling getting this from my sister. First, because losing the most important person in your life is not something you just shake off. Second, because I'm the one in our sibling relationship who's supposed to pass down the wisdom, the one with ten more years of life experience to draw from. Third, because Veronica is someone who doesn't like to waste time on silly things like feelings, so if she's trying to unpack mine, that tells me she's even more worried than I thought. And last, because she's absolutely right.

"You see," Veronica says. "There you go again, pondering."

This must be how I sound when I call to check up on her, which I don't do often enough. "I'm good, I promise. I don't know what else to tell you."

"Oh!" she says in a loud burst. "I saw the premiere last night! Gavin, you were brilliant. I mean it. It was a subtle performance but also frenetic, if that makes any sense. I couldn't take my eyes off you. And not just because you're my brother."

"Thanks," I say, relieved to be talking about the fictional me versus the real me. "You really liked it?"

"I *loved* it."

I didn't remember that last night was the premiere until I checked my phone this morning. Apparently it drew the biggest audience *The Long Arm* has ever had. The media credited the boost in numbers to what they called the "Gavin Winters fire stunt." It's true our ratings have never been stellar, which is frustrating because *The Long Arm* is a smart and gripping crime drama positioned prominently on a re-spected cable network, and Officer Beau Kendricks is by far the best character I've ever gotten to play. I just wish the show were succeeding on its own merits and not due to some scandal that will be forgotten in a week.

"There's one thing I don't get," Veronica says. "Are they trying to turn you into a bad guy? It feels like it's going in that direction. Would they do that?"

"That's actually —"

"No, don't tell me."

"— my evil twin brother."

"Shut up."

Syd was the same way. He forbade me to

share anything about where the story was heading. He wanted to wait like everyone else. We watched the entire first season together, Syd rewinding all my scenes with goofy pride in his eyes. Now he'll never know how the story ends.

"Even Mom gave it two thumbs up," Veronica says. "And you know she never pretends to like something if she doesn't."

"You spoke to her?"

"She called me, like, literally five seconds after it ended and proceeded to give her twenty-minute review. She even had her friends over to watch it."

I picture my mother, just an hour south of here, the lone holdout in that ancient house, sharing space with her own phantom love for the past thirty years. Veronica and I, meanwhile, got out as soon as we could.

"Are you going to visit her soon?" she asks.

"I'll get down there eventually."

There's a knock at my door.

"Hold on, V."

It's Joan, her hands behind her back, one Converse crushing the other. I've seen the same tossed-together wardrobe on hipsters in Silver Lake, though Joan's version seems far less intentional. Her hairstyle, if you can even call it a style, also appears to be an afterthought; her hair is uncombed and casually tucked behind her ears. But her overall chaos is grounded by the directness of her eyes. There's something confident and unflinching in them.

"Veronica, can I give you a ring later in the week?"

"Whenever. Just do me a favor and stay out of trouble."

Coming from her, the wilder child. "I will."

I toss the phone onto my bed and give Joan my full attention.

"Who was that?" Joan asks.

"My sister."

"Oh."

She brings her hands forward to reveal her journal, the one her doctor advised her to keep. It must be scary to have a child with a rare condition like Joan's. At the clinic, when Syd and I were planning for a child of our own, we provided our full medical histories. I knew Syd's father had died of heart problems but that was the first time I realized how far back the Brennett men had been suffering similar fates. My worry, upon learning this, was for my future child. I never considered worrying about the man sitting right next to me.

Joan is gazing down. "You know what? The hair on your legs looks like the kind of string that goes on a fishing pole."

"Thank you," I say.

I wait for more, but she's fallen into some sort of trance. I wave my hands at her. "Joan? You okay?"

She focuses. "I was just thinking about the time Grandpa took me fishing, which was Sunday, June fifth, 2011."

"That's amazing."

"What is?"

"How you do that. How you know what day of the week it was two years ago. I can't imagine."

She looks down at her journal as if hiding her face. I wonder if I've embarrassed her. "Do you like fishing?" I ask.

"No, because it's mean. Grandpa says fish don't feel pain like we do because they have small brains, but what if one of them has a brain that's different from all the other fish? How do you know you're not catching the one fish that feels a lot of pain?"

"I see your point." It dawns on me that I still haven't found out why she knocked on my door. "Can I help you with something, Joan?"

"Yes, you can, Gavin."

She hugs the journal to her chest and turns down the hall. I'm not entirely sure, but I think I'm meant to follow.

9

Gavin sits on the couch and I play my new song. I sing the four lines I wrote about Dr. M and I'm feeling proud but also embarrassed, because I hate the sound of my own voice.

"I'm done," I say so he knows he can clap.

He opens his eyes, which are bright but not wet. He stares at me and he says in a not-so-excited way, "Very nice."

"Did you cry?"

Gavin looks left and right and then straight at me. "Did I cry?"

"Yes."

"No. I didn't cry."

I make a low rumbling noise in my mouth so Gavin will know that he's supposed to ask me what's wrong, but he doesn't ask me, so I just tell him.

"I'm writing a song for the Next Great Songwriter Contest because I think it might be a good way to make sure I'm never forgotten."

"What do you mean? Why would you be forgotten?"

"Because everyone forgets everything. They forget the name of the second person they ever kissed and they forget about what happened to those twins who were taken apart as babies and they even forget their own grandchildren. And it's not fair because I would never do that."

"I believe you."

"But then I realized, it's not people's fault that they have crappy brains. That's what reminders are for. Mom never forgets to pay the bills because she has a reminder on her calendar. And Dad remembers to put new batteries in our smoke alarm only because it starts beeping. And no one forgets Martin Luther King because he has his own holiday every year. It works the same way with songs. Everyone remembers John Lennon, even Grandma, because his songs are reminders. My song is going to be a reminder to everyone that they should keep me in their brainboxes, and I have less than two weeks to finish it."

Gavin is frozen like a computer. It takes him a few seconds to get going again. "You've obviously spent a lot of time thinking about this."

"Yes, I have."

"But what does crying have to do with it?"

"A great song has to give you a strong feeling and one of the strongest feelings is wanting to dance. Even babies want to dance. The other strongest feeling is when you get sad and you cry because you hear a song and you remember everything that happened in your life. Which do you think is better for a song contest? Dancing or crying?"

Gavin hums like a humidifier and then he says, "Honestly, I don't think people care whether they're dancing or crying. A good song is a good song."

"I don't even know what that means."

"When a song is good, everyone knows it. You can't manufacture that. It's like magic. You just have to let it happen." He stops and thinks. "Actually, maybe you shouldn't listen to me. I haven't written a song in years."

"John Lennon said he doesn't believe in magic."

"He said that? When?"

"In his song 'God.' "

"Oh, right," Gavin says. "Yeah, I don't think he was talking about that kind of magic."

I look down at my journal and I wonder if there's magic on my page or not. Every once in a while Dad will play music from his college band and he'll say how much he likes Gavin's lyrics. He says Gavin was able to "capture life" with his words. There's one Awake Asleep song when Gavin sings *The night came to fight me,* and even though I don't know what the line means, I feel something when I hear it.

I hand Gavin my journal so he can read my lyrics about going to see the smart man in Arizona. He takes the journal carefully, like he's worried it's burning hot, and then he reads it and stays quiet for a long time after.

"Who's the smart man?" he says.

"Dr. M."

"Did Dr. M make you cry?"

"No. Why?"

He hands the journal back. "If that experience didn't make you cry, how can you expect it to make other people cry? What makes *you* cry?"

"Scary movies, anything with dogs, bad teeth —"

"Whatever it is, put it in your song."

I cried the day Charlotte moved away to Texas (Saturday, August 7, 2010), and I cried a few weeks ago when Mrs. Dresden said that time was up for our writing test but I wasn't finished yet (Wednesday, May 15,

2013), and I cried when it was time to say good-bye to Grandma Joan (Saturday, October 8, 2011) and I also cried when Pepper went to sleep (Wednesday, March 25, 2009). I've never actually cried over a song before but I've seen it happen to other people.

It was a Friday and Dad was driving. His phone was on shuffle and John Lennon's song "Mother" came on. Mom reached her hand to Dad's neck and she left it there, tickling his skin. In the narrow mirror, Dad's eyes looked shiny, and he stayed quiet the whole way home from Grandma Joan's.

And I remember Dad once saying, "If a song hits you deep enough, you never get it out of your system." That's what I want so badly, to have my song go deep into everyone's system, and that's why making people cry is a good way to do it because it worked for the song "Mother" with my dad.

Gavin is staring at me. "What?" I say.

"Sorry," he says, blinking his eyes. "I was just thinking about something."

"Me too. I'll tell you what I was thinking about if you tell me what you were thinking about."

He lets out a short little breath, almost like a laugh that never gets started. "I'm not sure I want to share, if that's okay." He stretches his arm over his head and his bracelet slides down his wrist.

"That's Sydney's bracelet, right?"

He drops his arm and looks at the bracelet. "It is."

Now I feel bad about asking him that question because I know just mentioning a certain name can put a person in a quiet mood. It happens with me when I hear someone say *grandma* and to Mom when someone talks about Sydney. Gavin is doing the same thing right now, just looking down and turning the bracelet around his wrist.

"When you see a memory," Gavin says, "how much do you really see?"

"It depends what I was paying attention to at the time. Why? What do you want to know?"

"Nothing. I was just curious."

"I don't mind. I love remembering."

He shakes his head, but I'm thinking maybe he's just trying to be polite, like when someone offers you the last piece of cake and you say, "No, thank you," even though you'd *love* an extra slice.

"I have an idea," I say. "How about I tell you the stuff I remember about Sydney and then you can help me with my thing?"

"What's your thing?"

"My song. Dad would normally help me but he's not here and the Next Great

Songwriter Contest says on their website that it doesn't have to be just one song-writer, it can be a team, like Simon and Garfunkel, or Tegan and Sara, or Lennon and McCartney. So you can be McCartney and I'll be Lennon. I'm the walrus."

"I thought the walrus was Paul," Gavin says.

"No, John was the walrus. You can be the blackbird because that's what Paul would probably be. I think we should have hand signals. Here's mine." I close my hand into a fist but I leave out my pointer finger and my middle finger and I hang them down like tusks.

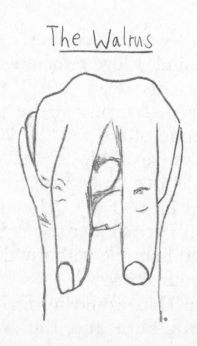

The Walrus

"What's yours?" I say.

He isn't sure what to do so I help him. I make it so his hands are stretched out and his thumbs are pressed together and I show him how to flap his palms like wings.

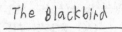

The Blackbird

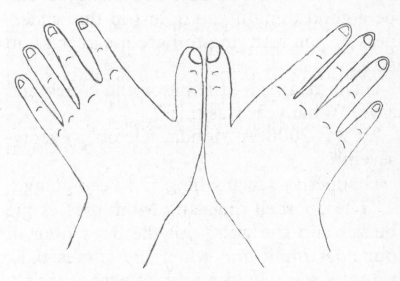

He drops his hands. "Look, Joan, I'm happy to help you however I can, but . . ."

I wait for him to finish his sentence, but he never does.

"Since we already worked on the song for a while, maybe we should do a memory now to make it fair," I say.

"Now? I have a few things I should probably take care of."

"We can start from the beginning, when I thought Sydney was a girl."

Gavin looks like he wants to leave, but he also looks like he wants to stay. I'm not sure what to say next. I'm wondering if this is one of those times when I'm *not letting up,* which is something Mom is always warning me about. But Dad says *not letting up* can be a good thing if you're lost in the wilderness or you're trying to have a career as an artist.

Gavin relaxes a little bit on the couch and says, "What year was this?"

"It was 2008. A Monday. October twenty-seventh."

He doesn't say anything so I keep going.

"The doorbell rings and Mom presses the buzzer and she walks out the front door of our apartment and when she comes back upstairs she's holding a box with a string. Sydney is standing behind her and I'm very surprised because when Mom said her friend Sydney was coming over for dinner, I was picturing a girl."

"What was in the box?" Gavin says.

"Macaroons. Not the coconut kind. They were some other kind that I don't like."

"*Macarons.* They're French. I didn't know what they were either until Syd introduced me to them." He seems interested now. "Go on. Do you know what he was wearing?"

"Yes. He's wearing a peach button-down shirt and it's tucked into his jeans and he has low-top brown shoes, the kind without laces, and his pants are rolled up and he isn't wearing socks."

"He never wore socks." He presses his back into the couch cushion like he's ready to get comfortable. "Did he say anything when he walked into the house?"

"He says, 'Hello, Miss Joan. I've heard so much about you. Paige, you said she had horns. I don't see any horns. Would you mind, dear?' and then he touches the top of my head to see if I have any horns and I say, 'I have a book about a unicorn,' and Sydney says, 'I love books and I love unicorns. How about you read the book to me after dinner?' and I say, 'I can only pretend-read,' and he says, 'I'll do the reading and you can be my page turner,' and then Dad comes into the room and Sydney starts talking to him."

"That's unbelievable," Gavin says, scrunching up his forehead like he's trying to figure out a very hard riddle. "That's really how he talked."

I feel like smiling, so I do.

"Did he read you the book?" Gavin says.

"Yes, and I don't even have to remind him

because he remembers by himself and I love when that happens. First he reads a page and then he makes a throat noise that means it's time for me to turn the page. When the story is over he tells me that he'd love to see a real unicorn one day and I tell him that that's impossible because unicorns aren't real and he says, 'How do you know?' and I say, 'People told me,' and he says, 'That's what I hear too, but what if they're wrong?' And that keeps me thinking for a while and I'm still wondering if there really is such a thing as a unicorn who lives far away where no people go and it makes me excited to think that maybe I'll see a unicorn one day."

Gavin nods like he's not surprised by what I'm saying.

"But all this happened after dinner," I say. "I'm jumping ahead."

I wait for Gavin to ask another question. I notice he's not like Sydney because he's wearing socks and his socks have three different color stripes — gray, green, and yellow. I like them and I want to borrow them.

"Hello?" I say, because the quiet is lasting a long time.

"I'm trying to picture his face," Gavin says with his eyes closed. "It's hard."

"Do you want me to draw it?"

He opens his eyes. "You can do that?"

I turn to a new page in my journal and begin to draw.

"People think I'm pretty good at drawing," I say, "but it feels like cheating to me since I'm only tracing the memories in my head. John Lennon drew pictures in his journal too."

Faces always take me the longest, so I stop halfway and ask Gavin, "How does it look so far?"

He sits up and takes my journal and lifts it to his face. He looks at it so long that I start to worry that I've drawn the wrong person. Then he places his hand on the page and he touches the side of the drawing's face and moves a finger over to the ear and he says one word in a low, low voice:

"Sydney."

10

Sydney had told me all about Joan, how uncanny it was that she could store so many details in her head, the monumental and inconsequential taking up equal space. I heard the amazement in his voice, but there was no way to truly appreciate her powers from afar. Now, sitting across from her, I finally understand. She is something close to miraculous.

We've been talking for over an hour, re-creating Syd's first visit five years ago. When we started I was wary, then enthralled, and now, as we're finishing up, I'm reluctant to stop.

"One more thing," I say.

Though Joan started us down this path, I doubt she knew what she was getting herself into. As she guided me along, my curiosity grew more intense until I was almost interrogating her. I didn't intend to push her so hard. I just kept asking questions and she kept having the answers.

My last question has to do with Paige and Ollie's attempt at matchmaking. "When your mom and dad were telling Sydney about me, did they say anything else? You said something about movies."

"Yeah, Sydney wanted to know what kinds of things you were into, like books and movies and stuff. Dad said you guys watched some movie in college and you'd always imitate someone named Zoro or Toro."

"Benicio del Toro."

"That's it."

In the film *The Usual Suspects*, Benicio del Toro would mumble so terribly, no one knew what he was on about. My impression of his character was always good for a laugh. Joan doesn't realize it, but this last detail feels like a tiny piece of gold.

She stands up to leave.

"Thank you," I say.

She smiles and picks up her journal. "I'll let you know when I come up with some good lyrics."

"Right, sounds great," I say, having briefly forgotten the agreement we made.

Part of me wants to end it here, since I know full well that I'm willingly stirring up feelings that should remain unstirred. But there's another part of me that just can't leave the past alone.

"I'm curious," I say. "How many more memories of him do you have?"

"He came back in 2009," Joan says, starting a count on her fingers, "and again in 2010. There was nothing in 2011. Then he came back in 2012 and once more in 2013."

"You saw him only once this year?"

"Just January twenty-sixth."

"I thought he visited you guys in April too."

Joan shrugs her shoulders. "Nope. He just came in January."

"Wait. Are you sure?"

Her brow tightens. I meant no offense. Actually, I trust her brain more than mine, which hasn't been too sharp of late. Still, I could've sworn. "I remember now," I say. "He took your mother out to dinner for her birthday. They probably met up in Manhattan," I say, satisfied to be tying up the loose ends.

But Joan is shaking her head. "No, I don't think so. My mom was sick on her birthday this year. She had a really bad stomach bug and she was home from work for two days. She didn't go out with anyone."

Her words are definitive, leaving me perplexed and more than a little disgusted with my own inferior memory. Granted, I shouldn't feel too bad; it was tough even for Sydney to keep track of his own busy schedule, which is why he had an assistant. "Sorry," I say. "I guess I was mistaken."

She nods and ambles up the stairs, humming a melody as she goes.

I retreat to my room and collapse onto the bed, half exhausted, half invigorated. Maybe it's best I wrap these blankets around me and take a nap. When I wake, rested and strong, I can look back at this morning's episode as a momentary lapse in judgment, a careless indulgence. I'm only strengthening Sydney's grip on me when I should be taking steps to extricate myself from him. Why else did I come all this way to New Jersey?

But maybe I'm tired of restraint. Maybe that fire ignited something in me that's still burning. In a sense, I was wrong about there being no way of building new memories of Sydney. They can be found, it turns out, in the minds of others. Joan isn't the only one who interacted with him when he was out here. There's also Paige and Ollie. And what about the project Syd was spending so much time on?

I couldn't sleep now if I tried. Instead, I shoot an e-mail off to Syd's assistant at Schiller Pierson, asking her to put me in touch with all the people Syd met with when he was working in New York earlier this year.

I jump in the shower, keeping my right arm clear of the water to protect the bracelet.

Joan's retelling made me feel as though I were somehow reconnecting with the real Sydney. I experienced that rush, that high, that merciful reprieve from the sorrow. She took me through the whole night. There were gaps in her story any time she'd gone to the bathroom or lost focus, but it hardly mattered. What was included was so vivid and idiosyncratic as to create the sensation of reality. For seconds at a time, I felt that Sydney really was here, that we were, for the briefest moment, together.

According to Joan, it was Paige who first mentioned my name at that dinner back in 2008. Sydney had just gotten out of a poisonous relationship and Paige was determined to help him find a good man. She's the one who looked to Ollie and said, "What about Gavin?"

I remember receiving the text from Ollie all those years ago. It must've been a few days after that dinner. Ollie wanted to gauge my interest in meeting Syd. I was tired of late nights in bars and clubs, of waking up next to strangers whose names I didn't know, of struggling to stay young and desirable. A blind dinner date seemed refreshingly traditional.

Sydney sent me an e-mail from his work account that began *Dear Mr. Winters.* I wasn't sure what to think about it. Did this guy want to hook up with me or sell me life insurance?

We met for sushi. He was almost entirely gray, making zero attempt to appear younger than he was. In fact, his hair made him look older than thirty-eight. There was just five years between us but it felt more like ten.

That same unabashed honesty he possessed about his age and appearance extended to all parts of his life. That first night, it was exhilarating, never off-putting, to hear him casually spill his guts about his family, his relationship history, and his career. I mentioned I had auditioned for a couple of commercials for his company, Schiller Pierson. Maybe he had seen me on tape at some point. He said it wasn't possible; he would've remembered me.

He asked if I did any impressions. When I told him impressions weren't really my thing, he said, *What about your Benicio del Toro?* How did he know about that? He pointed to the menu. The name of the

101

restaurant was Kobayashi, a blatant reference to *The Usual Suspects*. I asked him, *Does this mean you're Verbal Kint? Should I be worried?* He smiled devilishly.

Of course he had grilled Ollie and Paige about me. I had done the same. Joan didn't reveal anything I hadn't already known. But she did bring everything full circle, placing me right there at the Sully table as Syd vetted me.

I remember another thing from that first night. Syd asked me where I saw myself in five years. It was a question I might've laughed at if not for the gravity with which Syd asked it. At the time, I was close to quitting acting. Granted, I was always close, but at that point, after a series of painful rejections, I wasn't feeling optimistic about my career and was pondering alternatives. But here was this guy, this self-confident gray-haired man, asking a trite question with absolute sincerity. And so I dug deep for a worthy answer.

As an up-and-comer in my early twenties I dreamed of splitting my time between challenging pieces with auteur filmmakers and the occasional big-money role in a summer blockbuster. Now that I was in my early thirties, I had just one modest career goal: to work. I told the earnest man sitting across from me that in five years I'd be thrilled to have a steady gig on a TV show. Sydney nodded and said, *I can see that.*

I'm realizing that it all panned out. Four years later I landed a TV role on *The Long Arm.* If he were here now, Syd would assure me that it was no coincidence. He believed you could visualize almost any dream into existence. He'd meditate first thing every morning, never missed a day. I keep wondering what might've been different if he'd decided to skip his routine that final morning, just that one time. If I had held him in bed and never allowed him to leave.

I push the thought away.

The shower water is no longer hot. It could be a result of the boiler problem Paige mentioned or the fact that I've been lingering in here too long. I shut the faucet and relax my outstretched arm. Time to face the day.

Back in bed, I reach for my phone and check my in-box. Syd's assistant, Isabel, has already replied. For a moment, I consider deleting the e-mail without even reading it. Whatever buzz I felt before has now faded and with it my courage. To follow in Syd's footsteps around New York is a pointless quest. At the end of it, I'm still left with nothing.

And yet, I open the e-mail.

Isabel must be confused. She says Sydney didn't have any business in New York on the dates I mentioned. He took some personal days in February and again in April. She's not sure why.

I read her e-mail a second time, struggling to grasp the meaning. And then, entering my brain like vicious malware, is my earlier conversation with Joan. She contradicted what I was certain I remembered.

Isabel's phone number is listed at the bottom of her e-mail. I click it and soon she answers. "Gavin, hi."

"I just got your e-mail," I say. "This can't be right. Are you sure there was no project in New York? Can you ask around the office? Maybe there's some confusion. I know you guys hired some new people over there."

"Gavin, I don't know what to tell you. I'm ninety-nine percent sure. I can definitely double-check if you want, but —"

"How about travel? I drove him to the airport. He went somewhere. Did you book any flights or hotels for him during that time? Can you check on that too?"

"I did check," Isabel says, her voice increasingly more delicate. "I couldn't find anything. I'm looking at the calendar now and I have those days marked as personal days. He never said why he was taking them, and he didn't mention that he'd be traveling anywhere."

"He said he was going to New York. That's what he told me."

"That's all I know. I'm sorry."

"I don't understand." I didn't mean to say it out loud.

"I heard about the fire. It's been tough here too. Listen, if you ever want to get together, let me know, okay? Gavin? Hello?"

I move my lips, but this time nothing comes out.

■ ■ ■ ■

GIMME SOME
TRUTH

■ ■ ■ ■

11

I'm sitting on the edge of Harper's pool with my journal in my lap and my feet in the water. I'm all the way at the deep end while the other girls splash and jump and laugh in the shallow end.

I know I look weird sitting here all by myself, but I'm very close to finishing some lyrics that I think will make Gavin cry. I could go sit by the adults, but I can't listen to Mom talk about Costa Rica one more time. Sometimes I don't want to be a kid, but I don't want to be an adult either.

Even if I weren't working on my song right now, I'd probably still want to sit here by myself. Harper will always be one of my best friends, even though her family moved out here to the suburbs a few years ago, but some of the new girls she hangs out with are tough to be around. If I don't know a certain word, like *chiffon,* they'll look at me like I'm brain-dead, but if they don't know my kind of word, like *staccato,* then I'm a show-off or a know-it-all.

Harper calls out to me from across the pool. "Time's up, rock star."

She knows I like it when she calls me a rock star even though I pretend I don't. I wrap my journal safely in my towel and finally jump in.

I swim away from the girls and straight to Harper. "What word rhymes with *husband*?"

She pulls her wet hair into her mouth and starts chewing it. That's how she does her best thinking. "That's a tough one."

"It doesn't have to be a perfect rhyme," I say. "It just has to be close."

"How much money do you get if you win this thing?"

"It's not that kind of contest. I just want everyone to hear my song and know my name."

"Boring," she says, splashing water at me.

My best friends love me and my strange memory, but even they don't understand why I get so crazy about being forgotten. I guess we all have our own things to worry about. Harper stresses out about getting one wrong answer on a test, and Wyatt prays that the new Star Wars movie will be more like the books, and Naveyah gets totally depressed when the Giants lose a game. I suppose it just depends on what sorts of things you notice, because I didn't even know there were books for Star Wars.

I dunk my head under and come back up when I'm out of air. "Did you hear about that actor?"

"What actor?" Harper says.

"He's on a show called *The Long Arm.* He was on the news because he made a big fire in his backyard."

"I didn't hear about it."

"He's really famous."

"What's his name?"

I tell her Gavin's name and she promises to search for him on her new phone. She doesn't keep any songs on her new phone because she says there's no point when you have the Internet, but I'm hoping she'll at least put my song on her phone when it's finished.

She spits the hair out of her mouth and says, "Almond."

"What?"

"A rhyme for *husband.*"

"It doesn't really work," I say.

Harper drops her lips to the top of the water and starts blowing bubbles. "It would help if I knew what the song was about."

That's one thing I love about her: If you give her a puzzle, she won't quit until she solves it. I decide to give her a clue even though I know she's going to make fun of me.

"The song is about remembering."

It's hard to hear her, because her mouth is halfway in the pool, but I'm pretty sure she says, "Of course it is."

I'm ready to make Gavin cry but he's not in his bedroom or in the bathroom or in the studio. I peek into the courtyard and see the back of his head with Dad's studio headphones covering his ears. He's sitting at the table, staring down at his phone.

I grab the Gibson and step outside and tap Gavin on the shoulder. He whips his head around and grabs his chest. I think I frightened him.

I wiggle my walrus finger tusks.

"Oh," Gavin says and he flaps his black-bird wings, but only once. He looks back down at his phone. "What was the exact date that Sydney came in January?"

"He got here on the twenty-fifth. Why?"

He doesn't answer because he's busy typing. It seems like he's writing a book because he's typing so many words. He finally finishes and puts the phone on the table. "Sorry," he says, taking off his headphones. "What's up?"

It's time to get down to business, which means it's time to talk about what I want to talk about. "I thought about what you said about the song and I think I fixed it."

The other day when I showed Gavin the drawing of Sydney and I saw how sad he looked, I knew I should write the lyrics about Sydney. If these lyrics don't make Gavin cry, I don't know what will.

We were together, you and I
Our love reached up to the sky
When you left, my heart sank deep
Now I skip dinner so I can sleep

I think about the times we had
When we kissed I was so glad
I thought one day you'd be my husband
I can't believe what has happened

I can't go home 'cause you're not there
I'm all alone and really scared
All I have is a memory
A memory

I keep breathing but I have no air
I keep crying 'cause it isn't fair
All I have is a memory
A memory

I leave the last chord ringing and I wait for the clapping but there isn't any. His eyes look annoyingly dry. "You're not crying."

"You want me to be honest?" Gavin looks at me a long time and it makes me change the way I'm sitting in my chair. "The verses seem pretty generic. I would stay away from the clichés. They make the lyrics feel disingenuous."

"You're dissing generous."

"Sorry. I'm not saying it right. What I mean is I don't hear *you* in that song. You're singing about kissing and having a husband. I'm not sure what that's about."

"It's hard to find a rhyme for *husband.*"

"I think the chorus is pretty sweet," Gavin says. "The way the lyrics work with the melody and it feels personal, you know, because you're talking about memories. I think you should keep going with that."

I'm pretty sure he just gave me a compliment, which is my favorite thing to get. But there's one problem. "Are you sure you didn't cry?"

"Joan, I think you should forget about the whole crying thing."

I hate when people tell me to forget about things because it shows me that they really don't know me at all. But Gavin is giving me a friendly smile so I force myself not to be mad at him.

"How did you used to write *your* lyrics?" I say.

He picks up a pebble from the concrete and bounces it in his hand. He makes his palm into a tennis racket and swats the pebble against the brick wall. "I never played any instruments like you do, so it was different. Ollie and the band would give me the music and I'd just wander around with my Walkman."

I know what a Walkman is because Dad has one and that's how I listen to Grandma Joan sing her song.

"I would just keep listening to the music until something came to me," Gavin says.

"What if it took a really long time for something to come to you?"

He shrugs his shoulders. "I wasn't in a rush. I'm still that way, actually. It's not always a good thing." He stops talking for a second, like he wants to think about what he just said, and then he says, "It's just about relaxing and not overthinking things. Just letting things happen naturally."

But I can't relax because I *am* in a rush. I don't have time to wait for the best lyrics to pop into my head. I'm starting to wonder if I picked the wrong partner for the contest because whenever I think of an idea, Gavin

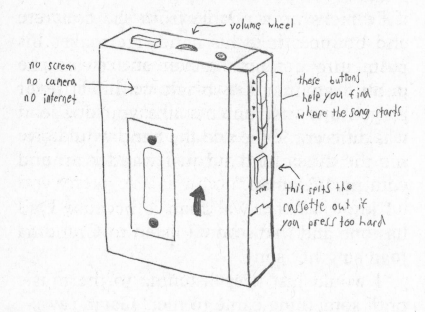

The Walkman
(or Walkwoman)

volume wheel

no screen
no camera
no internet

these buttons
help you find
where the song starts

this spits the
cassette out if
you press too hard

tells me it's no good. I thought Dad was a tough audience but he's usually tougher about the music than the lyrics.

Speaking of Dad, I haven't had a chance to show him my song yet because he's been getting home so late each day and then he's busy in the studio finishing up his projects. I really want to make sure I'm writing a song that will go deep into his system, because his system is a good test for other people's systems, because he's been doing music so long.

But right now I'm stuck with Gavin. He

said some nice things about my song and some not-so-nice things but I can only think about the not-so-nice things. I'm wondering if I can ever give Dad or Gavin or anyone else a strong feeling.

And now I'm hearing someone else's voice in my head. It's Gavin's voice and it's not just in my mind, he's humming a song, and it takes me a few seconds to realize that the song is mine, my chorus. It sounds so real coming out of his mouth and so pretty and it makes my arms tickle and the feeling goes up my back and into my head and all over my face.

"You're going to sing the song," I say.

"What?"

"When we're in the studio. You have to, it sounds so good, and I can't sing, not like you."

I've listened to the album Dad and Gavin made many times and it sounds very messy but Gavin's voice makes you feel like you're listening to something important.

"Joan, I haven't sung in almost twenty years. I don't think it would be any good."

"Dad's recording it, so it'll be great."

Gavin doesn't say anything else and that's fine, because I know that sometimes saying nothing is as good as saying *Okay* or *Yes* or *You know what, Joan Lennon, that's the best idea I've ever heard.*

"What color tie was he wearing?" Gavin asks.

He wasn't sure if he wanted to do another Sydney memory today, but I'm learning that if you want Gavin to do things, like help you write your song and also sing it, you have to keep pushing him.

"Black," I say. "Sydney is wearing a black tie."

Saturday, March 14, 2009: Mom and Dad and Sydney are dressed up real fancy and my babysitter is listening to Mom's instructions. Sydney looks at my pajamas, which have different color hearts on them, and he says, "Miss Joan, where did you get those?" and I say, "I don't know, my mom got them for me," and he says, "I have the same ones at home," and I say, "Really?" and he just smiles and that's when I know he's joking. I smell something minty and I see that he has gum in his mouth. I ask him for a piece and he hands me one and he says, "Five dollars," and that's another joke and this time I know it right away. But then I'm not so sure because Sydney says, "It's all right, you can owe me." He's holding a big white envelope that's too big for his pocket and this time he's wearing socks, but he doesn't seem too happy about it

118

because he keeps reaching down and pulling the socks up.

"I wanted to go to that wedding," Gavin says, after I share it all with him. "That's how you know you really like someone. You want to be their date at some stranger's wedding."

"Why didn't you go?"

"We'd been dating only a few months. Syd wasn't ready to show me off to his old friends. He didn't trust me."

"Why not?"

"Because men —" He stops. "We tend to change our minds a lot. He wanted to make sure I was serious."

"Like when I asked my parents for my own guitar and they wanted me to use one of Dad's guitars first to make sure I was going to stick with it and not get bored of it after a week like I did with the indoor trampoline Grandpa bought me."

"Exactly," Gavin says, winking, which I'm jealous of because every time *I* try to blink just one eye, both eyes end up blinking. "For the first few weeks Syd never let me sleep over. Every night, he'd kick me out."

"That's mean."

"I thought so. But it made it even more satisfying when he finally let me stay. Anyway, please go on."

I drink some more lemonade because I'm not used to talking for so long. I'm wondering how Mom does it, how she stands in front of her class and speaks all day. "Everyone says good-bye and then they leave for the wedding."

"Was it cold out?" Gavin says. "Were they wearing jackets?"

"Yeah. Sydney is wearing a long coat that has a belt attached, which I think is pretty cool. And he's carrying a pair of headphones, a kind I've never seen before."

I draw a little sketch in my journal so Gavin sees what I mean:

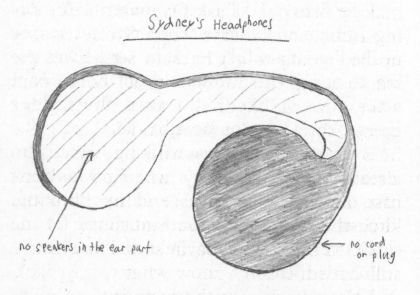

Sydney's Headphones

no speakers in the ear part

← no cord or plug

"Those weren't headphones," Gavin says, moaning a little. "His ears were always cold.

He'd wear that thing around Los Angeles. Can you imagine?" He starts laughing. "One time we were parking the car and the valet said, 'Sir, you dropped your headband.' "

He's cracking up now. I'm almost laughing too because laughs can be contagious, but I wish I knew what was so funny. When Gavin finishes his laughing party, he crosses his arms and closes his eyes and says, "When did you see him next?"

"The next morning it takes a long time for the grown-ups to get out of bed. Dad wakes up first and he cooks crepes and I'm very excited because Dad is very good at making breakfast. I ask Dad what we're doing today and he says when Sydney wakes up he's going to get back to setting up the studio, which is almost finished. Then Mom wakes up and Sydney wakes up too. He comes through the door and it looks like he's been up for a while because he's already dressed and he's wheeling his suitcase across the floor. He comes into the kitchen and he says 'Good morning.' "

"Good morning," Gavin says. His eyes are still closed. I don't know what to say back, so I keep going with the memory.

"And then Dad asks if he wants a crepe and Sydney says, 'I shouldn't —' "

" '— but I will.' "

Gavin is right. That's what Sydney said. "And then Dad asks how he likes his coffee and Sydney says, 'A splash of cream and a mound of sugar.' "

"You should really cut the sugar," Gavin says.

"What?" I say.

"Use the stevia," Gavin says. "You just have to get used to the taste."

I look around the courtyard but there's nobody else here and that's when I realize who Gavin is talking to.

"What time will you be home?" Gavin says.

I keep quiet and listen.

"We'll be shooting late tonight but maybe we can do breakfast. I'll bring it to you in bed. I don't want you to get up. You can skip it, can't you? Just lie there and don't move and I'll make you whatever you want. Would you do that for me? Stay in bed? Just this once?"

There's no answer, just some birds chirping. I raise my voice over them: "Gavin."

He opens his eyes. The light blinds him at first, but then he sees me. His face turns reddish from the sun and he reaches around for his phone and headphones and says, "I think that's enough for today."

12

I've lost track of what Paige is saying. I see her standing there, sprinkling freshly grated cheese on top of something in a baking dish, her lips moving. But it's as if someone has placed a pane of glass between us. I can't hear the words coming out of her mouth.

It's been happening more and more, ever since Syd died. I'll be in midconversation with someone and I'll lose the thread. By the time I realize I've drifted off, I've already missed so much.

"And we would obviously redo the flooring," Paige says, "so it's all the same."

That's right. She was explaining how she wants to knock down the half wall between the kitchen and living room to make their home more open concept. "That sounds great."

"She's been talking about this since February eighth, 2010," Joan says from her seat at the kitchen table.

"Yes," Paige admits. "But *now* we can finally do it."

I'm tearing up pieces of kale and dropping them into a wooden salad bowl. I enjoy cooking, but tonight my heart's not in it. Just handling this food reminds me how little I've cooked in the past month, how poorly I've been eating. And that leads me back to Sydney and the surreal conversation I had with his assistant.

I'm at a loss. I can't imagine why Sydney would lie to me about going to New York for business. On second thought, that's not true. I *can* imagine why and I have imagined it. It's just that I'd rather not consider those unpleasant possibilities. All I know is that he wasn't home with me.

"Here," Joan says.

I stare at the peeler in her hands.

"For the cucumber," she explains.

"Right. Thanks."

Again this afternoon I was unable to resist Joan's invitation into the past. Returning to the slow beginnings of my relationship with Syd reminded me that as open and honest as he was about most things, he could also be quite careful and deliberate. Especially with his heart, which had been badly broken before we met and which I had to prove myself worthy of being allowed to rebuild.

Considering how long it took to gain his trust, I find it hard to believe he would do anything to jeopardize my trust in him. That's what makes this whole thing so hard to comprehend.

I've done it again, drifted off while Paige is talking.

"I feel better putting money into the house now that the neighborhood is finally coming along," she says. "It still has a ways to go, but you should've seen it when we first moved here. The idea of having a farmers' market in Riverview Park was laughable."

From what I've seen of the neighborhood so far, it's mostly three- and four-story residential buildings with minimal commerce beyond a couple of bodegas and laundromats. This particular block features a real hodgepodge of exteriors, from brick to stucco to vinyl, the last of which adorns the Sully duplex.

"You can't beat the scenery," I say, gesturing out the kitchen window. The Sullys' house is perched on the far east edge of an elevated neighborhood known as the Heights, offering a nearly unobstructed view across the Hudson River to Manhattan.

"That's why we moved here," Paige says, only half joking. She slides the pan of eggplant Parmesan into the oven. "Obviously, at the time Ollie needed to be close to the city for his music."

"What do you mean, he *needed* to be close?" Joan barks. "Why do you say it like that? He still *needs* to be close."

Paige turns away from her daughter. She calmly shuts the oven door and gives me a deadpan look. "How about some wine?"

"Syd had this big yellow boat of a car," Paige says, her face glowing under the porch light. She and I are out back in the courtyard, bellies full and wine in our glasses. The sleepless city sparkles ahead. "I mean, it was *the* ugliest car I've ever seen. And like that wasn't bad enough, the turn signal had broken off, so he had to use a popsicle stick to work the blinker."

"No way."

"I'm serious," she says, the absurdity setting off a flurry of laughter.

I'm laughing too, but it's nothing like what Paige is experiencing. I'm jealous of the mental picture she has of teenage Syd and his ugly car. "Do you have photos of you guys from back then?"

"Somewhere. I'll have to dig them out."

The story Paige is in the middle of telling is one I've heard before. It's not like my

126

time with Joan, where I'm hoping to learn something new. Indeed, it's the opposite: I'm finding unexpected comfort in an old tale told by an old friend.

"He used to give me a ride home from school every day in that car of his," Paige says. "Then my sister broke up with him and started dating someone else. Syd said he'd keep driving me anyway, which really irked Lauren. She had to go back to taking the bus while her freshman sister was getting a ride with a senior. She was convinced Syd was just trying to stick it to her by driving me. But the truth is, he didn't seem all that upset about the breakup. He was never that into Lauren to begin with."

"Did you wonder about him?"

"The thought never crossed my mind," Paige says. "I was too busy falling in love with him. We were spending so much time together after school. My friends were jealous; they thought Syd and I were dating, and I let them believe it. I wanted it to be true. But it got to the point where I couldn't take it anymore."

"Is that when you kissed him?"

"Oh yeah," Paige says with exaggerated humility. "He saw me coming a mile away. I wasn't suave about it either. He basically just stuck out his arm and held me at a distance. He said I was like a sister to him. He drove me home from school the next day like nothing had happened. He would've kept driving me, too, if Lauren didn't tell my parents. They didn't like the idea that I was spending so much time alone with a senior. It didn't change anything, though. He still gave me a lift. He'd drop me off down the street from my house, and we still talked on the phone."

She pauses, bites the inside of her mouth. With her feet scrunched up on the chair, her whole body contracted, I have no problem picturing her as the fifteen-year-old girl with the older-boy crush.

"I went to his graduation. I have a picture somewhere. That summer I'd go swimming at the rec center where he was a lifeguard. I'd pretend to be drowning but he'd never save me. Then it was time for him to leave for Michigan. He said he'd call me and he did at first, but we lost touch. When we got close again, after college, he was dating Samantha. He was thinking about marrying her. I was so negative about it. I couldn't control myself. Of course, then he broke it off and told me why."

The crickets take over. Maybe it's just one city cricket. His chirp is so insistent, I barely catch Paige's next words.

128

"He was the best."

I stay quiet.

"I don't get it. He was forty-two, in perfect health."

She wants to know why. I've asked the same thing of the doctor, of Google, of myself. I received only theories, possible causes and effects. That's not what Paige is looking for, but it's all I have. "They say it was probably an arrhythmia that went undetected."

The same image flashes: his bare feet on the rug. I'd had a late night of shooting. If it had been another day, I might've woken up with him. On that morning, I didn't rise until after nine. By then it had been hours. They say it was quick. Still, I picture him lying there, all alone.

I place my open palm on the glass tabletop. She wipes her eye before taking my hand.

"I'm sorry," Paige says, her wet cheek shimmering in the low light. She sucks in through her nose, puts a period on her sorrow.

When it first happened, I couldn't stop crying. My food tasted like tears. Now, I couldn't cry if I tried. It's not a positive development, just a different kind of problem.

"Let's talk about something else," Paige says with perfect timing. "I'm trying to plan a family vacation."

"That'll be good. Where to?"

"Right now I'm thinking Costa Rica."

Another reminder. I have the pictures on my laptop: us in the hot springs, taking surfing lessons, at a coffee farm, on a remote beach. "We loved it there," I say.

"That's right. I forgot you guys went. I'm sorry I mentioned it."

"It's fine. Believe me, there's not much we can talk about that doesn't lead back to him."

"I just really want to make this vacation count," Paige says. "It's like, do we go somewhere with some history? Let Joan experience some culture? Or do we just plant ourselves on a beach somewhere? Personally, all I want is a piña colada and a trashy book. It's been a stressful few years."

"So the studio is really closing?"

She lifts her hair off the back of her neck and holds it in a clump on top of her head, giving her neck a chance to breathe. "We just thought it was time. Ollie's dad hasn't been the same since his wife died, and Ollie thought it was time to step in and help him. Obviously, if the studio were doing well, it would be a different story. But we can't keep going like this. Now Ollie can get a steady paycheck and we can rent out the space. We won't have to worry all the time."

Ollie has been pursuing music for as long as I've known him. He's outlasted so many others who showed early promise but quit when life took over or their passion ran out. Earlier tonight he wolfed down his dinner and slipped downstairs to record. Paige warned me that I might find him asleep on the studio couch. "How's he taking it?"

"He tries not to show it, but I know it's hard. At the same time, he's tired of putting so much of himself into these songs in the hope that somewhere down the line someone might pay him to use them. It's heartbreaking. You do all this work and nothing comes of it."

I get it. Until I landed *The Long Arm,* I was constantly going out on auditions, putting my heart into roles I ultimately didn't win. Still, as much as I've threatened to quit acting in the past, I can't imagine trading in the creative life for something like a construction gig or whatever it is Ollie's father has him doing. I haven't had a chance to ask him about the specifics. I just know that whenever I meet ex-artists, they always look half alive.

"As long as he's good with it," I say.

"Honestly, it's been tough, but I think he's also excited to have a fresh start and some peace of mind. We're all excited."

I'm not sure I believe that. "What about Joan? She seemed pretty edgy before dinner."

Paige sighs. "She blames me. But the truth is, I'm the only reason the studio has lasted this long. I don't mind having to work through the summer tutoring if I can put the money toward something like a vacation or fixing the house, you know. But to keep putting it back into a business that's just not working — I can't do it anymore."

Judging by how much she feels the need to explain, it seems she's harboring a certain amount of guilt. I wonder if Ollie knows everything she just told me.

"By the way," Paige says, "thanks for helping Joan with her song. She normally relies on her father for that stuff. We really appreciate you doing that."

"No problem. It's been sort of fun. I haven't worked on music in so long."

I stare off into the night. From here, Manhattan's soaring towers look quaint and manageable. My mind returns, as always, to him. "Can I ask you something? I was talking to Joan and she said Sydney last came here in January."

"That sounds right. Why?"

"He was supposedly back in New York in February and April. Did you see him then?"

She searches her mind. "No. I didn't even know he was in town."

"That's what's strange. I'm not sure he was." Just saying this stuff out loud makes it more real. "The reason he kept coming back was that he was working on some project. That's what he told me. He had so many things going on at once, I can't even remember what the project was. But the weird part is, I spoke to his assistant and she said Syd didn't take any business trips to New York this year. As far as she knows, there was no project."

Her forehead wrinkles with more than her usual concern.

"And there's something else," I say. "I specifically remember him telling me that he saw you in April and he took you out for your birthday."

Paige has always had the entire world's worry in her eyes. But when faced with a tangible problem, she, more than anyone, can be relied on to provide a level-headed solution. "No," she says. "That never happened. Ollie was supposed to take me out for my birthday, but we had to cancel. I got sick."

That's what Joan said. I was hoping these many discrepancies could be explained away as nothing more than an innocent misunderstanding, but that seems like wishful thinking at this point.

"When he was here in January, did he mention anything about work?" I say. "Do you remember what you guys talked about?"

"I'm not sure," Paige says, still processing it all. "I know he wanted to look at some property while he was here. I don't know if he did."

That's not surprising; we often spoke about moving back east. But what I can't fathom is the blatant deceit. It just seems unthinkable that my gray-haired man lied straight to my face.

I stare off. The city glows in the distance.

"What are you thinking?" she says.

"Nothing," I say, because I don't want to have to explain what I'm feeling. I can't prove it yet, but I know it in my heart: He's out there, Sydney, some leftover impression of him. And I really have no choice anymore. I have to give chase.

13

I'm lying on my bed in the middle of the day, using the Gibson as a pillow instead of an instrument and hugging my journal instead of writing in it.

Gavin told me to make my song more about me and my memories, so that's what I've been trying to do, but it's the hardest thing. I'll be thinking about one sad memory, like the day Pepper went to sleep in 2009, and I'll be back there in the lobby at the veterinarian's office while Mom and Dad are in the room with Pepper and the lady at the desk gives me a lollipop. And just seeing that lollipop sends me to another memory of being at camp in 2011 when I lose my lollipop and I find it stuck in Harper's hair. And that memory makes me smile and I come back to today and I realize that the contest deadline keeps getting closer but I still don't have a song that can spread around the world and be a reminder for everyone.

But I can't quit because Dad always tells me that he knew I'd be a musician when I was just a baby. He would play me songs on his guitar and I'd sit in my jumper and stare at him. I'd reach for the strings and he'd make different chords and let me strum. Dad says he realized back then that I had the music bug in me, the same bug he had and his mother had. I was too young to remember all this myself but I've heard him talk about it so many times, it's almost like one of my own memories.

But Dad can't help me now and I'm not getting anywhere on my own. I take my journal and grab the Gibson and walk past the kitchen, where Mom is busy teaching a boy, and I go down to the studio. Gavin's door is open so I walk right in and turn on the light. His naked arm is hanging off the bed.

"Sorry," I say. "I didn't know you were sleeping."

He sits up in bed and gives his blackbird hand signal and then he falls back down like he just used up all his energy.

There's a box of photos on the floor and on the top there's a girl I know looking up at me. "Is that my mom?"

He rolls over and sticks his face off the

bed and tries to see the photo. "Yes."

In the photo, Mom's hair is cut straight across and she's sitting next to a guy with yellow hair. "Is that Sydney?"

Gavin groans, which means I guessed right. I look at the younger Sydney and the younger Mom and I try to imagine what they were saying to each other when the picture was taken. But I'll never know and that's frustrating.

"Dad has pictures of Grandma Joan from when she was really young," I say. "I like looking at them but they also make me mad, because I wish I'd known her back then."

His eyes are squeezed thin, like he wants to see me, but the light is bothering him.

"She was one of my favorite people," I say.

He nods and looks down at the photo. I enjoy telling Gavin about my memories of Sydney, but I don't want to get into that right now because we have a lot of work to do on our song. "I've been waiting for a good idea to come, but nothing's happening. I need your help."

Gavin lifts himself up onto his elbow and looks at his phone. He nods like he agrees with what the phone is saying and then he tosses it onto the mattress. "I can't today. I have to take care of something."

He gets out of bed, as slow as an old man, and then he grabs the empty glass from the dresser and leaves.

Now I'm all alone in his bedroom. I kick a dirty sock into a pile of clothes in the corner. On the nightstand there's a cereal bowl, wallet, phone charger, and a few books from Dad's bookshelf, including *Songwriters on Songwriting*, which is a book full of famous rock stars talking about how they wrote their best songs. John Lennon isn't in the book. That's what gave me the idea to write my very own John Lennon's Ten Rules of Songwriting.

I grab Gavin's wallet and open it. On his driver's license, his last name is Deifendorf, not Winters, and his birthday is March 17, 1975. He's five foot eleven, which is the exact same height as John Lennon.

"There's not much cash in there," Gavin says. He's back and holding a full glass of water.

I toss the wallet onto the nightstand. "I was just looking. I don't know why."

He doesn't seem to care and now I'm focused on his stomach, which looks like a waffle maker but with bigger squares. I'm noticing he doesn't have any tattoos or hair like Dad has.

<u>Bodies</u>

Gavin

Dad

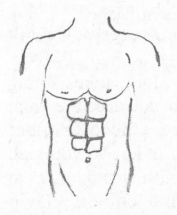

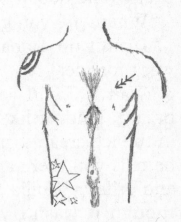

And now I'm focusing on his face again and it looks like he might be sick. "Are you okay?"

"I'll let you ask me anything as long as it's not that." He takes a long drink of water and when he's finished he makes a sound like he was very thirsty and the water was very good. "Sorry, I just don't like that question." He looks into his glass but there's no water left. "Have you tried a change of scenery?"

"I don't think so. What's that?"

"Go outside. Take a walk. Do anything but focus on your song."

That probably won't work because I have a really hard time getting my brain to think about what I tell it to think about. I guess I'm going to have to lose a whole day because Gavin is too busy to help me. I walk over to the door.

"Where are you going?" he says.

"I can't do a change of scenery. It won't work for me."

"Wait," Gavin says, and he takes a big breath, kind of like when you ask the man in the ice cream truck for a Choco Taco but he tells you there aren't any left so you sigh and order a vanilla cone with sprinkles, even though it wasn't your first choice. Gavin picks up one of Dad's books; I don't know which one. "Have you ever been to Café La Fortuna?"

"No," I say. "What's that?"

I open my drawers and pull out my clothes with the best memories: Sparkly shorts from when I won a stuffed animal on the board-walk (Thursday, August 2, 2012); fox socks from when Grandpa took me fishing and I caught a flounder and I threw the flounder back and promised never to go fishing again (Sunday, June 5, 2011); white button-down shirt from when the audience clapped for me at my piano recital (Friday, April 19,

2013). I'm being extra-picky because New York City is a special place where they have important events like basketball games, concerts, meetings, and award ceremonies for contests.

Mom hands Gavin some money, but he gives it back, and then I grab my journal and we're finally gone. We walk down the big hill near our house and through the town of Hoboken and each time we cross the street, Gavin holds my hand. His fingers are smooth like wet soap, not like Dad's fingers, which have calluses from playing drums and guitar.

We reach the train station and I want to tell Gavin that I was here once before with Sydney on Friday, May 21, 2010, but I don't say it right now because I don't want to slow us down. We walk down the steps and now we're underground. Gavin slides a card into a slot and we go through the gate and walk onto the train. I copy everything he does.

We come back up the stairs and now we're in the Big Apple, which is a name that's too strange to think about. There's so much to see, like a lady holding her phone far away and yelling into it and a man wearing a Beatles shirt who doesn't see that I'm holding up my hand for a high five and also a man who hands me a paper that says *20% Off All Apparel.* I don't know exactly what *apparel* is, but it seems like a good deal. Too bad we're not here to shop. I'm not sure why we're here, actually. We're on a Magical Mystery Tour.

Gavin looks down at me now with his sunglasses and his fuzzy cheeks, which are starting to look like Dad's. "Do you know how to call a cab?" he asks.

We stand at the corner and he lets me do the waving, but the taxis zoom by like yellow submarines.

"Try this." He lifts me onto his shoulders and we step into the street. I wave my hand until a taxi finally stops in front of us.

July 16, 2013. I called my first taxi.

The taxi lets us out at Seventy-First Street and now we're standing on the sidewalk and Gavin is checking his phone. We head over to a little store with a sign that says HARD-WARE and Gavin takes me inside. We go down a very crowded aisle to the back of the small store and then turn around and walk back outside.

"What are we doing here?" I say.

"We're soaking it in," Gavin says.

"We just walked in that store and walked

right back out."

"Yes, we did."

Now we're walking down Columbus Avenue and Gavin is looking at his phone again and we stop in front of a store called West Side Pharmacy. We go inside and Gavin heads to the counter, which is what you do when you want to pay for your item, but Gavin isn't holding any items.

"See anyone you know?" Gavin says.

I look at the man behind the counter who's busy helping another customer. He has glasses and a few pieces of hair and I know that I've never seen this man before in my life. But then I see another face behind the man's head and this face I know well because it's John Lennon's face. It's on a photograph that's hanging on the wall. The whole wall is covered in photographs and I know a few of these other faces too because they're famous and in some of the photographs I see the man behind the counter with his arm around the famous people.

"Can I help you?" the man behind the counter asks, and he says it like English is something he's still learning even though he's an old man.

"You like John Lennon?" I say.

He smiles and turns to the photo on the

143

wall. "The best."

"He's my favorite and he's also my dad's favorite."

"This was his pharmacy," the man says. "We were friends."

"No way. You're lying."

"I tell the truth."

"So you're saying John Lennon was in this store?"

He points to the floor right below me. "He stood in your same spot."

I look down. It's like I stepped inside one of John's memories, and now I'm afraid to move even an inch.

We turn off the busy road onto a quiet street with a few city trees, which are trees that grow out of little wooden boxes on the sidewalk instead of grass. They're nicer than the city trees we have in Jersey City because they don't have empty plastic shopping bags stuck in their branches.

I'm having a hard time believing that I just put my feet where John Lennon put his feet and I also met someone who knew John and his family. I ask Gavin, "How did you know that John went to that store?"

"I read about it in one of your dad's books. And you know that hardware store we went into before that? That used to be

Café La Fortuna. That's where John would hang out and drink coffee. He might've even written a few lyrics in there."

"That's so cool." It's like we're going through a John Lennon museum but the museum is the whole city and there are no signs on the walls telling you why each spot is important. I can't wait to tell Dad about this, but I'm also feeling pretty confused. "How is this supposed to help me with my song?"

Gavin walks with just the tips of his fingers sticking into the tight pockets of his shredded shorts. I want Mom to cut up my jeans the same way.

"Whenever I'm working on something," Gavin says, "I always do a lot of research. When I got the part of Beau Kendricks on *The Long Arm,* Syd and I flew down to Louisiana. That's where Beau is supposed to be from. I spent two days just walking around. Trying to see how he lived."

"Is that what we're doing? Research?"

"Sort of. I just thought it might help you to get out of your own head for a while. John Lennon didn't just sit at home and write songs all day and night. He lived his life. He walked around. Drank coffee. Shopped at the pharmacy."

"He kept making new memories."

145

"Exactly."

I think about that for a minute. "That's why you came to stay with us, right?"

He looks confused.

"To get out of your own head. That's what Mom said."

"Oh," Gavin says. "Yeah."

We keep walking and I watch my feet on the sidewalk and I think about how nice this memory will feel when I remember it later. But I notice that Gavin's feet are missing. They were right next to my feet a second ago and now they're gone. I stop and turn around and walk back to where Gavin is standing. He nods across the street at a building as big and pointy as a castle. "That's where John lived," he says.

The Dakota.

I remember when Dad first took me to Strawberry Fields in Central Park and he showed me the plaque that says IMAGINE. The plaque was covered with flowers and some of the flowers were forget-me-nots, which are my favorite kind, obviously. Dad asked if I wanted to walk over to the building where John and his family lived and I said yes, but then he told me the name of the building, the Dakota, and I changed my mind because I know all about the Dakota

— it's where the worst thing happened to John.

Gavin takes my hand so we can cross the street, but I pull back. "I don't want to."

He looks at the Dakota and then at me. The whole place makes me itchy, like when you walk through a spider web and you tear it off your body, but it still feels like it's all over your skin.

"Okay," Gavin says, turning me in a new direction. "Let's go visit Strawberry Fields instead."

I stand on the corner and look across a different street where the city just disappears all of a sudden. I know this place too. This is Central Park. I don't want to hurt Gavin's feelings because he's being so nice, but I don't want to go to Central Park either. "That's one of my dad's memories. I don't want to go there without him."

Gavin does a rock-star look for a few seconds, which is when your eyes stare at nothing and it seems like you're thinking about something important. It's the best rock-star look I've ever seen anyone do in person.

"I get that," he says. "Sydney would be jealous when I went to this one coffee shop without him. It's called Proof Bakery and they have the best croissants in L.A. Crispy on the outside and fluffy on the inside. We spent a lot of Saturday mornings there together."

"I wish he were here with us," I say, still thinking about Dad.

"Yeah," Gavin says.

Now it seems like we're both in a quiet mood and I didn't mean for that to happen. It's just hard to think about music stuff and not think about Dad. I really hope he likes my song.

"He will," Gavin says and that's when I realize I was just talking out loud. I'm not sure which parts Gavin heard but the dimple on his cheek is making me feel like whatever I said was the right thing to say.

Now we're facing a whole different direction and we're looking down a busy street with cars going both ways, but before we take just one step, someone stops us.

"Excuse me," says a lady with red sunglasses. She's standing with another lady who's holding what looks like a map, which is something we have hanging in our classroom but you hardly ever see anywhere else because everyone has maps on their phones.

I'm thinking the two ladies are lost, but then they ask a question that has nothing to do with directions. It's a question that makes me excited and jealous at the same time.

The lady lowers her sunglasses so she can see better and she says, "Are you Gavin Winters?"

We find an empty booth in the pizza restaurant and I ask, "Is this where John ate?"

"We're off the tour," Gavin says. "We're taking a lunch break."

"But I don't eat pizza."

"I know. Your mother told me. She also said you never tried it. I'll be right back."

I call after him, "Wait!" But he's already talking to the guy with the gigantic wooden paddle.

The two ladies who stopped us on the street both wanted to be in the picture with Gavin so I was the one who took it with the first lady's phone. Gavin stood with his arms around both of them and their shoulders fit right under his armpits. I looked at the photo before I handed the phone back and it was so easy to tell which one of the three people was famous. I hope one day I can stand out like that in a photo and I hope ladies will know my name and stop me when I'm walking down the street. I will be very nice to them, just like Gavin was.

He comes back carrying a tray. I see three

slices of pizza and two drinks.

"What's happening?" I say.

"If you're ever going to try pizza, you're in the right city." Gavin takes off his sunglasses and puts them on the table. "You ready?"

I look down.

"Just one bite," he says. "Remember, the more you experience, the more you have to write about."

I don't know how biting into this slice of pizza will turn me into John Lennon, but I don't want to let Gavin down. I lift the slice with two hands and bring it to my mouth. Gavin is watching me so I take the smallest bite and it's not as bad as I thought, but still not good. I hate cheese and it's so saucy. I shake my head.

"Hey, you tried," Gavin says. "That's all that matters. I'm proud of you. We'll stop somewhere else after this and get you something to eat."

"That's okay. I'm not even hungry," I say, washing out the cheesy feeling with water. I look across the table and it seems like Gavin wants to kiss his pizza slice.

"You're missing out," Gavin says, taking a huge chomp. "God, it's been so long since I've had real pizza. We don't have this in L.A."

"You don't have pizza in L.A.?"

"We do. But it's nothing like this. You've got this amazing city right in your backyard. You've got to take advantage of it. You can't even hail a cab in L.A."

He stops talking so he can do more pizza eating. He's humming as he finishes his first slice and he wipes his face with a napkin. "Is that related to the memory thing?" Gavin says. "You staying away from certain foods?"

I swish more water around my mouth. "With some foods, yeah. Like bananas, which I tried for the first time when I had a bad stomachache and now I never want to taste them again. But with other foods, they just have a look or smell that I don't like."

"I think I was pretty picky as a kid too."

"You don't remember?"

Gavin chews. "My whole childhood is a blur. Only the really big things stand out."

"What are the really big things?"

He looks down at the paper place mat, which shows a map of Italy. "My dad was gone by the time I was ten, about the same age as you. That was a huge one. My sister was just a baby. She never really had a dad, only a mom. And me." He stops for a second like he isn't sure whether to take another bite of pizza or keep talking.

I've been pretty bummed about Dad having to leave the house every morning and only getting to see him at night and on the weekends, but I guess it's better than what Gavin and his sister had. "Where did your dad go?"

"Sorry. I didn't explain that well. He didn't go anywhere. He got into an accident. A truck slammed into his car and . . ."

"Oh no," I say, and when I say it, I think about how it would be the perfect thing to put in my song to make Gavin cry, but I feel bad for thinking it. I should probably change the subject, which is something you do when something isn't fun to talk about.

"Anyway," I say, which is a good subject-changing word, "what's it like to be famous?"

He laughs but it doesn't sound like a real laugh. "I wouldn't say I'm famous."

"I would. You're on TV and you're on the news and people want to take pictures with you."

"That's just because I made an ass of myself."

"You mean when you started that fire and you were on TV in your underwear?"

He leaves his crust on the plate. "Yeah, that's what I mean." He tries to grab a napkin from the holder but instead of just one, a thick clump comes out, so he gives up and drops the whole wad on the table.

I pull a napkin out for him.

"Thanks." He takes it and folds it into a triangle. "From what I can tell, being famous is pretty shitty. Sorry — crappy."

"I'm allowed to say *shit.*"

"It would be one thing if I was getting attention for the work I've done. Who doesn't like that? But I'd rather not be known as the underwear-fire-starter guy."

"I didn't even know you were on a TV show until I saw you on the news, because it's a grown-up show and it's on past my bedtime. It was cool to see your name written out on the bottom of the screen. That's the first time I saw it."

He points to my plate. "You going to eat that?"

I slide my plate over.

"So, what you're saying is, I shouldn't care so much how people discover my work? I should just be grateful that they discover it at all?" he asks.

I'm not sure that's what I was saying but I nod anyway.

"You sound like my agent," Gavin says.

"Thank you," I say, because Gavin's agent must be smart or else Gavin wouldn't be working with him or her. "Do you get nervous when you're on TV and everyone's looking at you?"

"Yeah. But it's a good kind of nervous."

"I don't think I've ever had the good kind of nervous."

"Really? I live off that feeling."

I'd like to know what the good kind of nervous feels like because I've only ever felt the bad kind. "Thanks for taking me on this trip. I can't wait to go home and see if I can make the song better now."

"I meant to tell you. I've had your chorus stuck in my head ever since you played it for me."

I clap my hands together just one time. "That's amazing! That means it's in your system!"

"The thing is, I couldn't remember any of the lyrics."

I'm learning that when Gavin says something nice, there's always something else that comes after it, so I think from now on, I need to listen to only the first thing he says and then quickly run out of the room.

"I knew the word *memory* was in there," Gavin says, "but I didn't know how. You need something else to make it stick. Like Jay-Z's song 'Ninety-Nine Problems.' He doesn't have a *bunch* of problems. He's got ninety-nine of them. That's what makes it memorable."

Memorable is a tough word to understand. Everything feels memorable to me. How am I supposed to know what's memorable to everyone else? I want to lay my head on the table because I'm feeling very tired, but the tabletop is too sticky. "Where are we going next?"

I think I did it again, said the wrong thing, because Gavin makes his mouth very tight and he drops my half-eaten slice on his plate and tosses his dirty napkin on top. "There's one more stop I've got to make."

14

We wait for the broker on Thompson Street. Her name is Claire. After talking to Paige last night, I sent an e-mail to Syd's real estate agent in L.A., who wrote me back this morning and directed me to Claire in the New York office.

"Are you nervous?" Joan asks.

"No. Why?"

"Your foot is tapping really fast."

I look. Joan's right. I take a deep breath to compose myself. Perfectly timed, because here she comes, her high heels clacking down the sidewalk. She extends her hand well before actually reaching us.

"Claire," she says.

"Gavin."

"Pleasure." She gestures to Joan. "And who is this?"

"I'm Joan Lennon."

"Nice to meet you, Joan." Claire looks back to me for further explanation, but I don't offer any, just a broad smile.

We follow her inside. When we spoke on the phone earlier today, Claire confirmed that she did indeed show Syd a property in Manhattan. Not this exact property — the one they saw has since sold — but one just like it and in the same neighborhood. Also, it wasn't in January, like Paige had suggested, but in February. This is the first piece of proof I've obtained that Sydney really did travel to New York a second time this year.

Claire points out the doorman, mentions a gym. She keeps pitching, but again I'm missing words, too distracted by the possible revelations ahead. We reach an elevator and go up.

"How is he?" Claire asks, our three bodies pressed tight.

"Who?"

"Mr. Brennett."

I didn't get into it on the phone, didn't see the point. I simply asked Claire if she could show me more of what she showed Sydney. Now we're face to face, inches apart, and I've got a little girl peering up at me, waiting for my answer.

I grab Joan's hand and squeeze gently. "He's great."

Claire smiles.

The elevator lets us out and Claire guides us to a corner apartment. She's giving us the whole rap: square footage, river views, bedrooms, bathrooms, amenities, finishes. But Claire is wasting her breath. I'm not buying anything.

She leads us to the first of two bedrooms, then, after an apology, excuses herself to take a phone call. Joan has to use the bathroom so I send her into the en suite.

Alone now in the master bedroom, I take a seat on the queen bed. We have a queen at home. I wanted to upgrade to a king, but Syd wouldn't do it. He joked that we'd never see each other again.

It takes a lot of searching and luck to find a partner worthy of your bed. Sleep is so precious, and a partner cuts your space in half. They hog your blanket; they snore. But then you fall in love and you gladly invite one in. Over time your sleep patterns are no longer your own. The two of you form a joint routine. Years pass, and you barely remember the value you once placed in having a solitary bed. Until one day your partner travels for business and the bed is all yours again. You stretch out in every direction. When your pillow gets stale, you swap it out for the cold one. You sleep deeply that night. But then the second night arrives and it's harder to find peace. The balance of the bed is off. You can't achieve the right temperature in the room. Nothing you do fixes the problem. It's a bed for two, not one. Your partner returns. You're not so much relieved as stabilized. Things are back to normal. You tell him to roll over, he's snoring. A part of you wishes you were alone again. Until the day comes when your partner never returns. You realize how wrong you were for not always cherishing your shared bed. You forgot the earliest lesson of love: a little discomfort is a small price to pay.

Joan exits the bathroom. She notices we're alone and takes advantage of it. "Why did you lie about Sydney?"

I tell her the truth. "Sometimes it's easier to lie."

I'm not sure it's the right lesson to teach her, but what can I say? I'm doing my best to navigate an awkward situation. Besides, it was just a fib. I'm here to uncover the real lies.

I look around the room, searching for potential clues. Syd was never in this exact room, but he was somewhere not too far from here, perusing a similar space. What was he looking for? If it was intended for both of us, why didn't he let me know?

"I'm sorry about that," Claire says, return-ing.

I stand up from the bed.

"So, this is the master bedroom." She keeps her phone in her hand, pointing with a closed fist. "As you can see, the size is quite generous. You get gorgeous light through the window here. The closet is definitely roomy by city standards. And, of course, the en suite bath."

"It's very nice," Joan says.

Claire smiles and turns to me. "Any ques-tions?"

"Not at the moment."

Claire pushes on with the tour, leads us into a modest second bedroom. "This could work for an office or maybe a child's room. I know Mr. Brennett was envisioning a place suitable for a family."

She checks my face, waiting for confirma-tion. The charade is getting harder to pull off. I know I'm supposed to be an actor, but real-life performing is different. "Let me ask you, Claire. When you met with him, did he happen to mention *why* he was in town? Where he was coming from? Where he was off to next? Anything like that?"

"I don't think so," she says, flustered. Clearly these weren't the types of questions she'd been anticipating. She refers to her phone, hoping to find the answers in the client profile she created. When that doesn't work, she offers one resolute shake of her head.

I look over at Joan, who seems equally annoyed. No one is able to offer the level of detail she can. If only I could take her with me everywhere, I'd always have a complete vision of life instead of one riddled with holes.

Claire walks us through the kitchen and back to where the tour started. She's still talking up the apartment, but we're done listening. Joan looks bored out of her mind and I can't keep my performance going for one more second.

"Thanks so much," I say. "I'll let you know."

"Please do," Claire says. "And again, this apartment is a pretty close comp to what I previously showed Mr. Brennett. I'm not sure what you thought of that one. Sometimes the pictures don't do it justice. And honestly, I saw the pictures his photographer took and they weren't nearly as good as the ones my guy shot."

I'm not sure I heard her right. "What photographer?"

"The one he brought with him."

I glance at Joan, who looks just as confused as I am, but for different reasons. "Do you remember his name?"

"No, I'm afraid I don't," Claire says, retrieving the apartment keys from her purse. "And actually, if I'm remembering correctly, I believe it was a her."

High above us, the glass top of a building blends with the blue summer sky. Lower, a dozen trees sway in elegant harmony. Surrounding voices join in a soothing white noise. For a moment, I can almost be fooled into thinking the world is at peace.

"So, are you going to buy that place?" Joan asks. She's lying in the Washington Square Park grass, chewing on the soft pretzel I bought her from a street cart.

"No," I say, seated behind her along the concrete perimeter.

"Then why were we looking at that apartment?"

I have to question whether I should be sharing so much of my life with this ten-year-old girl. I keep forgetting that she's just a child, maybe because her parents seem content not to treat her like one. Maybe the fact that she is a child is what makes her so easy to talk to. Unlike an adult, she's eager to listen and not eager to judge.

"Syd and I had talked about moving out here," I say. "He thought if we were going to start a family, our child should have a relationship with its grandmothers."

The problem was I finally had a steady gig in Los Angeles and wasn't ready to move back east. Nor was I quite ready to be a father, even though I went along with the plan and participated in the process. Unlike Syd, I was relieved that we'd faced some setbacks on our journey to become parents. Actually, it was my own foot-dragging that caused part of the delay. And yet it would appear Syd couldn't stop himself from preparing for the day when at last we could start our family.

I'm not sure what to make of the news that he wasn't alone while he was looking at properties. I wouldn't know where to start in trying to figure out who the photographer was. Syd had a massive network of creative types to call on: filmmakers, composers, designers.

"You're being very quiet," Joan says.

"I'm sorry."

"Come sit on the grass."

I join her on the lawn. The bristly blades tickle my bare legs. She breaks me off a piece of pretzel but my stomach is already at capacity with all the carbs I just consumed.

"Why don't you tell me one of *your* Sydney memories?" Joan says.

And I was just getting comfortable. "Really? Right now?"

"Yeah. What's your best memory? Your absolute favorite one."

I think about it. And think some more.

"I don't know," I say. "I guess it would be just a regular night, him and me lying in bed, watching bad TV or something. I know it doesn't sound like much, but honestly, I can't think of many things I'd rather do right now."

She's not satisfied. "But what about one night that sticks out from all the rest?"

She's right. I should have an answer. I should have a hundred answers. The question should be difficult because I have too many great nights to choose from, not because I can't come up with a single one. All my memories of Sydney have been sucked into one swirling blur in my mind.

The disappointment on Joan's face is nothing compared to what I feel inside. "Sorry. I'll have to get back to you on this."

"Think about it."

"I will," I say, but I don't know if it's true. I'm not sure I can take any more thinking.

I'm still trying to figure out some way not to have to think at all. At least, not to have to think of him.

15

I don't see Gavin at all the next day. He never comes upstairs, not even for a snack, and when I go downstairs to check on him, his door is shut and there's no light glowing underneath. No matter how loudly I strum my guitar, he never opens his door.

Mom comes downstairs at one point and at first I think she's going to tell me to stop bothering Gavin but instead she asks me how the song is coming. I say, "Fine," and she says, "Can I hear it?" and I say, "No," because it's not ready.

And then Dad comes home for dinner and he also asks about my song and I tell him it's going great, even though it isn't. I still haven't written a song that will hit Dad deep and make him want to raise the volume to Spinal Tap 11 and make me always fresh in his mind.

That was yesterday. Now this morning I hear a knock and Gavin is standing in my doorway and he's doing his hand signal. His blackbird wings seem flappier today.

He walks into my room and pets my American Girl doll on the head (I don't play with her anymore but Dorothy is still a member of our family). He looks into my open closet and sees how I line up my Converse from heel to toe, but he probably doesn't realize I also line them up in the order I first got them:

| Tuesday | Sunday | Saturday | Saturday | Friday | Sunday |
| 8/30/11 | 12/25/11 | 2/25/12 | 7/14/12 | 11/23/12 | 3/31/13 |

Gavin sits down on my carpet between my bed and the wall. He looks too big to fit in that spot but there isn't anywhere else to sit in my room except on the bed with me. He reaches into my crate full of stuffed animals and pulls out Wally, my oldest walrus.

"I've had him since I was a baby," I say. "I can remember when Dad brought him home, but I don't know the exact date."

Gavin rubs his thumb on Wally's coat, which has gotten very rough over the years.

"Did you know there's a real live walrus on the loose?" I say. "He escaped from Sea-

World in Florida and I've been following him online. I wish I could meet him in the ocean and swim with him."

"That might be dangerous," Gavin says.

"But it would also be fun. I like to imagine things like that, swimming with a walrus or maybe —"

"Finding a unicorn?"

That's not what I was going to say, but I smile anyway because it's a good answer and it shows me that he was paying attention when I told him my memories of Sydney. Gavin looks down at Wally again and then he puts him back into the crate.

I have to ask. "Where were you yesterday?"

"Sleeping, mostly. Trying to." He scratches his fuzzy cheeks. "To be honest, I wasn't sure if I wanted to hear any more about Sydney. I wasn't sure if it was doing me any good. I'm still not sure."

I'm afraid of what might be happening right now. "Are you quitting?"

"No," Gavin says, his voice changing to something higher. "No, I'm not quitting. I still want to help you with your song."

I take a deep breath.

"And I still want to know whatever you can tell me about Sydney." Now Gavin is the one taking the deep breath. "For better or worse, I have to know." He leans back against the wall. "I think we were up to 2010."

He's right, so that's where I start.

"May twenty-first is a Friday," I say, making myself comfortable on the bed. "After school Mom drops me off at a guitar lesson that's supposed to be free this one time. If you come back another time you have to pay, but Mom never takes me back another time because my teacher isn't as good as Dad. After my lesson Mom picks me up and Sydney is with her and they have coffee cups in their hands that say *modcup* on the front. We start walking down Palisade Avenue. Sydney says, 'You've gotten taller, Miss Joan,' and I don't know if that's true or not because I never measure my height and I can't see myself grow. I try to see what's different about him but it looks like maybe he's exactly the same, except for one thing."

"What thing?" Gavin asks.

"He's wearing a new bracelet. The same bracelet that's on your wrist now."

Gavin touches the bracelet to make sure it's still there. "We both had them and then Syd lost his."

I'm ready to tell him more about the memory from 2010 but he isn't finished talking.

"We took a trip to Mexico. After dinner one night we were walking and we stopped at a street vendor. This woman was selling these leather bracelets with little animal shapes carved into them. They were really ugly. I made a joke that we should wear them to keep other people away. Syd never wore jewelry. He hated the feeling of having any extra weight on him. He wouldn't even keep his phone in his pocket. But he said he'd wear the bracelet for me. One bracelet had a fox and the other one had an eagle."

With his head leaning back against the wall and his eyes closed, Gavin looks like he might be sleeping, but his mouth is moving just enough to let the words out.

"The woman who sold us the bracelets had a story. She said the eagle was a golden eagle and that it was strong enough to drag a goat off a cliff. She gave me the golden eagle and she handed Syd the fox. She told him to be careful around me."

"And then the fox disappeared?"

"Yes."

"That's spooky," I say. "What happened to it?"

"He must've left it somewhere, I don't know. He'd always take it off. I was bummed when he lost it, not because I cared about the bracelet, just because I liked the idea of him having to wear it. It made him a little less perfect, less in control."

"So how did he end up with your bracelet?"

"He joked that he was going to hire a detective to go down to Mexico and find the lady who sold us the bracelets and buy a new one. But instead, he took the eagle bracelet from me and swore he'd never take it off. He wore it in the shower, to the gym; he slept with it. It started to have this funky smell. I told him he was off the hook, he'd passed the test, but he refused to take it off. And the thing is, he really hated this bracelet. I mean, he loathed it. When people asked him about it — and they did — he'd tell them how much he despised it. He'd play it up, how hideous it was, how much it pained him to have to endure it. He did that so they would know, and I would know."

"Know what?"

He swallows hard. "How much he loved me." His lips tighten and his head shakes back and forth. "To think I almost tossed it in the fire."

I understand why he'd want to throw the eagle bracelet into the fire because that bracelet is one hundred percent bad luck and also it's confusing to have an eagle on his wrist when he's supposed to be a blackbird. But the rest of it I don't understand. "Why did you want to burn Sydney's things?"

"Because it's too painful to remember."

I know this so well and it makes me feel so close to him, like maybe we're more than just songwriting partners, like we're on the same team in some other way. But I still don't understand. "Then why are you here now? Why are you talking to me?"

"Because it's even more painful to forget."

I never heard anyone say that before. I don't really know what it's like to lose a memory, but I guess it's true that I've seen people get pretty upset about it, like when Dad can't remember the name of an old club that one of his bands performed at or when he forgets the name of another kid's dad even though they've talked before at the park. I also saw it with Grandma.

"My grandma Joan started forgetting before she died. There was this sad look on her face all the time. She was always arguing with Dad and Grandpa. It was like she was trying to tell them something but she couldn't think of the right way to say it and she felt like no one could understand her."

Gavin lifts his knees and hugs them. "You think about your grandmother a lot, don't you."

"Yes, every time I see old hands on a piano or the baby blankets with the holes in them or when someone says *rascal*. And whenever I go to Grandpa's house and the front door opens, I still think Grandma Joan is going to be standing there with her arms open, ready to give me a big hug, but it never happens."

Gavin rests his chin on his knee. "I know what you mean. I'm reminded of Sydney everywhere I look. When there's a napkin folded into a rectangle, I always want to refold it into a triangle. That's what he would do. Or when I'm at a restaurant and they have Tabasco sauce at the table. Usually it's the brand that says *Avery Island* on it and Syd used to have a friend named Avery. Every time we saw that bottle of Tabasco sauce, I'd tease him and say, 'Look who's here.' I still say it to myself now."

Gavin shuts his eyes for a few seconds and then lifts his chin off his knee and says, "Should we keep going?"

Friday, May 21, 2010: Sydney says he has to catch a train back to the city but first he takes me out for ice cream. He and Mom don't order anything because they have their coffees and Sydney is asking me about my lesson and I tell him it was boring because I already knew what the man was trying to teach me. Sydney asks how I'm liking my chocolate ice cream and I say it's very good. He wants to know if I can guess his favorite flavor and I say that it's mint chocolate chip. He asks me how I know that and I tell him I took a guess because I remembered from the time he visited in 2008 that his favorite maca-ron *was the mint one and I also remember he was chewing mint gum when he visited in 2009. And then he asks me all types of questions about those other times he visited, like what day I met him in 2008 and what the weather was and what he was wearing and I tell him it was a Monday in October and the weather was chilly and he was wearing a peach shirt and shoes with no laces and he says, "That is amazing. You are amazing."*

And I say, "Thank you."

And he says, "I'm more of a future guy."

And I say, "What's that?"

And he says, "I like to focus on what's going to happen tomorrow. And the next day. I'm interested in where everything is leading. I'd rather just leave the past behind."

I tell the entire memory to Gavin, including the end when Mom and I walk Sydney to the train station. Sydney pretends that my high five broke his hand and Mom hugs him and she kisses him, and when I finish my story Gavin keeps quiet for a long while.

174

"Syd would get frustrated with me about that," he says. "If I didn't get a role, I'd be in a bad mood for days. But if his team didn't win an ad campaign, he'd just move on to the next one." Gavin rubs his eye like he's just waking up from a nap. "Anyway, it's not a bad song lyric."

"What is?"

"Leave the past behind."

"That just came to you?"

He sits up. "Well, Sydney's the one who said it. But *you're* the one who remembered it."

I'm strumming the Gibson and Gavin is walking around my tiny room. He's holding a piece of paper that he ripped out of my journal, which is not something I like to do but Gavin says it's not just about waiting around for an idea to come, it's also about knowing when the idea has finally arrived.

My arm is getting tired of strumming but Gavin wants me to keep going a little while longer. We have different ideas about what *a little while* means because he's been humming and scribbling forever and I guess for him it's like when you're dreaming and you think only a minute has gone by but you actually slept through the whole night.

"Okay," he says at last and his eyes are

bright and colorful like glass on the walls of a church. "What about something like this for the chorus?"

He sings along to my chords:

Keep running but I get nowhere
Keep swinging but I hit thin air
I hear you whisper in the back of my mind:
Start over, leave the past behind

Keep dwelling on what went wrong
Keep reaching for what is gone
I hear you whisper in the back of my mind:
Start over, leave the past behind

He stops singing and I stop playing and I feel ticklish all over. This is it, what we've been waiting for. I see something, the way he's waiting silently, something I haven't seen before but I know it so well because it matches how I feel inside: he wants so badly for me to love his words because *he* loves them.

"It's about Sydney," I say.

He gets a little shy. "It doesn't have to be."

But I don't mind because I can't always think of interesting things to write about and besides, the lyrics were already about Sydney even when I was writing them. I think it's good to write a song about some-one who isn't around anymore, like John Lennon did for his mother in his song "Ju-lia." And I'm missing Sydney too after spending so much time with him in my memories, almost as much time as I've been spending with Gavin, so I think it feels right.

"I guess I got in a flow," Gavin says. "I'm sorry. I know it's your song."

"No. It's *our* song."

I'm not even sure anymore which parts are mine and which parts are Gavin's and that's how it was with John Lennon and Paul McCartney when they wrote together in the Beatles. Dad says you can't tell where one of them ends and the other one begins because they were like one super-person instead of two regular people. Maybe that's why I like the songs they wrote together bet-ter than anything John ever wrote alone.

"You should finish the lyrics," I say, "and I'll take care of the music and it'll be half and half. I'll play the instruments and you sing."

He slides his hand through his hair either because he has great style or because he has a headache, I'm not sure which.

"The words are coming right out of you," I say. "It's magic. You already have the chorus. That's the most important part.

Now just write the verses."

He gives me a long look. "If that's what you want."

But he doesn't mean it like that, I can tell, because I say the same thing to Dad when he and I split up chores and Dad takes vacuuming and I take organizing and I pretend that I don't mind if we switch jobs but really I'm so happy I got organizing because that's something that makes total sense to me. So I'm thinking now that maybe Gavin wants to write this song just as much as I do.

And if people remember the name Joan Lennon because I teamed up with Gavin Winters, then I guess it's the same as someone watching Gavin's show because he started a fire in his backyard. I don't care why they remember me as long as they remember me, because I never want to feel the way I did when Grandma Joan forgot me. I just want to feel safe.

"One more thing," I say. "When we send our song into the contest, my name goes first. Joan and then Gavin. Deal?"

He shakes my hand. "I can live with that."

I open the fridge and look around until something excites me. I open the pickle jar and find the greenest one and I wrap it in a napkin because Mom hates when I drip pickle juice on the floor.

Mom's book is on the kitchen table. It looks like one of her schoolbooks because it has her yellow notes sticking out of the top, but it's something else:

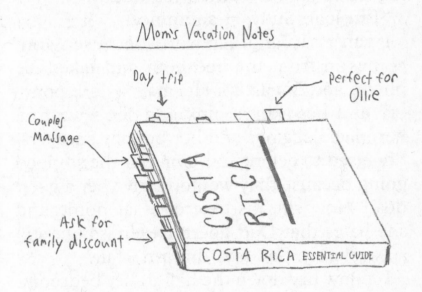

Mom's Vacation Notes

Day trip

Perfect for Ollie

Couples Massage

Ask for family discount →

COSTA RICA

COSTA RICA ESSENTIAL GUIDE

Seeing Dad's name messes up the good mood I was in. Dinner is the only time I see Dad lately, and that makes me want to take Mom's book and slide it through our paper shredder.

The phone starts ringing and I just want to shut it up so I answer it. "Hello?"

"Hello," a man says. "Is this Mrs. Sully?"

I decide to say yes.

"Oh, good afternoon, Mrs. Sully. I'm

sorry to bother you. My name is Robert Brickenmeyer. I'm the head neurologist at the Hollybrook Cognitive Research Center here in Summit. We're one of the area's premier research centers for Alzheimer's. As you might have guessed, I'm calling in regard to your daughter, Joan Sully."

"I'm Joan Sully," I announce.

I can't say another word because Mom comes in from the bedroom and takes the phone and hangs up. Her hair is in a pony-tail and her skin is pink and she's wearing her black leggings and her bouncy sneakers. She used to belong to a gym but she stopped going because they wouldn't give her a good deal. Now she just exercises at home and she hates that Dad doesn't exercise but still stays skinny. She says that isn't fair.

I follow her down the hall to her bedroom. "It was for me."

"I'm sure it was," Mom says.

"Why can't I talk to them?"

The lady on the television is frozen and Mom is about to unfreeze her with the remote but first she needs a few more seconds to catch her breath. She answers me in a quiet voice, which is her favorite move when I get loud. "Do you want to?"

I wasn't expecting that.

"Maybe we *should* set up a meeting,"

Mom says, shrugging. "They might finally stop calling. If it's something you really want to do, I have a whole list of people who are itching to talk to you."

"That man said something about old-timer's disease. That's what Grandma Joan had." I know it's called Alzheimer's but Dad calls it old-timer's instead because he says it helps to make jokes when life gets too sad.

"Yes," Mom says. "That's what your grandmother had."

I wish I had met Dr. M before Grandma Joan started forgetting because maybe he could have figured out how to capture all her memories and put them inside my brain so I could keep them safe.

"Maybe this Dr. Robert guy thinks I can help old people remember," I say. "Wouldn't that be great?"

She takes a long look at me. "Tell you what — write down the man's name and I'll give him a call." Mom pulls her ponytail tighter and gets back to her video. "By the way, I heard you and Gavin playing in your room today. The song sounds like it's really coming along."

I leave her bouncing in her bedroom and my legs take me slowly down the hall. The sun is shining through the blinds but it looks cloudy to me. I love thinking about my grandmother but I also hate it, because what happened at the end of her life makes all the other memories I have of her feel less special. It's like we were playing this great concert together and when we got to our last song of the night, she just left the stage and now I have to face the crowd by myself and sometimes I just don't feel strong enough to do it alone.

But I can't quit now, not when Gavin and me are finally getting somewhere with our song. Mom even said so.

16

The street is mobbed. Men, women, children, and dogs all crammed onto eight blocks of urban road for an arts fair.

Paige is with Joan in line for kettle corn. Looks like they'll be there a while. In the meantime, I'm browsing the offerings, or pretending to. Amid the funnel cake and brick-oven pizza is every kind of craft and tchotchke you could imagine. It's all a bit dizzying.

I wasn't going to come. I was planning on finally chipping away at the avalanche of e-mails smothering my in-box. My agent has been trying to get me to give an interview about the fire. My mother keeps asking when I'm going to visit her. Sydney's cousin wants my help in starting the Sydney Brennett Fund to benefit families who've lost loved ones to sudden cardiac death.

But Joan convinced me to join her and

her mother. She said if I had any hope of writing good lyrics, I had to keep having new experiences. Smart kid. Once again, she's coaxed me into doing something I didn't expect to be doing. First I'm facing Sydney head-on, welcoming his memory when I had sworn to outrun it. Now I'm writing song lyrics, something I haven't done in almost twenty years, and, what's more, writing about the very things I've been trying *not* to dwell on.

I pass by vendors of all types, surveying their wares from a distance, careful not to make eye contact with the artists. I feel too guilty not buying their stuff.

One artist's tent finally intrigues me. I'm particularly drawn to a painting of a woman surfing a wave. The ocean is achieved with haphazard strokes. In contrast, the woman and her surfboard are ultraprecise, even down to the thin strands of hair. I can't tell if it's the artist's style that's familiar or the feeling it evokes. Either way, I think it would make a nice gift for my sister.

On a table below the surfer painting is a box of prints containing smaller versions of the larger works hanging around the tent. Now I'm wondering if a bulky painting is too ambitious. I decide to look for an eight-by-ten instead. I leaf through the cards until

I find a copy of the surfer painting.

"Those are twenty-five each," says a voice. "The postcards are five."

It's a girl. A young woman, rather. Probably my sister's age, in her twenties. But there's something old-soul about her eyes, like she knows more than her years might suggest.

"Gavin?"

I've been recognized. Ever since my video aired on the news and gossip shows, I swear people have been looking at me funny.

"Sorry," she says. "You don't know me. I knew Sydney."

I remove my shades, turn again to the surfer painting. The loose ends start to connect. "We had one of your paintings in our house," I say. "The one with the forest."

The trees were a smattering of messy green jutting up against a starry night. The moon, meanwhile, was rendered with photorealism. It was a dramatic piece. The key word: *was*. I set it on fire.

"Mara," she says, reaching out her hand. "Nice to meet you."

"You too."

There were artists of all types at Syd's funeral, many of whom I'd never met before. Syd had championed their work, nurtured their creativity, and they all came to show their gratitude.

I hold up the eight-by-ten print of the surfer. "I'd like to buy this one for my sister."

"Awesome," Mara says. "Does she surf?"

"I don't think so. But she loves the beach."

She smiles. "It's a nice gesture."

I look again at the box of prints. "And do you have any postcards of the forest painting?"

Syd loved that painting, hung it in a prominent spot in our home. It took him several years to find something worthy of placing on that central wall.

Mara leafs through the box, keeps shuffling, seemingly without luck. Then, toward the back, she spots something. She reaches in and removes a card sheathed in plastic.

"On the house," she says, hesitating before adding, "I'm sorry about what happened. I didn't know him that well, but he meant a lot to me. In a weird way, he sort of made me realize how much I'm capable of."

I know the feeling. How unlikely to share it with a stranger on this day, in this random place. And I almost didn't come. Syd would say it was meant to be.

I tell Paige and Joan I'll meet them back at the house. I walk east until I'm up against the Hudson River, one hand gripping the railing. Below, the dark water sloshes against a concrete foundation.

In my other hand, I hold the two prints: the one for my sister and the copy of the painting Syd and I once owned. I torched the painting and somehow it returned to me. At first it seemed like a stroke of cosmic luck. But soon after, about the time Paige and Joan returned with their enormous bag of kettle corn, I was hit with an overwhelming despair. The forest painting that hung in our house hadn't been restored. I just had a smaller, cheaper duplicate of the real thing. The same can be said of Joan's memories of Syd. They might bring me closer to him, but they never truly bring him back.

And it only frustrates me more not to have full command over my experience of the past, the way Joan does. She asked me to share my favorite memory of Syd and I couldn't do it. Of course, I've got memories that stand out. The time he put way too much chili sauce in his pho and started dripping sweat and I couldn't stop laughing. Or the time we took a road trip out to the Salton Sea and checked into a dank motel where we discovered a suspicious hole in our window the size of a bullet; we held each other extra-tight that night. Or both of us shedding tears at the exact same moment while watching Sigur Rós perform at Hollywood Forever Cemetery. Or the time I had the flu and Syd took the day off from work and sat with me in bed with his laptop while I watched a ten-hour marathon of *House Hunters.*

I know there are a hundred better memories that I'm forgetting. I wasn't paying close enough attention when they were happening. I was too busy living, just enjoying our time together, completely unaware that it could all suddenly end. Now it feels like a distant dream.

And on top of that, to suddenly have doubts about Sydney when I never had them before. He lied to me, fine, but why? What was he doing out here? What was he hiding? Or is it still possible that this is all a misunderstanding? I might never know the answers.

I lean over the railing and stare down into the dark water. So tranquil. Sometimes I wonder if total blackness would be easier. When we were newly in love and totally inseparable, we hypothesized about what we'd do if one of us suddenly died.

The other will kill himself, I said.

Deal, he said. *Unless, of course, we have a child.*

I turn away from the water and start walking. Just moving my body helps to unblock my mind. It's been so long since I've done any kind of exercise.

I pick up my pace, the rhythm of my steps against the pavement creating its own kind of music. A skeleton of some larger composition. I flesh it out with the chords and melody that are foremost in my mind: Joan's. All that's missing now are some verse lyrics to go on top.

I think you've already sealed my fate.

I sing the brand-new line to myself as I walk along. It feels true, worth keeping. I repeat it over and over like a mantra.

Pretty soon another one comes:

I can't let you go, can never escape.

I've got two lines now. It's a start.

"Get your guitar," I say.

Joan hops off the studio couch.

"I guess you were right about me coming to the fair today," I say, holding a scrap of paper in my hand. "I have some lyrics for the verse."

She starts playing. I read-sing my handwriting:

Life began when you arrived

What came before was a waste of time

Now I'm wondering where to go
Some answers I'll never know
I could get up and flee this place
But no one leaves without a trace
I think you've already sealed my fate
Can't let you go, can never escape

I had forgotten how satisfying writing can be. Matching language to cadence. Flipping through the mental thesaurus. Seizing the perfect word, the one that packs meaning *and* feeling. I forgot how each vowel sings differently, alters tonality and emotion. I forgot how much music can help.

"That's all I have," I say.

"I love it," Joan says.

"That one line is weak. *I could get up and flee this place.* It's clunky."

"Are you saying you don't want to be here anymore?"

"I'm trying to say that wherever you go, you're never really gone. It's kind of like how you see people in your memories. They're still here somehow. Anyway, I'll keep working on it."

"Okay," Joan says. "For the chorus, you know how you say *Keep dwelling on what went wrong, keep reaching for what is gone?* What if one time you changed the second line to *Keep singing the saddest song?* Dad loves it when one chorus is different."

"Okay. I can do that."

"Also, I've been thinking a lot about a bridge. Wouldn't it be great to have a song that makes people dance and cry at the same time? One of Dad's all-time favorite songs is 'A Day in the Life.' It starts off really sad and slow and then the bridge gets fast and John sings about waking up and getting ready for the bus and then you totally want to dance."

"That's not John. That's Paul."

"What do you mean?" Joan says. "It's John's song. He read a story in the news-paper and he wrote the song."

"True, but that's Paul in the bridge. He wrote the middle part and he's the one sing-ing. You know, your style is more like Paul's than John's. Paul was a master of melody and he was the one coming up with the grand schemes, like *Sgt. Pepper's* and all that. That's you."

Her eyes narrow, ready to pounce. "Do you know how to talk with a British ac-cent?"

"You takin' the piss?" I say.

"What?"

"That's my accent."

"Oh. Okay. Say 'John Lennon' with the same voice."

"John Lennon."

"Did you hear it?" Joan says. "When you say it with a British accent, it sounds like you're saying *Joan* Lennon."

"So?"

"I'm just like John! Dad named me Joan *Lennon,* not Joan *McCartney.* I'm the walrus!"

I wait for her to sit down. "You know my last name is Winters, right? But my real name is Deifendorf."

"I saw that on your license. What's Winters, then?"

"I made it up."

Plenty of actors invent new monikers. For me, it wasn't just the fact that my birth name is clumsy and difficult to spell. I discovered I was only able to truly disappear into acting roles once I'd made my past disappear. Of course, it was just an illusion.

"Listen, you can call yourself whatever you want," I say, "but at the end of the day you're still you. There's no way around that."

She pulls out a loose thread from her pants and ties it around her finger. "What if that's not true?"

"What do you mean?"

"Well, my friend Wyatt told me I might lose my memory if I fell on my head again

192

in Home Depot. And if I lost my memory, then I wouldn't be like me anymore. I'd be like everyone else."

I want to laugh, but it's clear she's not joking. "Look, kids tell each other a lot of crazy stuff. I once told my little sister there was a half-bird, half-man creature who lived on our roof, and she was too scared to open her window for weeks."

She peeks up, cracks a smile. "I wish I had a sister or brother."

"Do your parents ever talk about having another child?"

"Yeah, all the time," Joan says. "But it's never going to happen."

I feel the need to offer an answer, though I'm not sure she's asking for one. "Having a kid is a really big decision. It's not something you just step into lightly. Maybe one person is ready and the other needs more time. And then, for whatever reason, it just doesn't work out like you planned."

I look up. Joan is doing her best to follow, but the thing is, she's not really the one I'm trying to explain something to.

17

The Hollybrook Cognitive Research Center in Summit, New Jersey, is nothing like the college where Dr. M works in Arizona. The college in Arizona is covered in trees and the sun is shining and happy students are sitting on the green grass.

But today in New Jersey it's all rain and clouds. The research center is just one brick building and it's got a parking lot around it with no trees, just telephone poles and wires stretching everywhere.

Inside the research center, it's even gloomier. Dr. M's office had interesting things to look at, like a model of a brain and a silver ball that never stopped swinging, but this room is just a table and chairs with nothing on the walls. Mom is allowed to stay with me, but she has to keep quiet during the tests.

We're waiting for the doctor to arrive and I'm playing my Nintendo DS, but I'm too nervous to pay attention. It's my own fault that we're here today. After Mom caught me answering the phone and I told her I wanted to help old people remember, she scheduled this appointment.

I reach my hand back to her. She takes it. "It'll be fine, honey. I'm here."

Dr. Robert Brickenmeyer is a skinny man with his hair combed like a dork. He puts a recorder on the table between us, but the recorder is nothing fancy, nothing like Dad's stuff. I guess doctors don't care how good things sound.

Dr. Robert reminds Mom not to say anything and he shows me a picture:

Then he covers the picture and he asks me questions:

What time was it on the clock?

— 3:25
— 2:35
— 1:45

What was directly above the ruler?

— chair
— cat
— football

196

Which hand was the teacher waving?

— right
— left
— neither

It's a really hard test because I was too busy looking at the cute little cat, but I try to ace it anyway. Then Dr. Robert reads me eight pairs of words:

car — puddle
fox — melon
computer — snake
diamond — chocolate
skateboard — gorilla
umbrella — corn
butterfly — plastic
teacher — buckle

Dr. Robert says *computer,* and I'm supposed to remember that it goes with *snake.* These tests are just like the ones Dr. M gave me until he realized that my memory doesn't work this way.

Then Dr. Robert takes out an iPad and plays a video. It looks like a TV show. There's a man and a lady sitting on a couch and then someone knocks on the front door and the man gets up and answers the door and it's another man. The first man lets the second man into the house and they all sit on the couch and then the lady goes into the kitchen and she comes back and the video is over.

"Okay," Dr. Robert says. He brushes his hair to the side, even though his hair is already as far over as it can go. "The first question: What magazine was resting on the coffee table in front of the couch?"

Magazine? What magazine? "I didn't see a magazine."

The doctor nods and then he asks more questions, like how many cups the woman was holding when she came back from the kitchen.

I answer each one and then Dr. Robert plays the video again and I see that I got every question wrong. The magazine that I didn't even notice was *People* and although I guessed that the lady was holding two cups, she actually wasn't holding any. She was holding a plate.

"That's not fair," I say. "It was a trick."

"It's part of the test."

I turn back to Mom and she smiles and it helps but I feel stupid because that's not how my memory works.

"Please face forward, Joan."

"I don't remember stuff like that."

"Well, that's just it," Dr. Robert says.

198

"We're not sure how your mind operates. We're hoping to figure that out."

"But I already did these tests with Dr. M. I don't want to do them again."

"You're doing great," he says, but he says it like a robot and I don't like robots.

"I want to go home." I turn around. "Mom."

She stares at me until she sees something and then she stands and slides her purse onto her shoulder.

"Excuse me," Dr. Robert says.

"I'm sorry," Mom says. "She's changed her mind."

I rush to her and Dr. Robert stands and he walks around the table and gets down on one knee. "If you come back another day, we'll have to start from the beginning. You don't want that, do you? You're doing a terrific job. Later you get to climb into a big machine."

"I'm not coming back."

Mom takes me by the hand and we find our way out.

I stare out the rainy window as Mom drives us away from Hollybrook and talks on the phone. It must be Dad she's talking to because he told Mom last night that he wanted to hear how it went.

"Not great," Mom tells him. "Yeah, she's okay."

I tried to tell Dr. Robert that it has to happen to *me* and in *my life* and I have to pay attention to it or else I won't remember it. Ask me what Grandpa got me for my fourth birthday (indoor trampoline). Ask me what day it was when I learned my first B minor chord on guitar (Monday, November 7, 2011). Ask me the color of the building where they sent Grandma Joan after she got sick (red brick). Ask me what Sydney was wearing when he arrived on October 27, 2008, but don't ask me what time it was when he came because I don't wear a watch and I never look at clocks.

The car isn't moving anymore. We're parked in a shopping center and Mom says, "How about a smoothie?"

Mom gets Berry Bananza and I get Nectar Nirvana and we sit near the front of the store and suck on our straws. The window is foggy so you can't see what's going on outside, but inside it's dry and cozy.

I like this smoothie shop because they have plastic cups, and plastic cups are better than paper cups because you can see how much smoothie you have left. Mom says plastic is bad for fish in the ocean but I know paper is bad for trees, so I guess that's why Mom says *you can't win,* which means there's no right answer.

After two giant slurps, I ask, "Are you mad?"

"No, honey, not at all," she says, shaking her head a zillion times. "It's my fault. I was afraid that would happen. That's why I was always against you doing this."

She's only ever let me talk about my HSAM to Dr. M. "So why did you let me do it this time?"

"Because you wanted to help people like Grandma and I thought I should at least let you try." I can tell she wants to say something else but isn't sure if she should. "Look, you've got a special thing and it's yours and I know that. When you're eighteen you can do whatever you want, but right now it's my job to protect you. People call me up with all kinds of requests and some of them offer us money and it just doesn't feel appropriate. You just have to trust that I'm trying to do what's best for you and your future. I don't always make the right decisions. But I'm trying."

I guess Mom is just like Sydney because Sydney was a future person and it seems like Mom is also a future person because she loves to plan everything out before it happens. I wonder if that's why they were such good friends.

"Do you miss him?" I ask.

"Who?"

"Sydney."

She puts her smoothie on the table even though there's a lot left. I know remembering hurts, just like Gavin says, but he and I both know that *not* remembering is even worse.

"Of course I miss him," Mom says. "I miss him a lot."

But she hasn't been crying lately, not like when it first happened. If she ever starts to forget him, our song can remind her. "Our song is about him. Gavin is writing the lyrics."

She thinks about this for a while. "I'm glad he's writing again. I wish you could've seen him and your father play back in college. They were pretty amazing to watch."

It annoys me that Mom gets to watch those memories but I don't.

"How is Gavin?" she asks. "Does he seem like he's doing okay?"

I'm only just getting to know him, so I don't know the way he's *supposed* to be. "He was pretty shy at first, and quiet, but he's not like that as much anymore."

"I can't imagine," Mom says. "Sydney was an important part of my life, but I only saw

him once a year at the most. But Gavin . . ."
Mom makes a whoosh sound like she's blowing out a candle on a birthday cake except she doesn't look like she's having any fun.

"How come you and Dad never had another baby?" I ask.

She turns her head to me. "Where did that come from?"

"Me and Gavin were talking and I told him I wanted a sister or brother and he asked me if you and Dad ever wanted to have another baby."

Mom is sitting up straight now. "And what did you tell him?"

"I said yes, you guys talk about it, but I didn't think you'd ever actually do it."

"Did he say anything else? Anything about becoming a father?"

"No," I say, and I'm not sure why she's asking. But then I remember. "Well, the woman in New York did say that Sydney and Gavin were going to start a family. Is that what you mean?"

Mom leans in. "What woman?"

"The woman who showed Gavin the apartment."

She picks up her smoothie cup, but she doesn't drink it. Actually, she's not doing anything right now. She's frozen.

"Mom."

Her eyes are aimed at me, but it's like she doesn't know what she's looking at. And then she says, "Sorry," and she takes a very slow sip of her smoothie. "I just remembered, I have to tell your father something."

She doesn't say what it is and that's okay, because she just reminded me that I have my own thing I need to talk to Dad about when he gets home later tonight. Today is Thursday, which means we're only two days away from the weekend and that's when Dad said he would record our song for the contest and I have to make sure he's not going to forget.

This may be one of the last times we ever record in his studio. I remember when Dad and I took out a bunch of keyboards and we used our fingers and toes to play eight different C notes all at once and when I asked Dad why we were doing it he said, "To see how it sounds." And I remember the day he taught me how to tune a snare drum by tightening and loosening those little metal knobs and I accidentally tuned the drum so low that it started to growl and that made me laugh so hard that I swallowed my gum.

Mom should be even more upset than I am about the studio closing because she has even more memories of Dad's music than I do. She's been watching Dad play ever since college. I look over at Mom and she's frozen again and doing something I've never seen her do before: it's her very own rock-star look. She's looking out the window, but she's not paying any attention to what her eyes are seeing. Actually, she's staring so hard it's almost like she forgot how to blink.

18

I'm deep in a digital daze — answering e-mails and skimming a heavy run of Twitter comments, the majority of which are complimentary, but a few contain alarming vitriol about everything from my lack of acting skills to my sinful sexual proclivities — when Paige throws open my door.

"Hello," I say, taken aback by the sudden intrusion.

"Sorry," she says. "I should've knocked."

I didn't see much of her yesterday. She took Joan to a doctor's appointment in the morning and then to an afternoon playdate that stretched into dinner. Without Paige here to care for me, I returned to my bachelor ways. I ended up eating Chinese takeout in bed while streaming a movie on my phone.

After scanning my unkempt room, Paige locks eyes with me. "Get dressed. You're with me today."

■ ■ ■ ■

We've been cruising down the turnpike for thirty minutes now (the same distance would've taken twice as long back home on the 110). Paige won't tell me where we're going, but I figure it out as soon as she veers off at exit 9. We're going back to college.

Finding a spot to park on the New Brunswick campus is even harder than it was fifteen years ago. We walk down College Avenue toward the parking lot across from Voorhees Mall.

It's clear from our trajectory, and the oily smell in the air, that Paige and I are about to dine at the Rutgers food mecca known as the grease trucks. It's an outdoor cluster of permanently parked vehicles serving exactly the kind of fare you'd expect: food normally devoured by drunk students at two in the morning. Today it will be consumed by us at the embarrassingly adult hour of eleven thirty in the morning.

"I can't believe these are still here," I say, salivating.

"I've dreamed of this day for so long," Paige says, possibly drooling.

"You've never been back?"

"Nope," Paige says. "First time since we

graduated."

"I know exactly what I'm getting."

She turns to me, wild with hunger. "Me too."

We sit on the curb with our massive sandwiches, just like we did all those years ago. A Fat Darrell for me and a Fat Sal for her. There can be no doubt — we'll be sick if we finish these sandwiches. Also true — we *will* finish them.

"This was a brilliant idea," I say.

She nods proudly. "Thank you."

Summer students pass by looking way too young to be attending college. Paige and I follow their movements, inspecting their clothes and affects.

"Everyone always talks about college being the best years of your life," Paige says. "Look at these kids. Can that really be true?"

I abandon any pretense of class and talk through the food in my mouth. "It wasn't true for me. But I imagine it's different for you."

"Why?"

I wipe my face with a too-thin napkin. "Because you met Ollie here."

She lowers her sandwich, waits until she's finished chewing. "Yes, but I still wouldn't want to come back to this. My friends talk about it like they'd return in a second, but they forget that we were poor, we had nothing, we *knew* nothing. I've done that already. I'm ready to be a grown-up."

She chomps down, gazes across the avenue at the students in the quad. Clearly there's a disconnect between what I see when I look at Paige and what she sees in the mirror. Even back in college, she seemed far more mature than the rest of us. Always focused and responsible, acing all her classes, somehow still able to make good decisions even while impaired and slurring her speech. And now she's a married homeowner with a kid and a steady career. If that's not a grown-up, what is?

And it's an especially odd comment for her to make while she's sitting on a curb, a girlish barrette in her hair, stuffing her mouth with a five-dollar sandwich packed with chicken fingers, mozzarella sticks, and French fries while the rest of society is stuck at work. In other words, while she's behaving like a child.

Then again, considering the satisfaction on her face, maybe that's her point. Being a grown-up isn't a matter of age or responsibility. For Paige, it's finally having the power to do whatever the hell she wants.

"Save some room," she says. "We're going

to Thomas Sweet next."

"What makes their chocolate chip cookie-dough ice cream so special," Paige says, "is that instead of just throwing a few chunks of cookie dough into vanilla ice cream, the ice cream *itself* is cookie dough."

We're at Thomas Sweet sharing a double scoop of what Paige claims is unequivocally the best ice cream in the world. What I assume has to be hyperbolic nostalgia becomes more plausible once I get my first taste. It's damn good.

The fact that I have zero appetite left doesn't stop me from sliding more ice cream onto my plastic spoon. It's been a carefree day of gluttony so far, but no matter how much I stuff in my belly, I can't fill the pit inside. "You were right."

"About what?" Paige wonders.

"Sydney was looking at properties in New York. But not in January; in February. I met with his broker. She mentioned that he was with a photographer. Some woman."

I hear a faint *hmm.* Not sure if it's in response to me or the ice cream.

"That's all I have so far," I say, putting down my spoon. "I still don't know if he actually came back in April. Or why he told me he was working when he wasn't. Or why he lied about taking you out for your birth-day."

She nods, swallowing. "So what do you think it all means?"

"Obviously, I hate to think that there could've been someone else."

She places her spoon on the napkin with mine.

"Listen," she says, checking the corners of her mouth for cookie-dough remnants. "You came all this way, back home, finally, and I've already seen such a change in you from when you first got here. I'd hate for this to take you backward. Trust me, what you and Sydney had was real and pure and special. You never once had reason to be suspicious the entire time you were together, right? Don't start doubting him now."

It sounds fair and logical and caring. It's probably even true. But I can't change how I feel. People don't lie because everything is fine and dandy. They lie because telling the truth is too hard. And though our relation-ship appeared to be solid, it seems even the best and most dedicated couples experience occasional periods of doubt. A one-night tryst I might be able to look past, but the thought of an ongoing relationship with repeated trips back and forth is a scenario that's just too painful to fathom.

"Can I ask you something?" Paige says.

Something in the way she says it, I know playtime is over.

"What took you so long to come back? I mean, we were all so close in college. You were a groomsman at our wedding. Then you just vanished, zipped off to California, changed your name. How come you never wanted to visit?"

I wasn't expecting to have to deal with this now, but I knew it was coming eventually. "It's not that. I wanted to."

I can tell from her face that it's going to take more than that. There's a stubbornness in her stare that reminds me of Joan. I'm suddenly very thirsty, but there's no water at the ready.

"Look, I had a really tough time in Los Angeles at first, leaving my sister and mother, being out there alone. I had to learn to push certain thoughts out of my head. I had to give myself permission to move on and not look back. I'm not saying it's right. It's just what I needed to do."

She's gearing up for a response, but I'm not finished.

"Then I came home for Veronica's graduation. She was just a little girl when I left and now she was this woman. My mother looked so much older, and all the guilt I felt about leaving came back, but this time it was even worse than before. It was hard on them, too, having me in their life again for this one brief moment. I remember flying back to California, telling myself I probably shouldn't go home again. It was just easier that way."

She winces at my words. "Thanks."

"I'm sorry. It wasn't about you guys. You know that."

"But your family still visited you in California. You handled that okay, didn't you?"

"For some reason, it didn't affect me the same way. Something about being home."

New Jersey had become synonymous with my father's death and all that followed. I can sense the same thing happening now with Sydney and California. Yet another forbidden zone on my trauma map.

"I meant to come back eventually," I say. "It's just, the longer I waited, the harder it got."

"You're back now. Is it so bad?"

"I don't know. No. But —"

"Listen to me. This stuff, whatever it is you have to push out of your head, you can't just ignore all that, because it doesn't go away. You have to deal with it eventually. There's no other way."

This sounds eerily familiar. "Did you and

Sydney talk about this?"

"Of course," Paige says. "I wanted to know where you'd been all these years." Her face softens. "Don't get me wrong, I'm glad you're here, even if it took a while. We just can't have you setting any more fires, that's all." She smacks my arm playfully.

I meet her eyes, which are unyielding but not unkind. "I don't care what you say. You've been a grown-up since the day I met you."

I mean it as a joke, but she responds in a solemn manner. "I know," she says, "just not in the way I want to be."

Joan finds me on the studio couch and notices the notepad in my lap. "Are those lyrics?" she asks.

After spending the morning with Paige, I feel lucky to have an outlet for the tornado of emotions spinning inside of me. "Trying," I say, underwhelmed by the progress I've made on the page. "How's your day been so far?"

She strikes a foreboding bass note on the piano. "Harper's mom took us to see a movie but I couldn't concentrate. When it was over Harper wanted to talk about how ridiculous it was when the alien showed up, but I didn't even know there was an alien. I guess I didn't see that part."

"It must not have been a good movie if you couldn't concentrate."

"No," Joan says, staring down at the piano keys. "It's not that. It happens with every movie. I'll see something that makes me think of a memory and then I just go somewhere else."

"It happens to me too."

She plops down next to me. "Can I see what you wrote so far?"

Now that the song has taken on a clearer shape, I've become pickier about what I'm willing to add to it. Most of the words on my notepad are crossed out. "I don't have much to show. I think I may need some inspiration. Do you think we could do another memory?"

"After this memory, we've got only one more left."

"I know."

Joan begins to tell me about Sydney's visit in 2012. She starts on September 9. The following day is when she saw Syd in his Ted Baker suit.

"We're in the courtyard," Joan says. "Dad is standing in front of the barbecue. He's dragged his studio speakers over to the back door so we can listen to music while we're outside. I don't know how many people are here but our courtyard is pretty crowded."

"What is Sydney doing?" I ask, eager to see him again.

"Sydney is sitting next to me at the table. He says he brought me something from California. He reaches into his pocket and then he makes me guess what's in his fist. I say, 'Candy,' and he says, 'No,' and I say, 'Earrings,' and he says, 'No. Give up?' And he opens his hand and it's a bag of guitar picks and each guitar pick has my name on it. It's definitely one of the top three presents I've ever gotten."

Syd was a talented gift giver. He'd always get me something I'd never buy for myself, intuiting what I didn't know I wanted or needed. One time it was a personalized book embosser. Another time a Santoku kitchen knife.

"Everyone's eating burgers," Joan says, "but Sydney is eating some type of rice thing. I'm eating watermelon, which Mom hasn't brought outside yet, but I snuck a piece out of the downstairs fridge when she wasn't looking."

"What does he look like?"

She describes him: V-neck, shorts, sandals, eagle bracelet. But it's all surface. She couldn't have known that our relationship had progressed drastically since she had previously seen Sydney in 2010. We'd left Syd's apartment in West Hollywood and bought a house together in Los Feliz. Talk about grown-up. It was the most adult thing I'd ever done and also one of the scariest. As big a commitment, I thought, as getting married. We didn't have a bed yet, but we were so excited to move into our new house that we slept on blankets on the wood floor. Maybe that's my favorite memory.

"The music on the speakers changes," Joan says, "and I realize that Dad is playing a song that we recorded together last week. My face is turning red but I'm also very excited that everyone is hearing it. There's no singing in our song, so no one knows whose song it is, but Dad gives me a wink and I think Sydney sees the wink because he says, 'You must really like this song.' And I say, 'I do. It's my song. I wrote it with my dad.' And then instead of telling me how much he likes my song, Sydney looks at Dad and he says, 'You have a really good father,' and I say, 'I know,' and Sydney says, 'I hope one day I'll be a good father too,' and I say, 'I bet you will,' and then Sydney says, 'I'd like to keep my name alive,' and when I hear that I'm really interested because I like when things stay alive and never die and that's when Sydney tells me that he's the last Brennett, but I don't know what that means."

Joan waits for me to explain. "It means that unless he had a child, he would be the last person to be born in his family. There would be no one else."

Her eyes cloud with sadness. "That's horrible."

For better or worse, I decide to confide in her.

"I've been thinking a lot about which is my favorite memory of Sydney. There are so many great ones and I can't really choose one over the other. But I know which is my least favorite."

She seems interested, so I go on.

"It was around Christmas last year — I can't remember the exact date," I admit, almost by way of apology. "We got into a pretty bad fight and it was all about us having a kid. That was Sydney's one big wish, to have a kid, and he was excited to move forward. I wasn't quite sure I was ready, but I went along with it. For a while."

Joan asks a good and obvious question. "How do two men have a baby?"

"It's complicated. You need a mother."

"Who was your mother?"

"That's sort of what the fight was about. We hired this company to help us through the process and we took all the beginning steps. We even had a mother in place, someone to carry the baby, but in order to get a baby, you need eggs. There was a list of people to choose from, but Syd didn't like the fact that we couldn't meet any of these women face to face, and I agreed. It was frustrating, because this was the person who was going to be responsible for what our child would look like and *be* like." It seems from Joan's expression that I've completely lost her. "Anyway, Syd had his heart set on someone and I wasn't sure about it."

"Who did he want?"

I've probably shared enough for one day, but it appears she's still curious. "My sister."

Now her brain is really working overtime. "He wanted your sister to be your baby's mother?"

I don't know how to explain it, so I just say, "Yes."

"But you didn't want your sister?" she asks, although I'm not positive how much of this she actually understands.

"It's not that I didn't want her. The whole thing was moving so fast. I just hadn't gotten around to asking her."

Using my sister's eggs was the closest we could ever come to having a baby that included a piece of both of us. I knew Veronica would've said yes without hesitation. That's the very reason I didn't want to ask her right away. Everything seemed to be moving too quickly. It was as if one night we'd decided to have a kid and the very next day we were cutting a hefty check to an agency and handing over sperm samples and selecting a surrogate. I wasn't trying to squash Syd's dreams. I was only trying to apply the brakes for a moment. I just needed more time. On this occasion, time ran out.

But the blame can't rest solely on my shoulders. "Syd could be very impatient," I say. "If he wanted something, he wouldn't let up until he got it. He'd wear you down. But the thing is, everyone works at their own pace."

She seems to understand. "I guess I'm like Sydney, then, and you're the other kind. You wait around until the magic finally happens."

She's talking about our song. That wasn't what I was referring to, but that doesn't mean she's wrong.

"What if your good ideas don't come fast enough?" Joan says. "We don't have much time left. Don't forget, we're recording the song *tomorrow*."

"Don't worry," I say. "We'll get it done."

I'm not sure if one approach is better than the other. Sometimes I wonder if Syd had an instinct, reinforced by his family's troubled health history, that his time was limited and that's what made him so driven. Whatever the case, there's one thing I do know: If I could go back and do that one night over again last December, I'd do it his way. I'd set aside my reservations. I'd grant him his wish.

19

I jump out of bed the next morning and run across the hall. I'm about to knock on my parents' door but Mom comes up behind me and whispers, "He's sleeping."

I put my arm down and follow Mom into the kitchen. She's grabbing eggs from the fridge and a can of beans from the pantry and there's chopped cilantro on the cutting board, which means she's making Dad's favorite breakfast: huevos rancheros.

On the living-room computer, I go to the website for the contest and click on the Rules page. *Entries will be judged on originality, melody, composition, and lyrics (if applicable).*

I grab my notebook and read through John Lennon's Ten Rules of Songwriting again. Rule no. 1: Get to It. On ten of the forty songs I studied, John starts singing as soon as the music begins, and on nineteen of the songs he starts singing within the first five seconds. He hardly ever waits more than ten seconds.

Rule no. 2: Repeat the Song Title. If John names his song "Sexy Sadie," that means you're going to hear him say *sexy Sadie* a lot during the song (twelve times). He loves to repeat the title: "Help" (sixteen times), "Julia" (fifteen times), "Lucy in the Sky with Diamonds" (fifteen times). His personal record is "Power to the People" (thirty-one times).

Then there's rule no. 3: Start with the Chorus. And rule no. 6: Lyrics Don't Have to Make Sense As Long As They Sound Good. And rule no. 8: When in Doubt, Fade Out. Now that I'm thinking about it, our song breaks almost all of John's rules. Maybe that's because our song follows rule no. 10: The Best Songs Sometimes Break the Rules. The best example of rule no. 10 is "A Day in the Life." Still, if we really want him to, Dad can give our song a fade-out, it's not too late.

Speaking of Dad, he's finally awake. I follow him into the kitchen. He sees what Mom is cooking and he pulls her forehead to his lips. He reaches for me too and squeezes us both, his two girls. I break away and do a little dance on the kitchen floor. "When can we start?"

Dad splashes sink water on his face and dries it with a dish towel, which is pretty gross. "I need a few hours, honey."

"How many?"

"Joan," Mom says, pouring the cracked eggs into the pan. I think she wants some of Dad's time too, which is fine, but does it have to be today?

Dad scoops coffee into his machine and I wonder if I should have coffee too because it's a very important day and I have a lot of work to do, but the truth is I don't need more energy and I also don't drink coffee.

I have to leave the kitchen because the smell of eggs is starting to hurt my nose. "I'll go see if Gavin's awake."

"He left," Mom says, swinging the spatula.

"What? Where'd he go?"

"He didn't say."

"When is he coming back?"

"I don't know," Mom says, and she says it like she wouldn't mind knowing the answer herself.

Dad is finally back where he should be, in his studio. All the lamps are glowing and the computer tower is doing its low hum and Dad has his roller chair set to his height. I know Dad has been the one missing but in a way I feel like I'm the one who's been gone and I just came home.

I sit on a stool in the Quiet Room and Dad tells me to tune up the Gibson while he sets up microphones around me. I'm so excited to be here with him, finally, but then I notice the Monkey Finger tattoo on his arm and I can't help but get sad.

Monkey Finger is the name of Dad's music company and it's from a line in John Lennon's song "Come Together." Once Dad shuts down the studio and stops making music for his company, it's going to hurt when I look at that tattoo. Sometimes reminders aren't a good thing. Gavin knows that too.

Before we start recording, Dad wants me to run through the song with him. I play my guitar part and hum the melody and my hands start to sweat because I'm nervous about what Dad will say.

He stares at the guitar a long time after I finish. "I'm sorry I wasn't around to help you more," Dad tells me, and he says it like it's a hard thing to say.

"Does that mean you don't like the song?"

"No, honey, I love it. I'm really proud of you."

After so many days of feeling like I was getting nowhere, it's so good to hear this from Dad, especially because I was worried

225

he might be mad that I wrote the song with Gavin and not him. Also because I went to all those cool John Lennon places in New York City without him and normally he's the one who shows me those kinds of things.

"I do have a thought, though," Dad says. "What if you walked up to the C on the chorus instead of going back to the E minor?"

He grabs another acoustic off the rack and plays the new part. I see what he means, so I copy Dad's fingers and I start practicing it. He puts the big headphones over my ears and tells me to keep playing. When he shuts the door, it gets super-quiet.

I want Gavin to watch me record my guitar part but he's still not home and I'm getting worried. He knows what today is. I can understand if he was having trouble finishing the lyrics and he wanted to go out and have more experiences, but we don't have much time left, only a few hours. But if this is something different, like Gavin deciding to do something else today because our song slipped his mind, then I don't know what I'm going to do. I'm probably going to cry, baby, cry, which is a John Lennon song and also something to do when you're completely out of ideas.

Dad's at the computer now but I'm too

short to see through the window. His voice comes through my headphones and it sounds like there's a tiny person living inside my ear. "Ready to try one?"

I've recorded with Dad so many times, but each time is just as exciting as the last. "Let's do it," I say.

I play the song once and Dad comes into the booth and moves the microphone closer to the guitar. He tells me to play the song again and again and again and then he tells me to stop and come into the studio.

I take my headphones off and leave the Quiet Room and I hear my acoustic guitar playing through the speakers. "You got really good at fingerpicking," Dad says.

It feels like I'm floating. Now I know what Mom means when she says Dad is in a cloud when he records his music.

"Do you want to add some bass?" I ask.

"Sure," Dad says. "You take the controls."

I take Dad's place in his roller chair and start recording for him. I see a large red bar move across the screen and black waves start to form as Dad's bass guitar follows along with my acoustic. He plays through the song a few times and then he asks me which parts I like. I like everything he does.

When Dad finishes recording the bass, he takes out a special little organ that he knows is my favorite because of the way it sounds and also because it doesn't have a plug or batteries. It works by someone blowing into a tube. Dad does the blowing while I hold down the organ keys that match my guitar chords. Then Dad plays the snare drum and hi-hat and after that I shake the shaker and tap the tambourine and then Dad tells me to hit the cymbal each time the chorus plays. The song keeps getting bigger and bigger. I feel like I'm getting bigger too, stretching out, like my body is too small to hold all the feeling inside me. I think I'd be happy just staying down here with Dad forever.

While he listens back to all the instruments and makes everything sound right, I sit on the couch with my journal. On the coffee table in front of me is the thickest book you could imagine. It's so thick because it tells all the secrets about how the Beatles recorded their music. Dad calls it his bible. Inside there are drawings of where each Beatle was standing in the Abbey Road studio when they recorded their famous songs because that's how important the Beatles were: people want to know exactly where they were standing when they made their magic.

If the song we're recording now does what

I hope it will do, then people in the future will want to see a sketch of how we recorded too and they'll want to know what Dad's studio looked like before it got shut down. I slide a piece of notebook paper over the book and trace the outline of one of the rooms at Abbey Road, and then I turn my outline into a sketch of Dad's studio:

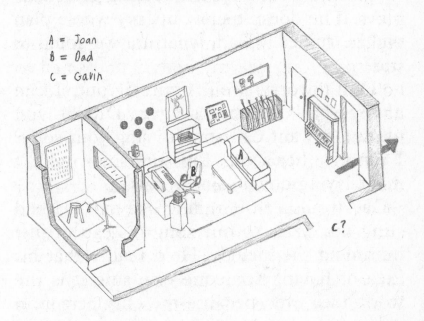

A = Joan
B = Dad
C = Gavin

I've got all the important stuff: the Quiet Room, Dad's roller chair, the guitar rack, and the arrow leading down the hall to Gavin's room. I've even got Dad and me in there. The only thing missing is Gavin.

"He's supposed to be here," I say.

Dad spins his chair around. "Listen,

229

honey, I just want to warn you. Gavin is going through a really rough time right now, and even at his best, he can be a little flaky."

"What's flaky?"

"He goes off the map sometimes."

"Which one is it? He's flaky or he goes off the map?"

"Never mind. I just want you to know that if he doesn't show up, it's nothing personal."

But if he doesn't show up, my whole plan will be ruined. "Dad, what are we going to do?"

"Don't worry. We'll figure it out. I can always call another singer. Didn't you originally want Christina to sing your song? I can give her a call. I'm sure she wouldn't mind laying down some vocals."

Dad wouldn't be smiling like that if I had sung the lyrics to our song instead of just humming the melody. He'd realize that his idea of having someone else sing it is the worst idea ever, because the only person in the world who should be singing those lyrics is Gavin. He's the only one who can put the true meaning into the words.

20

"Gavin."

"Hi, Mom."

She steps onto the porch, smothers me. I know instantly, standing here, holding my mother, that I was right to come today and wrong to have waited this long. I assumed she'd always be here waiting for my arrival. Given all I've been through, I realize it was never a guarantee. I'm lucky to be holding her right now.

But of course, this kind of grab-hold-of-life perspective never lasts long. Especially when your mother touches your cheek with no attempt at concealing her disapproval. "You have a beard," she says.

"So?"

"On the show you're so clean-cut."

"You've been watching."

"Of course I've been watching," she says. "I host a viewing party here every week."

I've purposely pushed the show out of my

mind. I'm proud of the work we did this year, but thinking about my second life on TV invariably reminds me of the video my neighbor leaked and the subsequent media storm, which, thankfully, I've caught only a glimpse of. I'm thrilled the show is finally getting the attention it deserves but I wish I could maintain my respectability in the process. My mother, however, would surely be tuning in regardless.

She welcomes me into the same three-bedroom ranch I grew up in but haven't stepped foot inside in the last ten years. I expect some bone-chilling melancholy to grip me as I enter, but the only overwhelming part of the experience is how surprisingly normal it feels. Even the nostalgia seems faint.

My mother wanders into the kitchen while I linger in the living room. The furnishings have changed, as has the layout, but the photos are all the same. The whole family is here on the wall, all the Deifendorfs, including our missing patriarch. Seeing him in these old photos, I feel a thousand competing things at once. I see a stranger and I also see a mirror. I am a heartless adult and a heartbroken child.

He was, like many fathers, quiet. If he wasn't leaning over a book, he was staring into space, always turning something over in his head. It was a shock to hear his students remark at his funeral how passionate an orator he was in his classroom. He seldom opened his mouth at home and yet he managed to take so much sound with him when he died; he was the only thing on our minds and none of us knew how to talk about him. I never quite learned how.

My mother appears at my side and stares up at the same wall of pictures. The difference between her and me is that she's smiling. She points to a black-and-white photo of me as a young kid, maybe five years old.

"Your first head shot," she says, handing me a cold drink.

I catch a distinct scent and notice the green leaves scattered throughout the glass. "Is this mint?"

"Yes, straight from my garden. One hundred percent organic."

I didn't realize mint was such a thing for Sydney until Joan pointed it out. It seemed from Joan's stories that even Sydney was unaware of how much he gravitated toward it.

We take a seat on the couch. She seems to have recovered from the sight of my beard. Her scorn has been replaced with an irrepressible smile. "I'm so happy you're here."

"I'm sorry it took so long."

She waves the notion away with her hand. "Don't worry about that. I know how busy you are."

Nonsense. If anyone is busy here, it's my mother. She's immersed in a thousand activities: her book club and mah-jongg and volunteering and jazzercise and crocheting and organic gardening and, new to the list, TV viewing parties. All that in addition to her job as an interior decorator.

That inclination to remain constantly busy is something I confused for indifference to my father's death when I was growing up. A normal person needs ample time to recover when her husband dies unexpectedly, leaving her alone with two children. Not my mother. She cried for forty-eight hours straight and then seemed to decide that was enough tears for one lifetime.

"Tell me when you're hungry," she says. "I made gazpacho."

"That sounds good."

"I also picked up some fresh corn. I bet you haven't had Jersey corn in a long time."

"I've had plenty of corn," I say. "I can't be sure where it came from."

"You used to cut the kernels off the cob

and eat them with a fork."

"I don't do that anymore."

"It's more fun to eat it off the cob, right?"

"Right," I say and start to laugh. We've had this exact same conversation so many times, about the way I eat corn and what produce I can acquire out in California. I know as the day progresses we'll repeat ourselves many more times. It's annoyed me in the past, but right now it's quite comforting to know that no matter how my mother and I talk — over the phone, video chat, text, or in person — or how long we go without talking, we pretty much always end up saying the same things.

"Was I a picky eater when I was little?" I ask.

"Of course," my mother says. "You know that."

"I wasn't sure how bad it was."

I'm on my second helping of gazpacho. My mother went all out: slices of avocado and sour cream to mix into the soup and rustic bread for dipping. She poured herself one tiny helping and as soon as she finished, she immediately put her dirty dish away.

"I gave up after a while and just let you eat whatever you wanted," she says. "But your father kept at it. He made you try everything at least once. That man had a lot of patience."

The word bowls me over: *patience*. It's a nicer term for what I'm always doing: delaying, procrastinating, waiting for things to fall into place. With a little calm and resolve, a character flaw becomes a virtue.

I remember as a child I'd ask my father a question, and if I received no response, I'd assume he either didn't hear me or was ignoring me. And then, after several moments of silence, he'd give an answer, and only then would I realize he had been thinking that whole time. These delayed reactions used to frustrate me greatly. And now, I'm pretty sure I do the same exact thing.

"By the way," my mother says, "Sydney's cousin e-mailed me. He wants to start a fund. I think it's a good idea. It's a nice way to remember him."

It makes me think of Joan and how she says songs are reminders. Another way of prolonging people's memories of you is to die and have someone name something after you. Of course, it's a far less gratifying option.

"I don't get it," I say. "Why is Syd's cousin e-mailing you?"

She shrugs. "He said he was having trouble getting in touch with you. I forwarded it to you. Whenever you have time. No rush."

No rush. Either she's trying to appreciate the fact that I'm in the middle of grieving, or she — like Sydney and Paige and now Joan — has lost faith in my ability to act swiftly on anything. Don't they realize? I'm just being patient.

But I can't help but return to the one decision in my life I'm most ashamed of not making with haste. In theory I wanted to be a father, but as Syd and I started taking the necessary steps to turn that into a reality, I became more and more crippled with doubts. Syd thought I was making parenthood more complicated than it had to be. *Most of it's just being there,* he'd say. But I knew that even that bare-minimum requirement was harder than it sounded. I haven't always *been there* for my family. In fact, much like my father, one day I all but vanished.

"Have you talked to Veronica lately?" I ask.

My mother, incapable of sitting still for too long, is already taking my bowl to the sink. "I talked to her a few days ago. Why?"

"I sent her something in the mail. I was just curious if she got it."

"Why don't you call and ask her yourself?"

Sydney would always ask me the same

thing. I still don't have a good answer.

My mother wants to go for a walk, another one of her hobbies. Before we can leave the house, she has to equip herself with ankle weights, a visor, and a wristband pedometer. "How far are we walking?" I ask.

"Around the block," she says.

It's not a stroll, it's a speed walk. Had I known, I wouldn't have eaten all that bread.

We go by the same houses I used to ride my bike past as a kid. Many have changed colors, some have added extensions, and a few seem to have been demolished and rebuilt. My mother waves to a couple I don't recognize and announces loudly that I'm her son. All of our old neighbors have moved away. Every single one of them.

"You never wanted to move, Mom?"

"Why? I like it here."

But I'm asking a slightly different question. "I mean, after Dad died?"

She doesn't break her stride. "I thought about it," she says between heavy breaths. "But where was I going to go?" Breath. "I had two kids." Breath. "One was just a baby." Breath. "I had to work and keep everything going. I didn't have time to sit and think about it." Breath. Breath. Breath. "Actually, that's probably what saved me."

I'm still going over those words when we come around the block and I spot our house up ahead. It doesn't look nearly as ominous as it did this morning, when it seemed to speak of only one single event: the news, arriving as a phone call, that my father had been sideswiped on the highway, all the relatives I barely knew suddenly visiting, pitching in, supporting, until the helping hands dwindled down to just four, my mother's and mine, caring for the baby who was soon walking and getting into things and whose welfare took precedence over my preteen needs and desires (and hurt) and, later, my teenage needs and desires (and hurt), and through it all, my mother was busy, busy, busy.

Now, I return to the house less as the put-upon boy who was convinced that he alone carried the family's sorrow and more as the man who's only now learning the many tricky shapes pain can take, who just heard his mother confess, finally, that it wasn't a given that she'd make it this far, that it had been a hard and daily struggle. And somehow she, unlike me, managed this feat without changing her name and while keeping the reminders on the walls and protecting the house from unruly backyard bonfires.

"I should get going," I say once we're back in the house. "I've got something I have to do."

"You finally come to visit and now you can't stay?"

There's the heartbreak I've always suspected she feels but rarely shows.

"I'll come back," I say. But then, seeing her face and doubting my own promise, I add, "Okay, a little bit longer."

While my mother brews coffee, I take an extended tour of the house. It's no longer the mournfully quiet place I remember. I find life's commotion in every room — in my old bedroom, where I thrash-danced to Nirvana blasting from my distorted boom-box speakers; in the basement, where I threw the keg party that led to a visit from the police, who seemed unconcerned about the noise because there was the more pressing matter of the Chevy Beretta that someone had parked on my neighbor's lawn; in the garage, where my high-school band rehearsed its unironic Bush covers; in the bathroom, where I read my gaming magazines on the tiled floor while Veronica's four-year-old fingers became wrinkled in the lukewarm tub.

And then, after sipping from our mugs in front of the evening news, my mother and I are back on the porch where we started this morning. She wants to give me a lift to the station, even though it's only a few blocks away. She says she has to pick up pies for the nursing home tomorrow. Why she has to pick up the pies right now, I don't know, nor do I ask. She's been living on her own for decades and doing just fine.

But that doesn't mean she never gets lonely. "You can always sleep here, you know," she says.

"I'll come back. We'll have a sleepover."

It brightens her. "You should drop in for a viewing party," she says on our way to the car. "My friends would absolutely die if you walked through the door."

"Hmm, yeah, I'll have to check my schedule. You know, I'm kind of a big deal now, so . . ."

"Hey," she says, pointing a stern finger at me. "I was the one who changed your diapers. Don't you ever forget that."

21

Dad wants to take a break so he can pick up dinner. I put on the TV but nothing excites me. I write in my journal but it only makes me think more. I ask Mom what else Gavin said before he left the house this morning, but she doesn't remember him saying anything. When the front door finally opens it's just Dad with dinner.

I'm not hungry but Dad says we can't finish recording until I eat something. He and Mom eat pizza while I force noodles into my mouth.

"I tried pizza," I announce.

"You did?" Dad says. "When?"

"In the city with Gavin. It was the same day he took me around to all those John Lennon places."

Dad nods and he takes a drink and now I'm feeling bad that I didn't want to try pizza all those times with Dad but I tried it with Gavin.

It feels strange without Gavin here because for two weeks now he's been eating dinner with us and he cleans up the dishes and takes out the trash and fixes the Internet when it stops working. I don't like what Dad said about Gavin being flaky and not showing up when it seems like Dad is the one being flaky because he's the one who hasn't been here lately.

I hurry up and clear my plate, but Dad needs coffee.

"How's it going?" Mom says.

"So far, so good," Dad says. "Just waiting on our singer."

I know Dad was only trying to help when he offered to ask Christina to sing our song, but I don't want someone else to sing it. Gavin isn't just my singer, he's my McCartney and he's the blackbird and he can't let me down. If he doesn't get here soon I might have to ask Dad to bring me to Home Depot for some important supplies so I can slam my head against the concrete and get rid of my special memory forever, because I don't think I'll want to remember this day.

Mom puts the leftover pizza slices in the fridge. "What time do you think you'll be done?"

"Hard to say," Dad says, watching the coffeepot turn black. "You know how this stuff goes."

She stands there with her arms crossed and she rubs her big toe along the gritty line between tiles. After doing her toe thing she takes two wineglasses out of the cabinet and puts them on the counter. She looks down at the two wineglasses and touches her chin and puts one glass back in the cabinet and fills the other glass halfway.

Dad's equipment looks like the controls for a spaceship. Right now he's putting a sound like a low siren in the background. "That's so sad," I say.

"Should I take it out?"

"No. Sad is good, right?"

He doesn't answer but I already know that Dad thinks sad is good. He leans back in his chair and lets the song play and when it ends he plays it again. "The bridge could be better."

I nod like I agree, but actually I want to bury my head between the couch cushions.

"Do you have any other ideas?" Dad says.

I play him the other bridge I wrote. It's much simpler.

"We can work with that," Dad says and then he sings it, *We can work with that,* to the tune of the Beatles song "We Can Work

It Out," which was written by Paul. I was pretty sure John wrote the bridge to that song but after talking to Gavin I'm not sure who wrote what anymore.

"Is it true that Paul wrote the bridge for 'A Day in the Life'?" I ask.

"Yes. It's amazing, right?"

"I never knew that."

Together Dad and I play through the bridge a few times and we try out different chords until the section feels right. It's hard to impress Dad, but when he finally gets excited, you feel like you've done something really special. "Okay," he says, "let's record that."

He leaves me in the Quiet Room and I practice playing the new bridge a few times and then I say, "I'm ready."

I wait for Dad's voice in my headphones but he doesn't answer. Maybe he went to the bathroom. I look around the Quiet Room.

Saturday, July 18, 2009: Uncle Nick and Grandpa are finished building the walls for the Quiet Room and now I'm helping Dad paint them. Dad has to go over my areas a second time because I moved my brush in every direction instead of up and down like he asked. Dad lets me sign my initials in silver Sharpie near the socket.

I slide off the stool and find my initials. Seeing those letters makes me smile but my smiling can't last because I start to think about what's going to happen to my initials when Dad shuts the studio down. What if the new people paint over my initials? What if they turn this downstairs apartment into a hardware store like they did to John Lennon's favorite café? I hate hardware stores.

I hear Dad's voice in my headphones. "Okay, honey. Go for it."

I climb back into place. I play the part until Dad is happy and he tells me to come into the studio. When I get there, I see someone on the couch. "Hello, *Joan Lennon.*"

He says it with a British accent and it's hard not to smile. But I'm also pretty annoyed. "Where have you been?"

"I took a train ride," Gavin says.

He sounds like Bob Dylan and I don't like that at all because Bob Dylan is the worst singer in the world, besides Tom Waits, and we're never going to win the contest with a voice like that. But at least he made it here in time. That's all that matters. Well, almost. "Did you finish the lyrics?"

He reaches into his pocket and pulls out a piece of paper. "I did." He unfolds the paper and says, "Let me hear the song."

Dad plays the song and we watch Gavin's face as he listens and reads the words on his paper. When the song is over he says, "It sounds great. The bridge is different."

"Do you like it?"

"Yeah," he says. "I need a pen."

Dad hands him one.

"Play it again," Gavin says.

Gavin listens to the song again and he writes more words. This time when the song ends he stands up from the couch, and, without saying anything, he walks into the Quiet Room.

I'm lying on the couch and staring up at the ceiling. Gavin's voice is coming through the speakers. I can hear when he clears his throat and when he does a little hum and when he coughs. The song starts and he sings his words, the new words he just wrote and the words he already had, and when it all comes together, it sounds like a song I've heard before, not in my room or in the courtyard, but on the radio or YouTube. It doesn't feel like my song but it is my song. Our song. Dad's song too.

Morning comes and you're not here
An empty bed but I feel you near

Such a mess you left behind
Not so sure I'll make it this time
I hate you more than you'll ever know
Just come back and I'll let it go
I feel the urge to cut and run
But you tied me up, can't get undone

Keep running but I get nowhere
Keep swinging but I hit thin air
I hear you whisper in the back of my mind:
Start over, leave the past behind
Keep dwelling on what went wrong
Keep reaching for what is gone
I hear you whisper in the back of my mind:
Start over, leave the past behind

Life began when you arrived
What came before was a waste of time
Now I'm wondering where to go
Some answers I'll never know
I could sail to the farthest place
But no one leaves without a trace
I think you've already sealed my fate
Can't let you go, can never escape

Keep running but I get nowhere
Keep swinging but I hit thin air
I hear you whisper in the back of my mind:
Start over, leave the past behind

Keep dwelling on what went wrong
Keep singing the saddest song
I hear you whisper in the back of my mind:
Start over, leave the past behind

How do I go back home?
How do I go back home?
How do I go back home?
How do I go back home?
Alone.

I don't know if it's memorable but it's beautiful and Gavin even used my line about singing the saddest song. After doing a few more vocal takes, he comes out of the Quiet Room.

Dad looks excited. "I forgot how rich your voice is."

Gavin paces around the room. "There's a line that's still bothering me."

It must be the same line from before. I notice he already changed it from *get up and flee this place* to *sail to the farthest place*. He's walking back and forth through the basement and I'm busy thinking about the farthest place I know.

Monday, November 12, 2012: Mom is helping me make a model of our solar system and she makes sure I get Earth's tilt exactly right so that the sun (an actual lightbulb) shines more on the North Pole than the South Pole.

Mom says, "This is just one solar system. There are billions of other solar systems in our galaxy. And there are billions more galaxies too. And each of those galaxies has billions of solar systems."

I try to picture it all but it's too much math.

Gavin is on the couch and he's out of ideas.

"What about outer space?" I say. "It's the farthest you can go and it rhymes with *trace*."

Gavin looks up and Dad spins his chair around. Nobody's talking.

And then Gavin says quietly, "Stars." He turns to Dad. "When we look at them, we're seeing the past, right?"

"That could work," Dad says.

Gavin's pen is moving fast. He jumps up off the couch and disappears into the Quiet Room. Dad gives me a wink and spins back to the computer. I lie down on the couch and shut my eyes and the song plays again and this time Gavin sings the new line:

I could sail into outer space
But even stars, they leave a trace

I'm feeling proud that Gavin used my idea even though the new line doesn't make as much sense to me as the old one. But if Gavin is happy and Dad is happy, then I'm happy too. Actually, this is just about as happy as I've ever been in my whole life.

As soon as I realize how perfect it is, my happiness sinks a little, because I know this night will never happen again. After this, I'll send my song into the contest and Dad will close the studio and Gavin will go back to California and I'll go back to being alone. I know I'll always have this night saved in my memory but memories are never as good as the real moment, just like a cover version of a song is hardly ever as good as the original.

But I have to tell myself to get out of my own head because the night isn't over yet. The song isn't finished. It's all still happening and I better pay attention.

I listen to the song play over and over again and I never get tired of hearing it. Gavin's voice sounds better each time. At one point, Dad says, "I like the double meaning of the word *stars,*" and Gavin says, "I didn't even think of that," and Dad says, "A guy at work asked if it was true that I knew you." Gavin sings more and this time on the last chorus he changes part of the melody. And later Dad asks, "Everything cool?" and Gavin says, "I miss this, I forgot," and Dad says, "What took us so long?" and

I wonder the same thing. I never want Dad to leave the house again, or Gavin, and I wish we could all live down here and Mom could bring us food to eat and I'd even learn to like pizza if that's what it would take. It's like we're a band, the three of us. We just need a name, something with a *the* at the beginning, like the Beatles.

And then Gavin goes back into the booth and he sings a harmony with himself and now there are two Gavins. The song gets fuller and fuller and it all plays like a movie that I'll never get tired of watching. The song is so large now, it's the most popular song in the world, and I see every baby and old man singing the words and the music is going deep into their systems. I'm above it all, watching it happen, floating in the clouds, or I'm on a city stage winning first place, or I'm in a golden slumber, I don't know, I can be anywhere, because with Dad home and Gavin's voice coming through the speakers, it's so easy to drift away. But I don't want to go too far, because this is exactly where I want to be.

■ ■ ■ ■

HELP!

■ ■ ■ ■

22

"He got to our house late on Friday, January twenty-fifth, 2013," Joan says. "But I didn't actually see him that night. I was asleep."

Joan is telling me about the final time Sydney visited the Sullys.

Last night was so pure and gratifying, such a culmination, finishing our song, hearing it come to life. But now, this morning, I feel the natural comedown of having accomplished this big thing we were building toward. There's an emptiness again and I'm not sure I'm feeling sturdy enough to tackle what I know is Joan's only remaining memory of Sydney. At first I was hesitant to hear her recollections. Now I'm anxious at the thought of having no more left to hear.

I start out on the studio couch, sitting up, but once Joan begins, I feel the need to lie down. Resettled, I ask, "When did you see him?"

"The next morning," Joan says. "I come out of my bedroom and pass my parents' bedroom and Dad is still sleeping because he was up late in the studio. I get to the kitchen and I see Mom and Sydney sitting at the table with a laptop and Sydney says —"

"Wait," I say. "Would you mind going a little slower? What does he look like? Tell me about his face."

"Okay, well, he has brown eyes like me and his hair is short and gray and his chin is a little bit like a ball."

"What about his ears? Do you see his ears?"

"No."

"He had very droopy earlobes. They were so long they'd almost swing."

Joan examines her own ears with her fingers.

"Sorry," I say. "Go on."

"Sydney says, 'Good morning, Miss Joan. Quick, what's today?' and I say, 'Saturday, January twenty-sixth,' and he says, 'What day of the week was January twenty-sixth last year?' and I say, 'Thursday,' and he says, 'What about the year before that?' and I say, 'Wednesday' and he says, 'Brilliant, absolutely brilliant, you should go on *Ellen,* she'd love you,' and I ask, 'Who's Ellen?'

and Mom and Sydney tell me who Ellen is and now I'm excited because I would love to go on a TV show. But then they forget all about Ellen and they go back to staring at Sydney's computer screen."

"Can you see the screen?" I ask.

"No."

I'm grilling her way more than usual. I have this savage thirst to squeeze every last drop of him from her mind. I know he's not really here — he's been gone for nearly two months now — but in a way it feels like I'm watching him leave a second time.

"What happens next?" I ask.

"I go into the fridge to get a drink," Joan says.

"What is Sydney doing?"

"Talking to Mom, but I'm not paying attention. I'm too busy thinking about how cool it would be to go on TV. I pour myself some orange juice and I ask Mom to tell me more about the Ellen show, but she says, 'Excuse me, I'm in the middle of a conversation.' Now I'm paying attention to their conversation because I'm waiting for a space so I can speak. When I find a space I ask Mom again about the Ellen show and she says —"

"Hold on. What about their conversation? What are they saying?"

"I have no idea," Joan says. "It's very weird. First Mom says, 'Personally I like wolf den,' and then Sydney says, 'Me too, wolf den or breakfast time. I'm also considering D and D.' "

It sounds like Joan is speaking in tongues. "Can you repeat that again slowly?"

She recites the same terms: *wolf den, breakfast time, D and D.* The words still don't register. I'm not sure if they're names or phrases or titles or what. But Joan is already moving on.

"And then Sydney walks into the living room to make a phone call. Mom asks me what I want to eat and I tell her I'm not hungry yet. I ask her what we're doing today and she says she's thinking about taking me ice skating."

"Do you hear Sydney talking on the phone?" I ask.

"Only the very last part. Sydney says, 'Perfect, see you at eleven. Looking forward to it,' and then he comes back into the kitchen and —"

"Stop." I'm sitting up on the couch now, hands out. This could be my best and last chance at figuring out what Sydney was up to in New York.

I make Joan repeat the whole thing and then I ask, "When he was on the phone, was he over in the corner, talking quietly? Did it seem like he didn't want you and your mom to hear?"

"No," Joan says. "He was walking around the living room, talking normally."

"And you're sure *he* made the phone call? Or did the other person call *him*?"

She takes much longer than usual to answer. "I don't know. All I know is that his phone didn't ring."

It wouldn't have rung. It wouldn't have made any sound at all unless it had been resting against a hard surface. He always kept his phone on vibrate.

"What happens next?" I ask.

"I ask Mom about the Ellen show again and she tells me Ellen's last name. I take my glass of orange juice to the computer and I look up information about Ellen and I watch some of her videos on YouTube."

"What are Sydney and your mom doing?"

"They're talking, but I'm not listening, and then Sydney goes down to the studio and that's the last time I see him."

"Wait, you mean . . . ever?"

Joan doesn't answer. She doesn't have to. I already know from her silence.

I sit on the couch, feeling impossibly tired. It's as if I've been made to stay awake for the past two months, and only now do I realize how badly I need sleep.

But Joan isn't finished. "He came back to the house later that day. I was out with Dad, I never actually saw him, but I did eat one of the mini-cupcakes he brought for us. It was the best cupcake I ever had because it had crushed Reese's Pieces on top and there was even one cupcake in a special container for Mom that didn't have any gluten in it because that was the week she was convinced she was allergic to gluten."

"And you have no idea where he went?"

She shakes her head.

"Joan."

"Yes?"

I fear the answer, but I have to ask. "Is there anything else? Anything at all you can tell me?"

She lowers her eyes, shakes her head again.

I sit there, staring. I feel an itch on my cheek but I leave it unscratched. I couldn't lift my arm if I tried. My mind has abandoned its post, rendered me motionless. All I can do is stare forward, past the girl in her father's desk chair, across the room, through the walls of the house, into open air, into space. I'm still here, my body is, but I'm so far away.

When my mind reconnects with my body, I

rise up off the couch and head for the stairs. Joan follows me up to her apartment. We find Paige stuffing a book into her bag.

"I was just going to call you," Paige says. "Can I leave Joan with you? One of my students was supposed to come here, but now she needs me to go to her. I can send Joan next door, but I know she'd much rather be with you."

Joan is nodding. "That's fine," I say, barely computing. "Are you leaving right now?"

Paige fills up a water bottle, screws the lid on, slings her bag over her shoulder. "Yeah. I've got to run."

"Before you go."

She pauses at the door.

"Joan was telling me about the last time Syd was here, back in January. She said Syd was on the phone talking to someone he was meeting later that morning. Any idea who that could've been?"

Paige contorts her mouth as she thinks it over. "Maybe a broker?"

"Maybe," I say, but it would have to have been someone other than Claire, who claimed she saw Syd only that one time in February. I find it hard to believe that Syd would fly out here three separate times just to look at properties and, on top of that, lie about it. It makes no sense. None of it does.

"Before that phone call, you and Sydney were looking at his computer and you were talking about something. Joan, what were those words again? Wolf den. Breakfast time. And what was the last one?"

"D and D," Joan says.

"Does any of that ring a bell?" I ask.

"D and D," Paige repeats, working it into her brain.

"It sounded like you guys were trying to choose between the three," I say, hoping to jog her memory. I've been spoiled by Joan.

"You know what?" Paige says, arriving at an idea. "Maybe he was showing me different ads his company was considering. He'd ask my opinion about that sometimes. But honestly, I can't say for sure. It was more than six months ago. I'm sorry."

I feel myself heating up. I know if I'm not careful I might end up igniting again. I left California in the hopes of cooling off and it almost worked. I've done my best to face up to the past, between the memories and writing the song and finally going home to see my mother, and I was nearly to the other side. *This* close to regaining some sense of control over my life. But now I've been blindsided again.

"Gavin." Paige has her hand on my shoulder. "Are you all right?"

"Yeah."

She inspects my eyes. "You sure?"

"Yes." It's some of my best acting.

She heads for the front door, opens it, turns around, says something about a family outing that she'd like me to be a part of.

"Sounds good," I say. But I barely heard a word she said.

Wolf den. Breakfast time. D and D.

I plug each of the three mystery items into Google and get a wide range of results. On the side of the results page is a list of nearby places whose names contain pieces of my search words. One place is essentially an exact match: a restaurant right here in town called D&D's. It's located near a stop on the Light Rail.

Joan and I are on the train before I have time to second-guess myself. I figure it can't hurt to take a quick trip downtown to see what we can find. On that day in January, Syd was back at the Sullys' by the afternoon and on a plane that same night, so he couldn't have traveled far that morning. Maybe he was looking on his computer for a meeting place. Maybe, just maybe, he chose D&D's.

It's a long shot, I know. I turn to Joan, seated on the bench next to me, and ask her to write down the three mystery items on a clean page in her journal. As the train glides along, the two of us stare down at the page, hoping for enlightenment.

"What were the exact words Sydney said when he was getting off the phone?" I ask.

" 'Perfect, see you at eleven. Looking forward to it.' " Joan turns to me. "What does it mean?"

I have no idea.

And unfortunately, D&D's is not going to provide the clarity I'm seeking. I know this as soon as Joan and I step inside. Syd would never set foot in a restaurant like this, if you can even call it a restaurant. It's a tiny takeout joint serving mainly fried chicken. The numerous chicken variations are pictured on an illuminated box and the only place to sit is a shallow counter facing the street.

Joan approaches the large woman manning the deep fryer. "Excuse me," she says, presenting her journal. "Do these words mean anything to you?"

The woman shimmies over, her puffed lips oozing annoyance. She sizes us up before deeming the journal worthy of her eyes. "Is this supposed to be your order?"

"No," I say. "We're not sure what it is."

The woman takes the journal from Joan

and holds it up to the light. Her coworker arrives and now they're both inspecting it. "What is it?" the new woman asks. The previous woman grunts and hands it back.

My next question is asinine, given our surroundings. "I don't suppose you keep a record of who dines here?"

She answers my question with a question of her own. "Huh?"

"Never mind," I say. "Thanks for your time."

I turn to leave, but then I notice Joan ogling the soaking fries rising out of the oil. I place my wallet on the high counter.

"We'll take a side of fries to go."

We're seated on a bench, waiting for the next train to arrive to take us home. Joan is munching on her fries, using her shorts as a napkin.

Now that my internal temperature has fallen, I see how ludicrous it was to come out here. All on a whim. And to drag poor Joan along with me. At least this time I was able to buy her some food she actually enjoys.

"You sure you don't want any?" Joan asks, proffering a soggy fry.

"No, thanks. I'm good."

But I'm not good.

"I'm sorry," Joan says.

"For what?"

"For not paying more attention to what Sydney was saying."

I look over at her. I mean, I *really* look. Her scrawny but formidable presence. Her clothes in a mishmash of colors. Her determined eyes. She's been a beacon for me this whole time. And I hardly noticed that somewhere along the line, I had adopted a trusted sidekick. That's how organic our alliance was. She deserves my best attempt at a smile.

"It's not your fault, Joan. Not at all. You've been a big help. Believe me."

"What time is the next train supposed to come?" Joan asks.

"One twenty-four."

"What time is it now?"

I take out my phone to check and get sidetracked by a new text message. It's from my agent. He wants me to call him. Following some gut instinct, I scroll past it, keep scrolling, moving backward in time, passing older and older conversations, until I find one name.

"Hello?" Joan says. "The time?"

"Sorry."

I give her the time and then I do something I haven't done since Sydney died: I

266

open our old message thread.

I had avoided this for the same reason I avoided all reminders. I feared the pain would be too extreme. But I've come a long way since setting that fire. Like Paige said, I can't put it off forever. And besides, now I have a reason to look.

I scroll down, down, down, until I arrive, finally, at the date in question: January 26 of this year.

Sydney (1:31 p.m.): *Mr. Winters. Plane gets in at 8:20. Can't wait to see your battered face!*

I feel that brief thrill, the past awakened. The words are unmistakably his.

The day before he left for New York, there was a minor accident on the set of *The Long Arm.* During a staged fight scene, another actor landed one of his pretend punches on my face and left me with a shiner on my left cheek.

Me (1:32 p.m.): *Meet you at the terminal. I'll be the one in the mask.*

Sydney (1:32 p.m.): *I got us a gift.*

Me (1:33 p.m.): *Sounds kinky.*

Sydney (1:33 p.m.): *Xoxo!*

I wonder if the line about the gift could be a clue. For the life of me I can't recall what it was that Sydney brought home with him. There were always gifts and souvenirs.

Between his clients constantly unloading presents onto him — everything from cheap swag to expensive booze — and his own love of shopping, Syd rarely returned home from anywhere empty-handed.

After that message, there's a break in our correspondence until I arrive at LAX. Then, just two more messages.

Me (8:39 p.m.): *Here.*

Syd (8:47 p.m.): *Coming out now!*

I shut my eyes, try to picture him walking toward me. A full memory of that night at the airport doesn't exist. This is something different, based in truth but fabricated. I see him in the distance, exiting the glass doors, but it's too dark to make out his face. He's too far away. He's moving, but not getting any closer, never reaching me. I'm still here, waiting. But for how long?

"Gavin."

I feel Joan's hand on my arm. Our train has arrived. The doors are open. Time to go home. Wherever that is.

23

I wake up with a very crummy feeling because every new day is also an old day and today's new day is also Grandma Joan's birthday.

Before I get out of bed I spend a little time thinking of my favorite Grandma Joan memories, like when she made pancakes and the flame shot high into the air and she didn't even notice and Dad called them hibachi pancakes (Sunday, February 3, 2008). And when she jumped around in the bounce house with me at the Italian festival and the man yelled at her to get out because she wasn't a kid (Saturday, May 9, 2009). And I think of when she played "Jealous Guy" on the piano and she changed the words to *I'm just a jealous wife* (Thursday, December 24, 2009). But all these memories only make me feel worse.

I spend half the day trying to fill up all my new free time. I watch TV and go with Mom to the supermarket and write in my journal, and I check where the walrus is swimming (Bald Head Island, North Carolina). Now I'm in the living room in front of the computer but I'm just staring at it because I haven't decided if I should listen to music or play a game or watch a video or if I should just get up and walk around. Nothing I do is anywhere near as fun as writing songs and sharing memories with Gavin, and both of those things are over now.

Gavin and I finished our song the other night and Dad sent it into the contest and now we have to wait a couple of months until we find out if we'll be selected as finalists and invited to the award ceremony in New York City. I was so busy trying to finish the song in time that I never paid attention to how long it would take for the contest people to get back to us. I don't know if I can wait that long because waiting is the worst thing ever invented.

It's especially hard now that Gavin and me have finished all my Sydney memories. It got a little annoying to have to sit there and tell Gavin every tiny thing, but now that it's over, I wish it weren't. No one has ever asked me so many questions about my memories or cared so much about what I have to say. Gavin never thought I was acting like a know-it-all when I was trying to be very careful about telling him exactly what happened. I wish we had a new project to work on so I could go downstairs right now and wake him up and tell him that it's time for us to get started.

My time with Gavin isn't the only thing I'm losing. It didn't really sink in that the studio would actually be closing until the other night when we were all downstairs recording and I had a feeling like I wanted to be doing that exact thing forever, making songs with Dad and Gavin, and that's exactly where I wanted to be doing it, in Dad's studio. It's almost August already, which means that pretty soon Dad will start moving all of his stuff out.

It's like when the school year ends and you clean out your cubby. The teacher takes all your projects off the wall and you stuff your projects and pencils and erasers into your backpack. You take it all home with you because next year you have to go to a whole new classroom, which I hate because I've got so many memories in the old classroom and I never want to leave. But this is even worse because there's no new classroom to move into. There's no new studio. Where will Dad record? Where will he put his piano and guitars and desk and

271

couch and drums? Where will he hang all his John Lennon pictures? Where will I write my new songs? If I win the contest — *when* I win the contest — my fans will want to hear more songs and I can't write here in the living room with Dad's smelly sneakers by the door and Mom working at the kitchen table and the mailman ringing the doorbell with a package and the phone always ringing like it is now.

Mom finally answers it. "Yes, this is Paige Sully," she says. "Oh, right, I'm sorry. Yes, I've been meaning to get back to you. I was going to talk it over with my husband. It totally slipped my mind."

Things don't slip Mom's mind too often.

"I see," Mom says. "So she would be in front of an audience?"

Now I'm really listening because I'm pretty sure *she* is me. I watch Mom reach into a drawer and pull out a pad and pen.

"And you're featuring only kids for this, right? Yes, it does sound interesting, but you know, the timing isn't great. I know. I realize that. Maybe there's a future show that would be right for her. I understand that. We'll just have to take our chances. Yes, we're going to have to pass on this one."

Mom moves her pen across the pad without lifting it off the paper even once.

"Yes, I'm positive," Mom says. "I'm sorry too. Thank you."

She hangs up the phone and I turn back to the computer, but I'm not even looking at what's on the screen because I'm watching Mom's reflection as it gets bigger and darts away.

After she's gone, I find Mom's pad in the kitchen drawer. On top of the page is my name and below that is a long list of other names and phone numbers and one of them is Dr. Robert Brickenmeyer. Somewhere near the middle of the page there's one whole line of information crossed out with Mom's pen. It's a person's name, a phone number, and all the way to the right it says: *The Mindy Love Show*.

I'm in front of the TV at exactly eleven o'clock. I've heard of *The Mindy Love Show* but I've never actually seen it before. I've got my journal open to a fresh page because I want to write down any ideas I have while I'm watching.

The first thing on the screen is a photo of a bald man in a suit. I hear a lady's voice: "Three years ago Arthur Ballibloc was living the American dream. As the CFO of a Fortune Five Hundred company, he could've had pretty much anything his heart desired."

As the lady speaks, the photos change. All the photos show the same man.

"But today, Arthur has no use for money. He gave it all away when he became a freegan. Now Arthur survives solely on what he obtains from his environment. We'll find out how a man goes from high roller to dumpster diver when I sit down with Arthur and the family he left behind, next on . . ."

The man's face is gone and now I see rows and rows of people sitting in a theater. A tall lady in a skirt shows up from behind a curtain and she walks easily in her high heels down to the front of the stage. Her smile is sweet, but not too sweet, which is how Principal Hershwin is. If the audience claps any harder, their hands are going to break off and fly away like butterflies.

The lady says, "Who loves you?"

And the crowd shouts, "Mindy!"

She waits for the people to quiet down and she tells us more about this Arthur guy. I can't get interested in Arthur because I'm more interested in the way Mindy is *talking* about Arthur, like he's someone really important. "Please welcome my guest, Arthur Ballibloc."

The audience whistles and cheers and claps and I want to join in but I have no idea what we're so excited about.

Arthur looks nothing like his photos. He's not fat anymore and his teeth are muddy and his beard looks like something a mama bird would try to raise her babies in.

I'm so focused on what's happening on the TV screen that I don't hear Mom walk past me on her way into the kitchen. "What are you watching?"

I grab the remote control and turn off the TV. "Nothing." I hop up off the floor and go downstairs. I hurry through the studio instead of taking my time because it doesn't give me the best feeling to be here anymore now that it's so dark and no one is using it.

Gavin's door is only a little open so I make it all the way open. He's in bed, staring up at the ceiling. I hop onto the mattress and crush his foot by accident. He seems annoyed, but beds are supposed to be jumped on and it's not my fault his legs are so long.

"Have you ever seen *The Mindy Love Show*?" I ask.

He speaks in a very lazy voice. "Isn't that one of those sad daytime talk shows?"

"No, everyone on the show is very happy," I say, opening up my journal in case I need to look at my notes. "Do you remember how Sydney said I should be on TV? Well, someone from *The Mindy Love Show* called Mom and it sounds like they want me to go on their show."

"Good for you," he says, but not like he really means it.

"I think you should come with me and we can play our song on TV."

Gavin smiles, but only because he feels bad for me.

"Think about it," I say. "It's perfect because this way even if we don't win the contest, people will still hear our song."

"I appreciate the offer, Joan. But I don't think I'm up for it."

Ever since we rode the train back home from the chicken restaurant yesterday, Gavin has been in one of his quiet moods, the kind he was in when he first came to our house. But I can't let him be quiet now. I need him to sing.

"You're lucky that people know who you are," I say. "I'm still trying to get people to know my name because they can't remember it unless they know it first. Don't you want to help me do that? I can't play the song without you. You're my partner."

There's something wrong with his face. He looks exactly like a blackbird today. There's a shadow all over him. "Yeah, well, I'm not a very good partner." He lets out a long breath, like I'm making him very tired.

"Yes, you are," I tell him. "You're a great partner. We just need a new project. We can't just lie in bed for the next two months."

"Two months?"

"That's when they announce the finalists for the contest and then later in the fall they have the ceremony in New York and they choose a winner and they put the winning song on their website so the whole world can fall in love with it."

I go into the studio and find the ad for the contest on Dad's desk and bring it back to Gavin. I can't believe I never showed it to him before.

He reads the front of the ad and turns it over to look at the other side but the other side is an ad for something else. "Joan, look, I think it's cool that we did the song. And I appreciate you letting me be a part of it. It came out great. I think you should feel really proud of it. I am."

It sounds like he's about to say *but.*

"But," he says, "I don't think you should get your hopes up about this contest."

"Why? You don't think we can win?"

"I'm not saying that." He tosses the ad onto the bed. "I just don't want you to get hurt. You're putting so much into this and sometimes things just don't go like you plan."

I remember him saying the same thing to me once before, back when we were talking about why he and Sydney didn't have a baby. And now he's turning his head to the wall and I'm turning my head to the door because I know exactly what's happening here: he doesn't want to have anything to do with me now that I've already shared all my Sydney memories.

It's like when the smartest girl in the class, Wendy Wang, asked to be my partner for the trivia game on Wednesday, November 14, 2012, and I thought it was weird because Wendy never seemed to pay attention to me before and all of a sudden she was acting so nice to me. But then after we lost the game she was bored with me again and I realized she wanted to be my partner only because she thought my memory would help her win.

I'm all by myself again and I'm surrounded by only sad things, the studio and Grandma Joan's birthday and Gavin, except the studio isn't something I can make be any less sad right now, and the same goes for Grandma Joan, but maybe that's not true about Gavin.

I slap my forehead very loudly. "Okay, I guess I have to tell you the truth now. I lied when I told you there were no more Sydney memories left. I actually have one more."

He rolls over. "What are you talking about?"

"I didn't want to tell you before, but now I'm ready to tell you."

"Joan."

"Let's get started. It's February fourteenth. No, I mean February fifteenth. Yes, February fifteenth, 2013. It's a Friday. Sydney is walking through the door. Look at him. He looks so nice with his shirt and his pants, they look like blue pants, yes, they're blue pants, and of course he's not wearing socks because he hates socks and there's his bracelet, which you're wearing now. Wow. He looks so great. His ears are very long too. I see that. They're so long. And do you want to know what he says? He says, 'Hello, Miss Joan,' and then I say, 'Hi, Mr. Sydney,' and he says, 'How are you?' and I say,

'Good. How are you?' and he says, 'I'm good,' and then I say, 'How is Gavin doing?' and he says, 'Oh, Gavin is home in California and he's doing great and I love him so much.' "

Gavin is very still.

"And then I say, 'I've never met Gavin. I'd love to meet him one day.' And Sydney says, 'I think you would really like him because he's nice and he's helpful and he's smart and he's tall and he's got very nice eyes.' "

"He says all that?" Gavin asks.

"Yes."

"Those are nice things to say."

"I think so."

He shuts his eyes a long time and then he finally sits up on the bed and he looks at me like Dad does when he's waiting for me to stop fooling around. "I know what you're doing, Joan, and it's really sweet, seriously. I don't even know what to say . . ."

I guess he's not lying when he says that last part because he doesn't say another word. He's not even looking at my face anymore. He's looking down at my hands. I look down too and I see my journal.

"Did you have that journal when Sydney was here in January?" Gavin asks.

"No," I say and then I realize why he's

asking — because he's wondering if my journal has something important about Sydney. "The journal I was using back in January is upstairs in my bedroom."

He nods like I should go get it right now, so I do. I run up to my room and grab the journal from January and by the time I'm back, I've found something.

"After Sydney left that day," I tell Gavin, "Mom asked me to go downstairs and strip the bed and empty the garbage. There was a paper bag sitting on top of the trash can and I knew it was from the cupcakes that Sydney brought home to us and I loved those cupcakes, so I drew the logo in my journal."

Gavin gets off the bed and takes the January journal from me. He finally has his energy back.

"Does this help you?" I ask.

He stares at it for a while and then he types into his phone. He reads his screen and he says, "It looks like there's only one Kroftman's and it's in Brooklyn."

"Is that good or bad?"

He squeezes his chin like people do when they're thinking very hard. "I don't know," Gavin says. "But I need to find out."

24

I pull Paige aside as we're entering the restaurant. "I need to ask you something."

She gestures for Ollie and Joan to go ahead in to where Ollie's father and brother are already waiting. We're here tonight, about to dine in some strip-mall establishment deep in suburbia, to honor the memory of Ollie's mother. Apparently it's a family tradition and apparently Paige extended the invitation to me yesterday and apparently I told her I'd be happy to join them. I have no memory of any of this. I was preoccupied at the time. I'm still preoccupied.

Paige stands under the ivy green awning, youthful in her spaghetti-strap dress. Her bony shoulders give off a girlish vibe, but her heavy eyes betray her years. "What's wrong?" she asks.

"He was in Brooklyn. Syd was in Brooklyn."

"When? What are you talking about?"

I undo one more button on Ollie's shirt. I didn't pack any formal wear. "When he was last here, back in January, you were with him in the morning. Then he went somewhere, he met someone, and when he came back he had cupcakes from a bakery in Brooklyn."

"So?"

"What was he doing there? That's what I need to find out."

Paige presses her palm to her forehead. I've exhausted her once again.

"I know what you're going to say, Paige. You think I'm turning this into something that it's not, but what if it's true? What if there really was someone else? It would change everything we had together. How am I supposed to go on with that question always in the back of my mind?"

She doesn't answer, so I keep talking.

"Certain things don't add up. Why wouldn't he tell me he met with a broker in February? Why keep that a secret? And why didn't he tell you he was here in February or April? Normally he'd go out of his way to come see you, right? He said he took you out to dinner but it was an outright lie. But you *were* with him that morning in January. Think about it. Was there something you

284

guys talked about that stands out? Anything? Please."

Ollie pokes his head out of the restaurant. "Table's ready."

"One minute," Paige says. She takes a deep breath but remains quiet, staring down at the pavement.

An elderly couple exit the restaurant and pass between us on their way to the parking lot.

I wait until we're alone again. "I tried to let it go, Paige. I did."

She finally meets my eyes. "What do you need from me?"

It's simple. "Help."

We're seated at a round table off in the corner. There are six of us: me, Paige, Joan and Ollie, and then there's Ollie's father, Jack, and his brother, Nick. Nick is older than Ollie and has one more kid and twenty more pounds.

I've been staring at the menu for five minutes now without actually reading it. When we were standing outside, Paige looked so frightened of me, like I was some paranoid patient who skipped his meds. I hope I *am* just being paranoid. Nothing would please me more. If Paige can just help me find some tangible proof for why my suspicions are entirely unfounded, I will happily return to the semi-rational man I used to be.

She's seated to my right now, studying her menu. Meanwhile, across the table, Jack hasn't even opened his. Something tells me he knew what he was going to order as soon as he woke up this morning.

The last time I saw Ollie's father was probably at Ollie and Paige's wedding. He's got a thicker build than his younger son, and a lot more to say. While Ollie is often introspective and restrained, his father can be rather outspoken.

Jack grabs a piece of bread from the center basket and winks at his granddaughter. "I heard you wrote a beautiful song, doll."

"Yes," Joan says, seated directly to my left. "Me and Gavin wrote it and Dad helped and I think it's good enough to win the whole contest."

"That's wonderful," Jack says. "So what are you up to for the rest of the summer?"

Joan smiles, as if she's been waiting all along for this exact question. "I'm thinking it would be a good idea for me and Gavin to play our song on a TV show."

"Wouldn't that be great?" Jack says. "I'm sure Gavin could help with something like that, couldn't you, Gavin?"

286

I told Joan earlier today how I felt about the idea. But of course, she mostly ignores the word *no*. Now I've got her grandfather staring me down.

Thankfully, Ollie saves me. "Dad, you can't just snap your fingers and get on TV."

"Actually," Joan says, "there's this one show called *The Mindy Love Show* that called the house. Mom already talked to them. It sounded like they really wanted me on their show."

Paige gives her daughter a stern look and then addresses the table. "Yes, I did speak to someone over there but —"

"Sounds like a great opportunity," Jack says. "Looks like we may have two celebrities at our table."

Joan is beaming.

"Mindy Love," Ollie says. "Isn't she a Dr. Phil type?"

"She's very nice," Joan says. "I watch her show all the time."

"Since when?" asks Paige.

"I'm sorry," Ollie says. "I don't think I can let you go on a show like that."

"Why not?" Joan asks.

"Because those people are predators. Why don't we make a video of you performing the song and we'll put it up on YouTube?"

Ollie knows full well that no one will see

that video. But I don't blame him for wanting to protect her from the media circus.

"Please, Daddy."

"She can handle it," Jack says. "Look at her. She's a tiger."

The waitress approaches, but I wave her off.

"Dad, she's a little girl," Ollie says.

"So what? I see little girls singing on TV all the time."

"There's a little girl killing it right now on *America's Got Talent,*" Nick says. And then, reading our faces, "I watch it with the kids."

"It's not her music they're interested in," Ollie says.

"Maybe not," Jack says. "But you have to take what's given. Your mother never got a chance to play in front of an audience like that."

The mention of his wife quiets the table and reminds us why we're all here tonight. From what I know, she was a weekend musician, never cracked her dream of being a full-time performer. Clearly that's where Ollie caught his bug. Joan too.

Jack continues, but in a more conciliatory tone. "What can they possibly ask her, Ollie? What day was August twenty-second, 2010?"

"Sunday," Joan answers.

"There you go," Jack says. "If she wants to do it, why not let her try?"

"She already did," Paige says. "I took her to see a doctor and it wasn't the best experience. Besides, it doesn't matter at this point. I already told them no."

"Then I'm not going on vacation with you," Joan says.

"That's fine. You can stay with your cousins."

"Everyone, calm down," Ollie says, considering the menu for the hundredth time.

I wonder how Syd and I would've handled this situation as parents. Ultimately, I think I'd be the one forbidding it. Out of fear, what else.

Taking advantage of the break in conversation, Jack leans over to Ollie. "So when's this vacation happening?"

"Next spring."

Jack kneads his chin. "Yeah, that might be tough, bud. That's our busy time."

Paige drops her elbows on the table, leans in. "What's that, Jack?"

"Nothing," Ollie says.

"I was just saying that spring may be a problem," Jack says. "Especially if Ollie is taking over scheduling."

"I can handle it while he's gone," Nick says.

"We'll figure it out," Ollie says, locking eyes with Paige. She turns away, not liking what she sees. I know how much the vacation means to her. Back at the house she's got half a dozen travel guides stacked up on the coffee table.

The busboy arrives and delivers flutes to the adults. The waitress, right behind him, fills each glass with champagne. When the servers have left, Jack raises his glass. The rest of the table follows.

"I'll keep this short." Jack's broad shoulders rise with a breath and sink back into place. "I met Joanie at my friend Marvin's wedding. She sang a song with the band and I was smitten. I was just a kid compared to her, but our ages didn't matter. I asked her to dance, and the rest is history. We had forty-one beautiful years together. Even the last couple. I'm counting those too. I know you're up there now, looking down on us, and I just want you to know I love you. I miss you. We all miss you. And there's not a single day that goes by when you're not with me. I mean that. Happy birthday, dear."

Paige dabs her eye with a napkin. On my other side, Joan seems lost in one of her time warps, her body frozen, her hand gripping her water glass.

My mind drifts too. Syd's favorite restaurant was up in Laurel Canyon. I can't imagine ever setting foot in that place again. I don't know how Jack manages, how he can come back to this place after coming here with his wife for so many years. As inspiring as it is to witness his resilience, the way I feel now, it's hard to believe I'll ever get to that point. Especially not after this latest setback.

But there will always be setbacks. There will always be reminders. Every calendar year there's another birthday, another anniversary. The streets I walk down, the restaurants I eat in, the triangle-folded napkin resting on my lap, they all speak of the past. Sydney is everywhere, always.

I finish my champagne and nod to Jack in appreciation. He's not the only one who's made it through to the other side. My mother is right there with him, and so many others. Maybe the trick, when I'm finally ready, is to quit treating these reminders like treacherous chasms to leap over. And to one day, maybe, see them as good reasons to stop and celebrate.

25

I hold my key-chain flashlight in my mouth and shine it on my journal. It's dark in the Quiet Room and I don't want to turn the ceiling light on because then this place won't be a good hiding spot anymore.

The Quiet Room is the perfect place to go when I'm feeling extra-lonely because only good memories have happened in here. It's where I sit when Dad records my songs. As soon as you step inside this little room it's like you're the most important person in the world because every sound is blocked out except the sound you're making.

Right now the only sound I'm making is with my pencil against the paper. There's so much to write about and think about, like how Gavin doesn't want to be my partner anymore now that we finished our song and we handed it in. I finally know how bummed the Beatles must have felt when they broke up and they had to do all those shows and interviews all alone without anyone else to share the spotlight with. It must have sucked.

And then there's Dad, who I used to think understood me better than anyone else, because he's the only one who listens so closely to music and the only one who remembers all the artists who were once big but aren't anymore and the only one who knows how powerful one song can be. But it seems like he's forgotten about all of that now.

It just won't be the same without the studio. Enough has changed around here already. People think I shouldn't miss things because I always have the memories of them saved in my brainbox, but the memories only make me miss the things more. That's why it was so hard to act normal tonight in the restaurant while everyone drank out of their fancy glasses, because I actually *saw* Grandma Joan sitting at the table with us. I wanted to talk to her and tell her about my song but I couldn't because she wasn't really there.

Gavin should know what I'm talking about. When I shared my Sydney memories with him, it was like he got confused sometimes and thought Sydney was actually sitting there in front of him. I guess that makes us even closer than I thought, because we both know what it means to lose someone special.

Dad says Grandma Joan is a spirit, and Aunt Lauren says she's in heaven, and Grandpa says she's an angel, and my older cousin says she's in a box with worms. Mom has students who believe a grandma can turn into a different animal and come back to life, but I have my own idea. I think Grandma lives inside a cassette tape and when I listen to the cassette tape and I hear her sing and play piano, it almost feels like she's singing and playing just for me.

I turn off my flashlight and close my journal because now I want to find Grandma's tape. I want her songs to remind me how good it feels to be around her. I push open the heavy door and it seems like someone just pulled earplugs out of my ears because now I hear voices: Dad's and Gavin's.

"You remember?" Gavin says. "You wrapped your hand up, but the bandage kept unraveling. You tore it off in the middle of the song and it landed on my head."

"That's right," Dad says. "I cut it on that stupid lock we had on the trunk." He sounds much happier than he did at dinner. "How about the show in DC when you walked on the pool table?"

"I was out of my mind back then," Gavin says.

"Was?"

They both laugh.

Then Dad says, "How's it been going?"

"It?" Gavin asks.

"You. How are you?"

"Some days are okay. Some days really aren't."

"It sucks, man. I'm sorry. I don't know what else to say."

"Yeah."

It gets quiet. I'm starting to sweat in here. Dad made it so the air conditioner doesn't flow so well in the Quiet Room because it's too noisy when he's recording.

Now Gavin is asking Dad if he remembers anything about the last time Sydney visited us in January and Dad is doing what he always does if the subject isn't music: forgetting. "Sorry," Dad says, which is another thing he always does: apologizes for forgetting. "Did you ask Paige?"

"She didn't remember much."

"Really?" Dad says. "That's surprising. She usually holds on to that stuff. She can still remember what we ate for dinner each night on our honeymoon. It's amazing. I can barely recall what we had for dinner last night."

Gavin doesn't say anything and Dad just keeps talking.

"I've always thought that's where Joan got her memory from. But the doctor said it doesn't work like that. Who knows."

Dad finally shuts up and everything stays quiet for a long time. I climb onto the stool and crouch on my knees and peek through the window. Dad and Gavin both have glasses in their hands. Dad has his feet up on the couch. His eyes are moving all around the studio and I have to duck in the window so he doesn't see me. I hear him say, "It'll be hard to tear this place down."

Gavin still isn't speaking.

"But hey," Dad says, "I lived out my dream. Almost twenty years."

"Are you sure it's the right move?" Gavin says finally.

"I think so. I'm tired of scrambling. It's too much, having everyone sacrifice just for me. I should be the one taking care of them."

"But you are."

I raise my head slowly. Dad is staring into his glass like he found an eyelash or a fruit fly.

"It doesn't have to be all or nothing, right?" Gavin says. "Why don't you set up a little spot for yourself upstairs?"

"I don't know. I sort of feel like it does have to be all or nothing. I'm like an addict. If I see an instrument lying around, I have to play it. Before I know it, hours have gone by. Honestly, right now it feels like maybe my music days are over."

I hear the loudest cymbal crashing in my ears and rattling my bones and I almost fall off my stool. Not really, but that's how it feels. That's how much Dad's words shake me. He told me he was closing the studio, but he never said anything about not making music anymore. That's a whole different thing.

I want to jump out of the Quiet Room and run to Dad and beg him to keep the studio open and to quit working for Grandpa and to just leave everything the way it's always been. We already lost one musician in the family, Grandma Joan. We can't lose another. I'll be the only one left.

But Dad already said no to me once tonight and I don't want to hear it again. I decide to stay in the Quiet Room and think this through. It seems like Dad is doing the same thing he did after our dog Pepper died. Once Pepper was gone, Dad took Pepper's bed and toys and food and he threw it all in the garbage. It's like he was purposely trying to forget Pepper and now he's doing it again with music. It's what Gavin did when he burned all of Sydney's stuff. But Gavin didn't *really* want to forget Sydney. He wanted to hold on to him and I helped him do that. Maybe I can do that for Dad too, help him hold on to what I know he loves.

But how? I can ask Grandpa to fire Dad, but I don't think he'd ever do it. I heard him saying earlier at dinner that he named his business Sully and Sons because he wanted both of his sons to be working with him and now they finally are. And Mom already told me weeks ago that she's tired of having to pay for the studio, so she's definitely not going to help.

Actually, that's not all Mom told me:

Tuesday, July 9, 2013: "If you want to pay for the studio, be my guest."

Maybe I'm the one who has to do it. If I can find a way to keep the studio, then Dad won't be able to forget, because all his instruments will still be here, and if they're still here, he'll see them, and if he sees them, he said it himself, he'll have no choice but to play them.

The next morning, when the house is very quiet, I open the drawer in the kitchen and

I find the phone number that Mom crossed out the other day. Next to the number is the name Felicia Dufresne.

I know I shouldn't do it, but I can't just sit around anymore and watch Dad become a different person. I have to remind him who he really is.

Mom said that some of the people who call the house about me want to give us money, and I'm hoping *The Mindy Love Show* is one of them.

I dial the number and a lady answers.

I whisper, "Is this Felicia?"

"Yes, this is Felicia. Who is this?"

"My name is Joan Sully."

"Can you speak up, ma'am?"

"I'm Joan Sully," I repeat just a tiny bit louder. I don't want anyone to hear me. "I think you spoke to my mom, Paige Sully?"

She must have hung up, that's what I'm thinking, but then her voice comes back. "You're the girl with the memory."

"Yes. That's me."

"Joan Sully. Well, well, well, we've heard some incredible things about you. Let's see, what day of the week was December sixth, 1923?"

"I don't know."

"You don't?" Felicia says, sounding angry.

"I was born in 2003."

299

"Oh, right. Of course. How can I help you, Joan?"

"I'm calling about *The Mindy Love Show.*"

"Yes, you know, we were *really* hoping to feature you on our whiz-kid episode. We've got an eleven-year-old premed student, nine-year-old twins who are chefs, and an eight-year-old herpetologist."

"That's great because I have good news. My mother changed her mind. I can go on your show. Just tell me when you want me to come in and I'll be there."

"Oh," Felicia says, turning that one small word into a whole song. "That's a shame. I wish you would've called sooner. I'm afraid it's too late now."

"Too late? No, it's not too late. Why would it be too late?"

"We're shooting the episode tomorrow."

"That's okay. I don't have anything to do tomorrow."

"No, you don't understand. We're completely booked."

"But you called my mother just the other day!" I say too loudly.

"Yes," Felicia says. "We were holding a spot for you. But now that spot's been taken."

"I want my spot back. You have to give me my spot back."

Felicia laughs like I've told the funniest joke, but no one ever thinks of me as a funny person. "This isn't some web series, okay? This is network television. I can't just add you to the show at the last minute."

I ask myself: *What would Mom do?* She's a master on the phone because she always gets the cable company to fix our bills. "Well, I guess we'll just have to go with Dr. Phil, then."

"Dr. Phil?"

"Yes. He wanted me really badly."

"Is he doing a whiz-kid show too?"

"Um, yes. I'm pretty sure he is."

"No," Felicia says.

"Yes. I better call him right now and tell him I'm ready. I wonder where my mom put his phone number."

"Let me speak to your mother. I really should be discussing this with her. I'm sure she and I can figure something out."

"My mom said I should do this by myself," I say, which isn't a complete lie. "You can talk to me."

"Joan, listen to me. *Dr. Phil* is on at the same time as us and we have way more viewers, so if I were you, I'd definitely want to be on *our* show, not his. Plus, you don't want to fly all the way to California. That's just ridiculous. It's such a long flight and it's so hot out there in the summer. Let me see . . . oh, look at this! It appears we have some room at the top of the show. Why don't we just slide you right in there? How does that sound?"

"It sounds good. But what about the money? Do you pay a lot of money?"

"Oh my," Felicia says. "You know, I'd prefer to discuss that with your parents. But yes, our pay is industry standard."

I'm not sure how much Dad needs to keep the studio open but *industry standard* sounds like a lot. "And you're in New York City, right?"

"Yes, and I see you're right across the river, so that should be a piece of cake. What do you say? Are we all set?"

I don't want Dad's music days to be over. I just want everything to go back to normal. I want him to be downstairs right now playing his instruments and not to miss any more trips to New York City, and while all of that is happening I'd also like to play my song for thousands of people on TV and have it go deep into their systems so they'll never forget me and I'll finally feel safe inside their boxes. I don't even care if Gavin is with me or not, because I can still sing a little bit and a little bit is better than no bit. Besides, Mom already said that I could do this if I really want to.

"Yes," I say.

"Excellent! I'll go ahead and send your mother the paperwork. It'll have our location and your call time. Have your mother sign the last page and bring that with you tomorrow. Do you have her e-mail address handy? I'll zip it right over."

I tell Felicia to send the paperwork to our family e-mail address. I say good-bye and I'm about to go on the computer to get Felicia's e-mail, but just as I'm hanging up, Dad walks into the kitchen. I'm worried that he heard me on the phone, but probably not, because he hasn't had his coffee, which means he's not totally awake yet.

"I thought you'd be working today," I say.

"I'm going in late."

"Where's Mom?"

"She had to run out." He pours a big glass of water and drinks all of it. "Have you had breakfast?"

"No."

"How about crepes?"

I miss Dad making breakfast, but I can't stick around. "No, thanks. I'm not hungry."

I try to leave the room.

"Joan," he says. "Sit down."

It takes Dad almost twenty minutes to get

breakfast ready, because he's still waking up and also because he takes his crepe-making very seriously. He fills my crepe with Nutella and strawberries that he cuts paper-thin. Then he folds the whole thing up, sprinkles powdered sugar on top, and puts it in front of me. Before he's had a chance to sit down at the table with his own crepe, I'm already halfway done with mine, that's how good it is.

"So," he says, putting down his coffee mug and cutting his crepe with the side of his fork. "Are you going to tell me what you were doing in the studio last night?"

I didn't plan to, but I fell asleep in the Quiet Room. Dad and Gavin just kept talking and I was too scared to leave the vocal booth. Then somebody said my name and the door pushed open and Dad carried me to my room and covered me with a blanket. When I opened my eyes, my journal was waiting on my nightstand.

"Writing in my journal," I answer.

"Why down there?"

"I like it there."

He stops chewing his crepe, which is filled with yucky bananas and some type of gooey cheese. "I know you do."

He watches the table and I watch too, thinking there might be something to see, but the movie he's watching is playing only in his head. I know how that is.

"When I was your age," Dad says, "Uncle Nick and I asked Grandpa to make us a tree house. He wanted us to build it ourselves. He did most of the work, but we had our hands on the tools. We held the wood in place. We felt like we were building it. At the end, we had this thing that we helped make. We could put our hands on it, touch it. You don't get that from a song. It exists in the ether."

"What's the ether?"

"The air. You can't see it. It's mostly in our minds. Music involves a lot of faith."

Memories are that way too. That's why I like keeping a journal. It makes all my memories feel more real.

Dad's arm is resting on the table and his Monkey Finger tattoo is staring right at me. "I like it better when you're home," I say.

He takes his thumb and wipes Nutella off my cheek. Even after the Nutella is gone, he keeps staring. "I know it's hard, Joanie. It's hard for me too. But when you go back to school in September, you won't even notice I'm gone."

But that's not true.

Wednesday, May 1, 2013: I walk in the front door after school and I drop my book bag on the floor and grab an apple out of the fridge and I walk down to the studio and Dad is at his computer. I grab the Gibson off the rack and I start playing and Dad is working and I'm working too and we're not even talking to each other but it's perfect.

That school day is pretty much like every other school day, except the songs are different and our clothes are different and sometimes it's a nectarine in my hand and not an apple and sometimes I'm not even playing music because I'm doing my homework instead, but I'm still down in the studio with Dad.

And now Mom comes through the front door wearing her sunglasses. I look at her hands, thinking she might have gone food shopping or maybe she got her nails painted at the salon. But her hands are empty and her nails look dull and clear. She's not even carrying her purse, which is weird, and her hair is up in a ponytail, which is even weirder. Mom hates her ears, so she puts her hair up only if she's really hot, like when she's exercising. But right now she's in her normal clothes, not her workout clothes.

"Where were you?" I ask.

"I went for a walk," Mom says, which for her is even weirder than not having her purse or wearing her hair in a ponytail. "Is

306

Gavin still sleeping?"

"I think so," Dad says.

Mom opens the studio door and heads downstairs.

Dad and I watch her go and then Dad turns to me in his chair and reaches out his arms. "Come here." He pulls me in and the hug makes me feel even worse because it only reminds me how happy I am when he's around. Sometimes I forget things too.

"I'm sorry about the whole *Mindy Love* thing," Dad says into my ear. "I'm just trying to do what's right for you."

I'm trying to do what's right for me too. And while I'm doing that, I'm also trying to do what's right for him.

26

In the dark, a familiar voice calls to me, whispers my name. I lift my head, open my eyes, squint against the light. A figure stands in the doorway. I wonder, for just a moment, if it might be him. Have I finally woken up from this long nightmare?

"You awake?" the figure says.

It's not Sydney. Of course, it's not Sydney. It's Paige.

I drop my heavy head back to the pillow. "Yeah," I answer.

"Get up. Get dressed."

"That may take a while."

"Please," Paige says. "We need to talk."

She leaves and shuts my door.

"This was his favorite spot," Paige says.

We're in Riverview Park, just a few blocks from the Sully house. We're seated on a concrete foundation that used to be the floor of a gazebo. According to Paige, the gazebo's top blew off during last year's superstorm.

"I don't think he thought much of the neighborhood," Paige says, "but he loved the view from up here."

Our legs dangle off the side of the foundation, our eyes forward. The concrete is warm under our thighs. Out ahead, a blinding sun rises up over Manhattan.

"There's something I haven't told you," she says.

My heart revs up, adrenaline focusing my mind. I had wondered, after some of the things Ollie said to me last night about Paige's uncanny recall, if it was possible she knew more than she was letting on.

"I didn't think it would do you any good. But I see now you're never going to let it go and I don't blame you. If what you were saying yesterday is true, then Sydney was keeping things from me too."

I didn't want to be right about this. I desperately wanted to be wrong.

"Did you know Sydney asked me for my eggs?" Paige says.

"No."

"A few weeks before he visited in January, he called me up and sprang it on me. I didn't know what to say. I told him I'd think about it and get back to him." She pauses.

"I'm pretty sure that wasn't the response he was hoping for."

"I don't understand," I say. "Why would he ask you? We were going to use my sister. That was the plan."

"I know," Paige says, staring ahead. "But that plan didn't work out."

"What are you talking about?"

"Syd reached out to Veronica on his own."

"What? When did this happen?"

"Around New Year's."

I think back to that night in December, how frustrated Syd was with me for wanting to put the brakes on parenthood.

"Veronica said she'd be happy to do it," Paige says. "But there was a problem. She had just started dating this guy and she thought it might go somewhere. The timing wasn't right. Syd didn't want to count on that relationship going sour, so he began working on a backup plan. I guess that started with me."

I still can't get past the first part. "I was the one who was supposed to ask my sister. I was going to."

"He knew that," Paige says, adopting a motherly tone. "He knew you'd come around eventually. But he also knew how involved the whole process would be. He wanted to get started while you were figuring out whatever you had to figure out."

"It's so patronizing."

"No, it wasn't like that. He didn't want to rush you, that's all. He wanted to give you the time you needed, but he also knew he couldn't wait forever."

Syd's sense of urgency about the future had often felt obsessive and irrational. And yet the way Paige describes him makes him sound clairvoyant. It's like he carried an hourglass in his pocket and knew exactly when his time would be up. In truth, it's simply a matter of Syd's fears being as influential for him as mine are for me. The difference being his fears propelled him forward while mine continue to hold me back.

"What does this have to do with all those trips he took to New York?" I ask.

"I'm not sure." She stands up. I watch her pace around the concrete foundation. "What I'm about to say is just a theory, okay? It's just a hunch. I didn't want to tell you this from the start, because I'm not even sure it means anything."

I stand up with her and cross my arms, bracing myself. "Go ahead."

"When he visited in January, he never brought up what we spoke about, the possibility of using my eggs. I had been giving

it a lot of thought. I was seriously considering it. But he was already on to the next
thing."

"Which was what?"

"Another woman. I didn't know who she
was, but he swore he felt a connection with
her. I told him I didn't think it was a good
idea. You can't go up to a woman, basically
a stranger, and just ask her for her eggs. I
told him he should go home and talk it over
with you. I thought you guys would be better off going back to the agency and finding
a donor that way. But I don't think he was
hearing me. We were right here, looking out
at the city, just like we are now, and I swear
I had this feeling like whatever I was saying
just wasn't sinking in."

"What did he do?"

"I don't know," Paige says, letting out a
long sigh. "Maybe nothing. I have no proof
that anything came of it. But knowing Syd,
he might have decided to go for it anyway.
If he came back two more times and it
wasn't for work, then . . . I don't know.
Whatever it was, after I discouraged him, I
guess he didn't feel like confiding in me
anymore. I'm sorry. I never meant to keep
it from you."

Syd hated the agency process. The large
majority of egg donors prefer to remain

anonymous and understandably so; they don't want their offspring coming to find them later in life. But Syd couldn't understand how we were supposed to make such an important life decision based on a list of stats and a couple of images. He insisted on "knowing" the person.

"Who was she?"

"Some kind of artist. That's what he was showing me on the computer that morning. He wanted to know what I thought of her work."

"Do you remember her name?"

"Yes," Paige says, knowing full well what I'll do with the information but unable to stop it now. "Marigold Hallowell."

We return to the house and I assure Paige that I'm not angry. I understand. With Syd, if you refused to get on board, sometimes you got left behind.

She goes upstairs to the apartment and I head in through the studio, where — surprise, surprise — Joan is waiting for me on the couch.

I ask, "Have you ever heard the name Marigold Hallowell?"

"No," Joan says. "So you're babysitting me tomorrow morning, right?"

"I am?" I say, heading off to my bedroom.

Joan follows behind. "My mom says you guys talked about it last week."

"Right. What about it?"

"I just wanted to double-check that you remembered. Are you sure you still want to go solo?"

"I don't know what you're talking about, Joan."

"I'd rather be a duo, but it seems like you'd rather go solo. I really have to know because I have a very important gig coming up."

We've reached my door. My brain is worthless. I can barely keep up with my own thoughts, let alone hers. "I don't know what you mean, Joan. What gig?"

"I can't say. It's a secret."

I don't have time for any more riddles, not now. I excuse myself as gently as I can and close my bedroom door. I'm about to do a search for the name Marigold Hallowell, but I never reach my phone.

I spot something on my dresser. It's Sydney's forest painting, the postcard version that I bought at the arts fair. It's been here the whole time, right in front of me. I destroyed the original, but the painting somehow found a way back into my life. I didn't know why at the time, but I see it now. How could I forget? The gift Sydney mentioned in his text message, the one he was supposedly bringing home from New York. I remember now. He didn't actually have anything with him when he landed at LAX. It came in the mail about a week later. It was the forest painting. I had never heard of the artist. He called it an investment.

I flip the postcard over. The artist's name is Marigold Hallowell. Mara.

All her contact info is listed. *Brooklyn, New York,* is crossed out. Above it she's hand-written a new address in New Hope, Penn-sylvania.

Mara's website shows all her work, includ-ing the forest painting. The piece is actually called *Woods.* She has other paintings. Among them: *Wolf Den, Breakfast Time, D&D.*

At first I plan to hop on a train, but I opt for a rental car instead. I plug the address into my phone and let the GPS guide me.

I haven't driven a car since I arrived in New Jersey. It's a relief to be behind the wheel again, moving at whatever pace my heart dictates. In this case, it has me racing down the left-most lane of the turnpike. My arms are stretched out ahead, the bracelet swinging from my wrist, the eagle staring at me.

My instincts were correct. He was lying to me. Just not for the reason I suspected. He was looking for an egg donor.

I don't know if all of this ends with Marigold Hallowell or if it involves others. All I know is that Mara was the one Syd was meeting in Brooklyn in January. He acquired a painting from her and had it shipped home, where it hung proudly on our wall until it was thrown into a fire. The rest is a mystery, including what else he was doing in New York in February besides checking out properties and what he was doing there on an April trip that I've yet to learn anything about.

I'm startled when the GPS orders me to take the next exit. I've been on the road for ninety minutes, but it feels more like twenty.

I've left behind the skyscrapers, industry, and congestion. I take a ramshackle bridge over a sleepy river and pass through a modest downtown. I'm winding along a country road, arching trees casting shadows onto the pavement.

I turn onto a side road. The house, according to the GPS, is still up ahead, but I stop here and exit the car. Birds and bugs make animal music around me. I peer up, hoping to put a face to a chirping sound. A blackbird is perched high above. My spirit animal, according to Joan. Finding it here, in the middle of a journey like this, feels like a good omen. But upon closer look, I see it's no bird at all, just a shadow. I search the trees for other melody makers, but all the musicians are invisible.

I reach the mailbox by the curb and confirm the address. I start up the driveway, which is occupied by a single car, a hatchback. Somebody is home.

As I approach, I hear a low roar, constant and steady, something man-made. It's coming from the detached garage situated some thirty feet from the side of the house. The overhead door is lifted. Inside are canvases propped against a wall.

I walk closer. In the garage, someone squats over a can, stirring with a stick, back turned to me. A large industrial fan blows against a white T-shirt; long hair is tucked under a cap. My shoes crunch as I leave the driveway and start down the gravel path to the garage. She turns her head and rises.

She's not entirely surprised. There's a sense of reckoning in her creased forehead.

She drops the stick into the can and wipes her hands on her stained jeans. After adjusting her hat over her pile of hair, she opens her arms to everything around her, the makeshift studio, the woods, the whole world, and says, "Welcome."

27

We're shuffling through hangers, looking for something special. I'm also listening to the music playing through the store and I'm not feeling very impressed. Mom thinks we're here to shop for school clothes but the real reason I need a brand-new dress is that I'm going on television tomorrow.

Mom reaches her hand into a rack and she pulls out a dress. I feel like I've done this exact same thing before. I think I'm having déjà vu, which is when you feel like you've got a memory of doing something but the memory isn't actually real. I've never actually had déjà vu before, so I wasn't sure at first, but now I'm definitely sure, because I know this is the first time Mom has ever taken me to shop at this store.

Mom usually shops at the kind of store that has lots of different things to buy, like clothes and notebooks and toilet paper and furniture and food, and you put everything you want into a shopping cart. But this store sells only clothes, and none of the clothes have fallen onto the floor or been put back in the wrong rack or been thrown into a sloppy pile on a shelf. Everything is perfect. And also, there are no shopping carts.

The dress Mom is holding up has stripes, which I like, and it's sleeveless, which I also like. I close my eyes and picture myself on television, and the dream is almost perfect except that my partner isn't by my side. I open my eyes and Mom shakes the hanger and makes the dress dance in the air. "Well?"

"I like it."

"But do you love it?" Mom says.

"I don't know."

"Let's keep looking."

I had to think of something to do today because today was feeling like the longest thing there ever was, longer than the lines for roller coasters at Six Flags and longer than the black-and-white movie Dad makes us watch every year at Christmas.

Mom is shuffling from hanger to hanger. "About this *Mindy Love Show*," she starts to say.

My stomach gets tight. "Yes?"

"I know the idea of going on TV seems

exciting," Mom says, "but right now your father and I think it would be best to have your HSAM be more of a private thing."

"Why?"

"It's different with your friends and family. They know you. But you have to remember — sorry, you have to *realize* that what you have is extremely rare and if you go on TV, suddenly there are going to be a whole lot more people wanting to talk to you. Our phone will ring way more than it's ringing now. Do you understand?"

That sounds amazing. But I know Mom doesn't see it that way and it makes me wonder if the secret thing I'm trying to do is really worth it.

And now Mom is making me feel even worse because she just found a dress that is so great it would normally make me want to jump into the air but instead I just smile like a clown. Clowns have big smiles painted on their faces but they still don't look happy.

"You don't love this one either?" Mom says.

"No, I do."

It reminds me of a superhero costume but also a police uniform and also the phrase about wearing your heart on your sleeve.

I smile for real now and so does Mom. She hands me the dress and walks away to

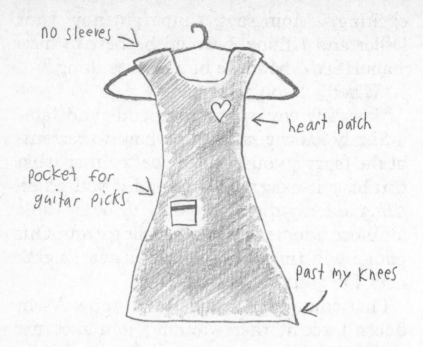

no sleeves

heart patch

pocket for guitar picks

past my knees

shop some more. I hold it up by the end of the hanger and I notice the price tag. Normally Mom buys me clothes with prices that start with a number 1, like $12 or $14 or $18, but this dress is $52.

I follow Mom into the adult section so she can look at pants. There's a girl my age and she's also with her mom. Her mom holds up the same white pants that Mom is holding up, but her mom's pants are much bigger and it makes me look again at Mom's thinner legs and smaller waist because sometimes you see the same thing so many times that you forget what it really looks like.

"Are you going to get them?" I ask.

"You're not supposed to wear white after Labor Day," Mom says.

"When's Labor Day?"

"In a few weeks."

She holds the pants higher and she looks at the front and the back but she never looks at the price tag, which is usually the first thing she looks at.

"Why not," she says, hanging the pants over her arm and leading us over to the dressing room.

I'm wondering what's going on here, why Mom took us to this fancy store and why she doesn't seem to care about price tags, even though she says we don't have enough money to pay for the studio. Now I'm not feeling so bad anymore about what I have to do tomorrow because if Mom would rather shop at fancy stores and go on fancy vacations than save Dad's studio and keep him playing music, then I really do have to do this all by myself.

And now I'm thinking about *The Mindy Love Show* again and also my partner. We're in the dressing room and Mom is staring at the mirror to see how her legs look inside those white pants. I'm wearing the dress and it seems to fit well, but I'm focused on something else. "Do you know Marigold

Hallowell?" I say.

We look at each other in the mirror even though we're standing side by side. "Where did you hear that name?" Mom says.

"Gavin was asking about her before he left. Why? Who is she?"

Just a few seconds ago, Mom seemed happy with how the white pants fit her. But now, from the look on her face, she doesn't seem so sure. "She's an aspiring artist."

"What does *aspiring* mean?"

"It means she wants to be a real artist someday, but she's not quite there yet."

I guess I'm an aspiring artist too, but not for much longer, because after I play my song on television and win the contest, I'll be right where I want to be.

"What else did Gavin say?" Mom says, putting her normal clothes back on.

"Nothing, really. I reminded him about babysitting me tomorrow when you have tutoring."

We leave the dressing room and get on line to pay. She's decided to buy the pants but she still has that unsure look on her face. "Maybe I should cancel my session and stay home with you."

My secret plan isn't going to work unless Gavin is the one watching me. "You can't cancel. What about your students? They need you, don't they?"

"Since when do you care about that?"

I shrug.

"I guess I can always send you to Naveyah's tomorrow," Mom says.

"But I thought Gavin is supposed to watch me."

The clerk asks for the next person in line. "I know," Mom says. "But that was before . . ."

"Before what?"

Mom steps up to the counter, puts our clothes down in front of the clerk, and digs through her purse for her wallet.

"Before what, Mom?"

She runs her credit card through the machine and presses a few buttons. "Nothing, honey."

But that's not good enough for me. "I would like to know what's going on with Gavin."

She slides the card back into her wallet. "So would I."

28

The waitress brings our drinks and leaves our menus. Maybe I'll eat later, but for now, my stomach is already busy eating itself.

"When we met at the fair," Mara says, "I wasn't sure what you knew."

When I ran into her that day, I saw Mara only as an acquaintance of the man I'd loved and an artist whose painting we once displayed in our home. But this woman sitting across from me now is someone entirely new. She's a person on whom Syd was willing to bet our entire future.

It's hard not to examine her every move and attribute. Rainbows of paint nest under her fingernails. Her eyes are hypnotically blue, extra-pronounced against her dark brown hair and fair skin. She's got decent bone structure in the face, nothing too striking. On the whole, there's something undeniably warm and welcoming about her, as if she's subtly smiling even when she's not.

And then, when she actually smiles, her face seems to expand, and a grand dimple forms on her right cheek.

I take a swig of beer. "Please, start from the top. How did you two first meet?"

Mara begins her story at a house party in Park Slope. She was invited by a friend of a friend. It's unclear how Sydney ended up there.

"I was peering up at a bookshelf and he just came over," Mara says. "He thought I was looking at the books, but I was actually looking at the shelves. The entire wall of this house was built-in bookshelves. I told him someday I was going to have a house with built-in bookshelves. And he said, 'I believe you.' " She pauses, reflects. "It wasn't the response I expected."

I wonder how I would've reacted if Syd had approached me randomly at a party instead of us meeting on a prearranged date. Would I have taken him seriously? On looks alone, probably not. His allure was most apparent when he got you one on one. It was then that you discovered his special gift; he had a skill so rare that when people experienced it, they found themselves opening up to him fully. It was simple: he listened.

They talked more about bookshelves and

then about books. Syd noted that *The Art of Looking Sideways,* which was placed horizontally on a shelf, would be better displayed vertically so the shelf peruser would actually be forced to look sideways in order to read the title. At that, Mara wondered if all books should be placed with their spines inward so that you would never know what book you were reaching for. Syd asked if this was some extreme interpretation of the old adage to never judge a book by its cover.

"It wasn't what I meant," Mara tells me. "I was just thinking it would be more fun that way. Like a little adventure every time you wanted a book. Syd liked that."

This first meeting between them happened back in September. It makes sense timing-wise. As Joan already shared with me, during that same New York trip, Syd also attended a barbecue in the Sully backyard where he talked to Joan about not wanting to be the last Brennett.

"What did you think of him?" I ask.

She takes a moment. "Put it this way — before he came over I was bored out of my mind and ready to leave the party. But after we started talking, I sort of lost track of time."

"What else did you guys talk about?"

"He was really interested in hearing about

my art." She almost flinches when she says it.

"What?"

"Nothing. I hate talking about what I do. I'm much happier just doing it." She pulls her hand off her beer glass as if only now realizing how cold it is. "That's one thing I don't miss about Brooklyn. It just seemed like some people were more interested in saying they were artists than in actually making art. But anyway, I didn't mind talking about it with Sydney. It was nice."

Syd was great at that, making us artsy types feel important. He truly believed in the power of art to inspire, guide, and change. He also knew how effective it was at getting people to buy into something. Selling was, after all, his vocation.

"And I assume you knew he wasn't trying to pick you up?"

She smiles gently. "He mentioned you pretty quickly. I thought it was really sweet how he was bragging about you. He was telling me all about the show and your role in it and insisting that I watch it. I told him I didn't really watch TV and he said something like, 'Well, darling, you better start.'"

She says it with this wistful look in her eyes. I saw the same look when she was speaking about Sydney at the arts fair. The remembering-Sydney look isn't hers exclusively. I've witnessed a similar expression in Paige and many others when they talk about Sydney. And now, realizing this, I know it's a mistake to treat Mara as a stranger or adversary or someone to merely extract information from. Because now I know, I see, that she, like the rest of us, loved him.

"I don't know why," Mara says, still with that look, "but he just had this calming effect on me."

"I know what you mean," I assure her. I long for the calm he gave me. I'm pretty sure Mara and I would both welcome a dose of it right now.

She takes her first sip of beer, leaving a faint smudge of lipstick on the rim of the glass.

"How did you guys leave off that night?" I ask.

"He told me . . ." She trails off. Her bag is ringing. She looks at her phone and debates whether to answer. She ignores it and apologizes. "Syd said he was going to check out my stuff online. Most people say that and you never know, but a couple months later he called, out of the blue."

"When was that exactly?"

"Early January. Right after New Year's."

After our December fight.

"He said he wanted to buy one of my paintings," Mara says. "He wanted to know if he could visit next time he was in town. I was literally dancing in my bedroom, just freaking out. I'd never gotten a call like that in my life. I thought it was too good to be true. But he called again to set a date. I was really inspired after that. By the time he got here, I had a bunch of brand-new paintings to show him."

"You were living in Brooklyn back then?"

"Yeah," Mara says. "He came to my apartment. He brought, like, five different kinds of soup."

"Why all the soup?"

"I couldn't figure it out at first either. Then I remembered I had written on my Facebook page that I loved soup." She lifts her beer, as if Syd's thoroughness deserves a toast. "He obviously did his research."

I think back to my first date with Syd and the knowledge — gained only recently through Joan's memory — that he had chosen that particular sushi restaurant based on a crude impression I'd done back in college. It seems there's still plenty more to learn about the lengths Syd would go to when he really wanted something.

"We sat in my apartment and ate soup and talked. He asked me all sorts of questions,

but it never felt like an interview or anything. It was really natural and easy, like we
were old friends. He asked surface stuff,
like what's my sign, to —"

"What *is* your sign?"

"Leo."

I nod knowingly.

"What?" Mara asks.

"Leos and Libras are the best signs. That's
what Syd always said. He thought they
made for the most solid people."

She reflects on it and then pats her stomach. "I could definitely stand to be more
solid."

I smile and lift my beer in agreement.

"He asked about deeper stuff too," Mara
says. "He wanted to know about my grand
plan, which I had to laugh at. I didn't have
one. I told him I had a hard time believing
I could really have a life as an artist and he
basically told me, Hey, if that's the way
you're going to think, you should stop now."

"He was definitely all or nothing."

"I get it," Mara says. "I'm trying to be
more like that."

Syd got into her head. I don't mean that
in a negative way. He got into mine too. He
made me realize that I was falling short of
my potential and that it wasn't too late to
correct that. Honestly, when he first gave

me that speech, I thought it was a bunch of bullshit. But then, to my surprise, it actually worked. It seems he was trying to teach Mara the same lesson. How to believe.

"Is that when he bought the forest painting from you? *Woods*?" I ask.

"I was asking two fifty," Mara says. "He said my price was too low. He gave me twenty-five hundred for it." Her arching eyebrows tell me she still can't believe the amount.

"Did you wonder, like, who is this guy?"

"Totally," Mara says. "But as far as I could tell, he was completely legit. He handed me a check right then and there. I didn't want to cash it right away. I remember just staring at it for days. It meant so much, more than just money. And believe me, I *needed* the money."

"Then what? He took the painting and left?" I say.

"He gave me a big hug." She drops her gaze, fixes on a spot between us. Then, peering up with a brave smile, she says, "I didn't realize how much I'd been starving for it."

"The hug?"

"The reassurance," Mara says. "Someone to say, 'Good job, keep going.' My parents wouldn't pay for art school. They never really got it, you know."

I know how powerful it can be when someone puts his faith in you. I'm trying to find the right words to say next, but the waitress arrives and shatters the moment.

I order fries for the table, just to get something in our stomachs, even though we both claim not to be hungry, then excuse myself to the bathroom. I rinse my face with cold water but it doesn't help. It doesn't wake me from what feels like a dream. Sydney had forged an entire relationship with this person and though I was aware of it peripherally, I had no appreciation for how substantial the bond was or how much was riding on it.

I wasn't prepared for Mara the person either. She's bright, witty, humble, thoughtful, and, from what I can tell, solid. I should've known that Syd wouldn't have devoted so much time and energy to someone who wasn't really worth it. But I just didn't expect the woman who had built a secret partnership with Sydney without my knowledge or approval to be so likable.

There are so many questions that only Syd can answer, about his mind-set and intentions and emotions. But all I have is Mara's one-sided narrative. I suppose I should be used to it by now, after doing it so many times with Joan. Still, hearing about Syd only makes me wish all the more that I could hear *from* him.

I return to the table and find the fries there already and Mara hunched over her phone. Not merely passing the time, but dealing with something. She puts the phone away, resets in my presence.

"I'm glad we're doing this," she says, almost confessing it.

"Me too."

She's once again hypnotized by the spot between us. It's not the table she's focused on. She's staring at my wrist. At Sydney's bracelet.

"I just feel terrible," Mara says. "The whole thing didn't go how I thought it would."

It's a reminder. No matter how her story unfolds, the ending will always be the same.

A few weeks after purchasing her painting, Syd called Mara. He was planning to return to New York in late February and wanted to meet up. Syd claimed he had an easy photography gig for her, that he'd pay twice her daily rate at the gallery if she could take the day off from work. She said she would.

He met her at the corner of Charles and Washington. Mara brought along her camera. They found Claire, the broker, upstairs.

"Syd wanted me to take photos of the space," Mara says. "He said they were going to be used for a brochure or something."

I can only assume Syd invented the job for her, because as far as I know, nothing came of the pictures. Yes, he hoped we'd eventually move to Manhattan and was interested in finding us the right property, but it seems his prime objective that day was simply to spend more time with Mara.

"He took me out to lunch afterward," Mara says. "He handed me an envelope with five hundred dollars cash. I started tearing up." She looks down at her lap, as if still clutching the envelope all these months later. "It had been a rough couple of weeks. Even with two jobs, I was barely covering my bills. The money he'd given me for the painting was already gone. And again, it wasn't just about the money. I had been working so many hours, I hardly had time to be creative, and that's always been a release for me, you know?"

"I do."

"And here I was, getting paid just to take a few photos, something I would've done for free. It was like he came to see me at the perfect time, just when I was thinking about moving back here to New Hope, which I really didn't want to do. It felt like admit-

336

ting failure or something. But he helped me put it in perspective. He asked me what was more important, living in Brooklyn or being an artist? I knew the answer, but it took a few more months before I could really accept it."

She finally grabs a French fry from the plate we've both been ignoring. Now that she's partaken, I follow suit, lifting a lukewarm fry and inserting it dispassionately into my mouth. We each stop after the one.

"We went for a walk after," Mara says. "I don't know what it was, maybe just the fact that I had opened up to him at lunch, but all of a sudden he started telling me everything that was going on with you guys. All the baby stuff."

It feels like the French fry is caught in my throat, even though I'm certain I've swallowed it. I listen as Mara rattles off all the troubles Syd and I were facing. The lack of control a couple has when neither party has a uterus. The inconsistent laws from state to state. The sifting through databases, having to judge egg donors based solely on short videos and résumés. The fact that we (really, Syd) had already exhausted the obvious donor options, namely, family members (at least one of them, Veronica) and friends (Paige, possibly others). And, finally, our desire to have a satisfactory answer when our child asked about his or her mother, the peace of mind we could offer if we had a person who wasn't a mystery but someone with whom we had an intimate bond.

"I could see how much it meant to him," Mara says. "He looked so tortured. I wanted to comfort him the way he always comforted me, but I wasn't sure what to say. And then at one point, I don't remember when, he just asked me straight out if I'd ever thought about donating my eggs."

It's exactly what Paige advised him not to do. Just hearing it secondhand makes me squirm. "What did you tell him?"

"The truth," Mara says. "The thought had never crossed my mind."

I stare down at the plate of fries, wondering if I should shove them into my ears instead of my mouth so I wouldn't have to endure the rest of this story.

"That was it," Mara says, as if intentionally sparing me. "He didn't mention anything else about it. He flew back to L.A. and that's when it hit me: Did this man just ask me for my eggs? I didn't know how to process it. I felt so many things at once. It was shocking and also kind of flattering and definitely overwhelming and even disturbing. I felt a connection with him, sure, but I was imagining more of a mentor/protégée thing. And then I started to wonder, Who is this guy, anyway? I Googled him, dug as deep as I could. I saw the pictures he posted of you two together, and I felt the love there, it was obvious, but these were my eggs we were talking about."

"Of course. It's a huge deal."

"I knew I wanted kids of my own someday. I mean, not anytime soon — I'm only twenty-five — but eventually. I wasn't sure how that would work. So I started researching what it was all about."

She watched YouTube videos of donors describing the procedure: the doctor visit; the screening process (Ever paid for sex? Ever taken anti-depressants? Recreational drugs? More than two male partners in the last six months?); the daily hormone injections; the needles in your belly and thighs; the side effects; the ultrasound visits; the abstaining from sex, alcohol, and medication other than Tylenol; finally, the surgery.

The women in these videos were just like her. Some in their teens. Most in their twenties. A few nearing thirty. Typical compensation ranged between eight and ten thousand dollars. The money went to pay off debt, college tuition, daily expenses, even vacations. Many of the women had donated half a dozen times.

Some donors had personal relationships with the intended parents. Most did not. The majority preferred to remain detached from the act, to treat it like a job, albeit one that gave them a feeling of doing good in the world. They all took comfort in the fact that they were helping people. Giving life.

"It was kind of beautiful," Mara says. "I totally understood why someone would want to do it. But I couldn't imagine doing it myself. I couldn't get past the idea of having a kid out there, in the world, existing, feeling, thinking. And what if you guys decided you really did want to move here to New York? The kid would be right around the corner. What would my future husband think about that? As much as I adored Sydney, I had only just met him."

I can't argue with anything she's saying. Had Syd included me in the process — had I made him feel I was ready and willing to be included — I would have encouraged him to take a step back and slow down.

"I sent his next call to voice mail," Mara says. "His message didn't say anything about babies or eggs, nothing like that. He was just checking in, saying hi, seeing how I was doing. Part of me wondered if I had imagined the whole thing."

An entire month went by before they spoke again. It was now April, four months since Syd and I had had our December fight, which, as far as I was concerned, had put our parenthood quest on hold. It seemed to me then, based on what I knew, that Syd was respecting my wishes to slow down a little. The agency was still sending us updated donor lists, but Syd rejected every single one. The plan, in my mind, was still for me to ask Veronica, when I was ready. By April, I knew what Syd had already learned back in January, that Veronica had started dating someone. I didn't think much of it then. I figured this new relationship, like her previous ones, wouldn't last long (I was wrong about that). Besides, I needed the extra time. I was so busy with *The Long Arm* during those months that I had mostly pushed the notion of fatherhood out of my mind.

But Syd, I now know, had never stopped thinking about it. He flew back to New York in April and asked if he could take Mara out to dinner in Manhattan. After some hesitation, she accepted.

"He seemed a little off from the start," Mara says. "He didn't have that usual calm about him. We chatted for a good half hour, talking about art, New York, everything, and then, I remember, he just looked at me and took a deep breath and said, 'Oh, Miss Hallowell . . .' "

My whole body tightens, bracing for some imminent crash.

"I asked how things were with you two and he started to go into it a little bit. He said you had found a few donors that looked promising. Then he stopped himself. He wanted to say more, I could tell. I encouraged him, made him feel safe, and then he told me everything. He said at first he didn't have a picture of who the ideal mother was, but that changed when he met me. He said I was a little bit of him and a little bit of you, that I was smart and focused and imaginative and beautiful. I was kind but also edgy. Confident but also self-deprecating. A realist but also a dreamer. No one's ever done that before, spent all that time thinking about just me and who I am and what I'm made of. It was intense."

She relaxes a moment, reminding me to do the same.

"He got quiet and then he apologized for spilling his guts like that. He didn't want me to feel pressured by anything he'd just said. Honestly, I didn't know how to feel or what to say. I cared about him. I cared about him a lot. But . . ."

342

She pauses.

"I really wanted to help him," Mara says. "I just couldn't."

It took her several weeks after their last dinner in New York to gather the strength to tell Sydney that. She called and left him a message saying she wanted to talk. She was surprised when several days went by and she still hadn't heard back. She decided to check his Facebook page. Everyone was saying such nice things about him. The sorts of things people say when you're no longer alive.

We're outside now, Mara pacing alongside the restaurant with her phone pressed to her ear. Her hushed voice suggests drama unfolding over the line. She must've checked her call log a half a dozen times back at the table.

I'm standing twenty feet back, allowing her privacy. The parking lot is dusk-covered, the tops of cars resembling rolling hills across a blue horizon. My rental car is here somewhere. I forget what it looks like.

I watch Mara walk, her summer dress falling shapelessly around her. The canvas shopping bag on her shoulder should be carrying groceries, not personal items. Back in the restaurant, she filled in all the pieces

I was missing. And yet, I've never felt emptier. Yes, he went behind my back. Yes, he "fell" for someone else. But he did it all for us. He loved me until the very end. What the hell am I supposed to do with that?

Mara finally finishes the call and strides over with a hearty sigh. "I could use a cigarette."

"I'd love that."

She slips inside the restaurant and returns with two smokes and a matchbook, all of which she'd bummed from the bartender, a guy she went to high school with. She strikes a match. The flame dances in the air, clings to the white edge, glows orange.

Now seems like the right time. "I set your painting on fire," I say.

"Excuse me?" Mara says from behind a puffy cloud.

"I burned Sydney's things."

"Right," she says, swiping at the air. "I heard about that."

"I'm sorry."

"Don't worry about it. I've often wanted to burn them myself."

I light my cigarette. The smoke swirls in and tickles all the right places. She lowers herself onto the curb and I join her. We sit for a while, smoking in silence. It feels like we've just hiked up some impossible mountain and now we're resting at the top, taking in the view, surprised at how we got up here.

"Can I ask you something?" Mara says.

"Sure."

"What Sydney said he felt about my art — do you think it was sincere?"

Inhale, exhale. "I understand why you'd ask that," I say. "Honestly, there were times I wondered the same thing. Did he truly think I was a good actor? Or was he just biased by his emotions? But you know what? I don't think the two things are separate, you and your art. They're part of the same thing. And the whole point with art is that we try to make people feel something, right? And you did that. Really. That I can say without any doubt."

She leans back onto her elbows, gazes skyward. Her smoke joins mine, forms a supercloud above us. I follow the smoke as it rises, wondering how far it will travel, imagining it will somehow reach Sydney. If he's up there watching, I'd like him to know I approve of his choice, even if I disagree with his method. I just wish he hadn't felt the need to keep it from me. I wish I hadn't made him feel like he had to.

"I should probably go," she says, crushing her cigarette into the pavement.

It feels too soon. I just found her.

"My boyfriend's been calling," she explains. "I was supposed to meet him a few hours ago."

This is the first I'm hearing of a boyfriend. "How long have you been with him?"

Mara seems to know why I'm asking. "Believe me, it had nothing to do with my decision. We've been together only a few weeks, but we dated in high school. When I came back here to New Hope, he was still here. It's been a huge help to have him around, actually."

It's good to hear. For some reason, I feel invested in this girl's future now. "Do you think you'll ever go back to Brooklyn?"

"I don't know, maybe. I don't see myself staying here long term, but I think I needed to come back for a little while, just to recharge."

I know what she means.

We both stand and face each other. "I'm sorry for just showing up like this," I say.

"I'm glad you did."

I hug her, hold her like I'm holding him. It's hard not to think of what might've been.

When I finally let go, I tell her, "I think Sydney would want me to keep an eye on you, if that's okay. You know, just to make sure you're not slacking."

"Please do," she says. "I'd really like that."

346

29

The next morning Gavin finally comes upstairs. Mom is leaving for her tutoring session and Gavin asks her when she'll be home because he really needs to chat.

Mom leaves and Gavin makes coffee. He offers to make me breakfast but I say no and then he offers to squeeze me fresh OJ with the present we got Dad for Father's Day last year and I say yes because I'm afraid that if I say no to every single thing, he'll know there's something fishy going on. But the OJ is a mistake because it makes my stomach feel extra-nervous.

And then my stomach feels even more nervous when Gavin asks me why I'm wearing a dress. I tell him I'm going to make a video on my iPod in my bedroom and he believes me. He finishes his coffee and says he has to use the bathroom. He goes downstairs and that's when I pull the note out of my pocket and leave it on the kitchen table:

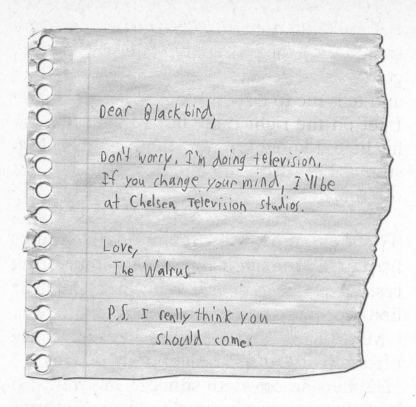

Dear Blackbird,

Don't worry, I'm doing television.
If you change your mind, I'll be
at Chelsea Television studios.

Love,
The Walrus

P.S. I really think you
should come.

Finally my memory is good for something. I
go the same way Gavin and I did the day
we went into the city, down the big hill and
through Hoboken. It gets trickier when I
reach the underground train because Gavin
used a yellow card to get us through the
gate but I don't have a yellow card. I
thought of everything else. On my back I
have Dad's Gibson and inside its soft case
I have all my supplies: my journal, change
purse, the Sydney guitar picks, bubble gum,
and the papers that Felicia sent over. But
no yellow card.

A nice man in a Mets jersey sees me standing by the gate and asks me where I'm going. He slides his yellow card into the gate and tells me to walk through. He makes sure I get on the right train and I thank him for his help. I know I'm not supposed to talk to strangers, but I'm not supposed to do a lot of things.

The train lets us out underground. I walk past a man on a bench who's bent over so far it looks like he might fall onto the tracks, but I don't have time to help him. It smells like the toilets at the Riverview Fair and I have to follow the people up the stairs until it's bright and I can finally breathe.

There are so many people and they're knocking into my guitar like they can't even see me. Suddenly I realize where I am: I'm in New York City and I'm all alone.

This place is very dangerous because it's hard to tell who's crazy and who's normal and that's what happened to John Lennon. Mark David Chapman looked like a nice guy, but he was really a fanatic (which is totally different than just a really big fan, like me and Dad). Mark David went to the Dakota and he walked right up to John and he shot him with a gun, even though earlier that same day John gave Mark David his autograph. I don't know why Mark David did that because John was being so nice to him. It makes me think of that photo Gavin took with those two women (Tuesday, July 16, 2013). Dad says Mark David wanted to be famous by hurting someone famous and so for just this one time, I'm happy to be nobody special.

But not for long, because today I'm going to be on television.

I walk to the corner and reach my hand up as far as it can go, but the taxis just zoom by. I wave and wave and the guitar is getting heavy on my back and the shoulder straps are digging into my skin.

I'm still waving my arm when I hear a man's voice behind me: "Just you?"

The man has a mustache, but it's not bushy like a cowboy's, it's thin and neat. He sticks his arm way up high and a taxi stops. The mustache man puts me in the backseat and I tell him I want to go to Chelsea Television Studios. He tells the driver where I want to go and I ask the mustache man, "Do you watch *The Mindy Love Show?*"

"Never heard of it."

"Well, I'm going to play a song on the show. You should watch."

He says, "Good luck," and he taps his hand on the taxi roof, and the driver starts driving. I see the driver's dark eyes in the mirror and he says, "Hello."

And I say, "Hello. My name is Joan Lennon."

I wait for the driver's eyes to get big because he is amazed by my name, but his eyes stay the same size and he says, "My name is Adisa."

"Do you like the Beatles?"

"No, no beetles. Where I am from, this is no good."

"The last time I was in a taxi was July sixteenth, which was a Tuesday."

"I like Fridays the best. Do you agree?"

"I do like Fridays," I admit.

The car turns. "We must go all the way to the river," Adisa says. "I have wondered what this looks like inside, the studios where they make the television programs."

"Me too."

"You have never been?" Adisa says.

"No."

"This is a special day. I will pray for you."

Sunday, February 20, 2011: Grandpa brings me to church because he says if he doesn't bring me then no one will, because Dad doesn't believe and Mom is Jewish. He says we're here to pray for Grandma Joan, but he never tells me how to pray so I just close my eyes and listen to the lady singing. I like how in church you can sing softly but your voice

351

fills the whole room.

I wish Grandpa could see me on TV today, but he's busy working and also it's a secret.

Adisa stops at a red light and he taps a beat on the steering wheel, just like Dad, and I ask Adisa, "Do you play music?"

"I play the djembe," Adisa says, tapping away. "But only in the car."

"That's like my dad."

Adisa turns his head around and his white teeth glow behind the glass. "Your father drives a taxi?"

"No."

He turns forward and we start moving again. "What is his job?"

"Well, he used to make music for commercials."

"What commercials?" Adisa says.

"Have you ever seen the one where the Coke bottle turns into a telescope?"

Adisa turns around, but he's still driving. "This is your father? I love this commercial! They play it on the TV in Times Square. This is a very nice commercial. Wow, I am very lucky today."

So am I. I'm glad to have Adisa as my driver because he knows how special Dad's old job is and it makes me feel even more sure about my secret mission.

Adisa drives fast, the same way Dad always tells me he drove after I fell in Home Depot. I have to hold on to the handle because it feels like we're going to crash into other cars. Adisa likes to honk the horn and I like to hear it.

Through my window I watch people walk past a man sleeping on the sidewalk. I wonder if the man's family knows where he is. Maybe he's sneaking around like me. I think about reaching into my guitar case and throwing the man some coins, but Adisa speeds away before I get a chance. I wonder if the sleeping man drinks coffee like Dad does when he wakes up because Dad says the city has the best coffee.

Tuesday, July 16, 2013: Gavin says New York City has the best pizza.

Now the car isn't moving and I can see the river out my window.

"We are here, little girl."

I don't think Adisa remembers my name, which isn't very nice. He presses a button and points to a sign with bright red numbers. "Seven forty-seven, if you please."

I open my change purse and count my coins and Adisa watches me through the glass. He gets out of the car and opens my door. "Okay, this is no problem." We make a pile for each dollar and Adisa lines up all

353

the piles on the seat. "You saved up this money? This must be a very important day."

"Yes, it is."

I have no more coins left in my case. I look at the piles on the seat and there are only six.

"Okay, little one," Adisa says. "This is very good. Have fun on the TV."

He holds up my guitar case and I crawl out of the car and Adisa slides the straps onto my shoulders and points to a building along the river. "This is where you go. I wish you good luck."

I look at the building and the river behind it and I see New Jersey. I wish I could see my house from here because I want to show Adisa where I live and how far I've come. But when I turn around, the taxi is gone.

30

I was away for five minutes and now she's gone. Joan is gone.

I call out her name, go from room to room, check both apartments. She's nowhere.

I return to the note I found on the kitchen table. It's not a game. It's true. Joan went to New York City all by herself.

At least I know where she's headed.

I grab my wallet and phone, calling Paige as I race out the door. The call goes straight to voice mail. It's for the best. I hang up without leaving a message. This happened on my watch. I have to be the one to fix it. And quick.

I run down the hill, sprint to the train. I nearly trip over my untied shoelace. Pedestrians pay me no attention as I speed past them.

Down the stairs, through the turnstiles, onto the idle train. I take a seat and then change my mind and stand up. I can't sit, not now, not with this burning in my chest and my heart stabbing. The other passengers wait patiently while I scan for the conductor. There must be someone who can get this train moving. Someone who can act in a time of emergency.

But there's no help coming. I force myself onto a bench and manage a deep breath. A pair of women's flats appear next to my feet. "Excuse me."

I look up.

"You dropped this," the woman says.

She hands me a piece of paper. Joan's note.

The sight of her handwriting puts a shiver in me. She had asked me to go on this dreadful TV show with her but I refused. How could I know she'd resort to this?

I shut my eyes and picture her cowering through the city all alone. My chest can't take it. I don't know how Paige and Ollie live like this, how any parents do. How they let these tiny pieces of themselves out of their sight for even a second. I suppose it's no use. We can be close by and watching like hawks, and those we love can still slip away. Even the ones who are supposed to be old and wise enough to take care of themselves.

It's happening again, someone escaping from my grasp. Nausea comes over me as the train finally jerks forward. I'm not sure I can hold it back, the sickness. I barely had time to process what happened last night with Mara and now this. I shut my eyes, try to talk myself through the dizziness.

The rest passes like a dream: off the train, up the stairs, into a cab. I lean forward in the backseat. "Please," I tell the driver. "As fast as you can."

31

The man in the lobby tells me to take the elevator to number nine, which is a spooky number because of the Beatles song. I'm floating up and when the doors open I see a lady wearing headphones that cover just one ear.

"Joan Sully? Felicia Dufresne. Oh my, you cut it close. Follow me."

It's hard to keep up with Felicia because she walks like she talks. She says something into a skinny microphone that's hanging off her head-phones: "She's here."

Felicia looks younger than I imagined she would, with blond hair in a long ponytail. I thought I was pale, but Felicia is so white I can see the blue veins through her skin.

"Are your parents downstairs?" she asks.

"No."

"Where are they?"

"They're not coming."

"What do you mean, they're not coming?

Who's coming?"

"I don't know. I'm hoping Gavin will come."

"Is he camera-ready?"

"I don't know."

"This way to your room."

On the walls I see pictures of people I know from TV and I wonder if they're all in the building right now. I also wonder if Gavin works in a building like this when he does his TV show.

"Quickly, Joan!"

It's hard to catch up to Felicia with the Gibson on my back. She puts a key in a door and brings me into a room. It's bigger than my bedroom at home and it has a leather couch and a coffee table and my very own bathroom. There's even a mirror with those special lightbulbs around it.

"Did you bring the paperwork?" Felicia says.

I sit on the shiny couch and reach into my guitar case and hand the papers to Felicia. I stay very still while Felicia looks them over. I drew Mom's signature in pencil first and went over it with pen.

"Who's Gavin?" Felicia says. "Is he a member of your family?"

"Pretty much."

"Is he an uncle, grandfather, what?"

Felicia waits for my answer. "Uncle," I decide.

"It'll have to do. And when exactly will he be arriving?"

"I don't know. Soon, maybe."

Felicia looks like she smells a fart. It wasn't me. "Do you have his phone number so I can give him a call?"

I shake my head and now Felicia is looking at me the way Mom does when I tell her something bad and she hopes I'm lying. "Your parents sent you to New York all by yourself? Why am I not surprised?"

I have no idea.

She fans her face with her hand and writes something on her pad. "Okay, I'll be right back and we'll do your pre-interview and then we'll get you off to hair and makeup. Are you hungry?"

"Yes. Very." I should have let Gavin make me breakfast.

"We'll get you something from craft service," Felicia says, walking to the door.

"Wait. When do I get my money?"

"Your uncle can fill out the forms later," Felicia says. "You'll receive your check in six to eight weeks."

"Son of a bitch."

"Excuse me?"

"Johnny Cash."

Felicia shuts the door.

In six weeks the studio will be gone and it'll be too late. I need to get paid right now.

I shove a piece of bubble gum in my mouth and start blowing bubbles. It's all about watching the bubbles get big and then hearing them burst. I blow and pop, blow and pop, and then I remember: I'm hanging backstage in my very own dressing room before going on a real television show.

I'm nervous but I think it's the good kind of nervous, the kind that Gavin was telling me about. I'll play my song and after people hear it, everything will change and no one will be mad at me anymore because they'll be too busy smiling at me and what I've done. Something special. Something to remember.

THE MINDY LOVE SHOW

ANNOUNCER

And here's your host, Mindy Love!

[Cheers and applause]

MINDY

Who loves you?

CROWD

Mindy!

MINDY

And I love you back. Today on the show we've got an extraordinary group of youngsters whose talents will surprise you, delight you, and, in one case, maybe even save your life. We'll be talking to an eleven-year-old premed student who'll receive his MD before his friends are halfway through high school, a set of master-chef twins who count Mario Batali and Geoffrey Zakarian among their many fans, and an eight-year-old reptile expert who just returned from an expedition in Honduras and already has a new species of snake named after him. But first, it's my pleasure to introduce a special young lady with an extremely rare condition known as highly superior autobiographical memory, or HSAM. There are fewer than thirty people in the world with this condition and the person you're about to meet is the youngest one by about twenty years. She's only ten years old, and this is her very first television appearance. Please welcome a truly one-of-a-kind guest, Joan Sully!

[Cheers and applause]

MINDY

Well, hello, Joan. Aren't you adorable. Thank you for coming on my show.

JOAN

Actually, I like to be called Joan Lennon. Not Joan Sully.

MINDY

Like John Lennon, the musician?

JOAN

Yes.

MINDY

And I see you brought your guitar.

JOAN

Yes.

MINDY

Joan, tell us about yourself. Where are

you from?

JOAN

Jersey City, New Jersey.

MINDY

Any brothers or sisters?

JOAN

No. But my parents always talk about having another kid.

MINDY

And what about Mom and Dad? Do they have good memories?

JOAN

My mom has a great memory. My dad doesn't.

MINDY

Just like *my* husband. [Laughter] And what do Mom and Dad do for a living?

JOAN

Like, for a job?

MINDY

Yes. What are their jobs?

JOAN

My mom is a teacher. My dad used to make music for commercials and movies and stuff.

MINDY

Dad doesn't work now?

JOAN

He does. He works with my grandpa and my uncle. Not the uncle who might be coming here today, the other one.

MINDY

I see. And where are Mom and Dad now?

JOAN

My mom is tutoring. I don't know where exactly my dad is.

MINDY

Are you alone a lot?

JOAN

I guess so. Kind of.

MINDY

That must be hard. Do you use your memories to escape?

JOAN

I don't know.

MINDY

What I mean is, do you find it easier to think about your memories than to think about what's happening around you?

JOAN

Um. I don't know.

MINDY

What's your favorite memory?

JOAN

Probably when I recorded my new song with Dad and Gavin. I mean, my uncle.

MINDY

When was that?

JOAN

July twentieth. It was a Saturday.

MINDY

That's amazing. Do you always remember the day of the week?

JOAN

Oh. Yeah. Starting around age five.

MINDY

So let me understand. You remember every day of your life, including the day of the week, from today all the way back until you were age five? Is that right?

JOAN

Yes.

MINDY

Incredible. And how about before age five? Do you remember anything before that?

JOAN

Most of it. I just don't know all the days. The movies aren't so clear from when I was a baby.

MINDY

You say movies. What type of movies are we talking about?

JOAN

When I think of the day, I see a movie of what happened, but I'm not *in* the movie, I'm watching it.

MINDY

Tell me, what day of the week was December ninth, 2011?

JOAN

It's a Friday and I'm at school and Ms. Dudley is teaching us about penguins that live all the way at the bottom of Australia. She puts us in groups, but I don't like my group because Tracy is in it and I don't like Tracy.

MINDY

Did Tracy bully you? Did she pick on you?

JOAN

Tracy is a boy. He doesn't pick on anyone. Everyone picks on him because he smells.

MINDY

Okay, well, I'm sure Tracy is a nice boy. How about August third, 2006? Can you tell me about that day?

JOAN

I'm not sure. I was probably home that day. Maybe we went to the park? I was only three.

MINDY

Let's try a later date. How about March twenty-sixth, 2009? What day was that?

JOAN

A Thursday.

MINDY

Is something wrong?

JOAN

[Inaudible]

MINDY

Oh, Joan. There's no need to get upset. Did something bad happen that day? What happened on March twenty-sixth? Take your time.

JOAN

It's the day after Pepper died.

MINDY

Who's Pepper?

JOAN

My dog.

MINDY

I'm sorry, honey. Do you miss your dog?

JOAN

Yes.

MINDY

Losing a pet is very tough, I know. It must be even harder when your memories are so vivid. Is it painful to think about your dog Pepper? That's all right, honey. Take your time. We'll be right back.

[Music and applause]

MINDY

Welcome back. I'm here with Joan Sully, a special little girl who happens to have a near-perfect memory. Before we move to our next wunderkind, I'd like to get some input from Dr. William Satcher. Dr. Satcher is a neurologist at the Weill Cornell Medical Center here in New York City. Dr. Satcher, tell us, what causes HSAM?

SATCHER

Well, first, I must say that I'm no expert in HSAM. But to my knowledge, there is currently no known cause.

JOAN

My friend Wyatt says I got HSAM when I fell on my head in Home Depot.

[Laughter]

MINDY

Did you really fall?

JOAN

Yes.

MINDY

Tell us what happened.

JOAN

Well, it was when I was two. Dad was pushing me in the cart and I fell out and hit my head on the concrete.

MINDY

How terrible. That must have been very painful.

JOAN

I don't know. I think so.

MINDY
Were you wearing your little seat belt?
JOAN
No. Dad let me stand up in the big part.
MINDY
Your father wasn't watching you?
JOAN
He was. He said he was going to put me in the seat but then one of his songs started playing in the store and that's the first time he ever heard his music playing while he was shopping. I think he was just really excited, that's all.
MINDY
Were you mad at your daddy for letting you fall?
JOAN
No. It was my fault. I shouldn't have been leaning over.
MINDY
It's not your fault, Joan. It's not your fault.
JOAN
Okay.
MINDY
Dr. Satcher, can a fall like the one Joan describes cause HSAM?
SATCHER
No, I don't believe so. From the research I've seen, none of the people with

HSAM show brain trauma of any kind. One of the first places we look is the hippocampus. Damage to the hippocampus would result in a compromised memory. We see that in Alzheimer patients, for example. But with HSAM, the opposite is true. We actually see brain regions that are in fact seven times larger than what you'll find in the average person. We also see far more white matter connecting gray matter, which results in better communication within the brain. But with regard to the original question, without knowing more about Joan's accident, I can't speculate about what might have occurred as a result of her fall.

MINDY

Did you see a doctor after you fell, Joan?

JOAN

Yes. She gave me a lollipop.

MINDY

You're a brave little girl.

[Cheers and applause]

JOAN

My grandmother had that.

MINDY

Had what, dear?

JOAN

What he said. The old-timer's disease. The one that makes people lose their memories.

MINDY

Yes, Alzheimer's. So your grandmother is no longer with us?

JOAN

She sings to me from a cassette. I was hoping maybe I could help old people like her remember better.

MINDY

That's an interesting idea. Dr. Satcher, can Joan's condition tell us anything about diseases like Alzheimer's?

SATCHER

It's possible. But we have a long way to go.

MINDY

What if I'm a parent watching at home and I think my son or daughter has a particularly strong memory, like Joan here? What should I do?

SATCHER

As we've discussed, HSAM is very rare, so the chances of your child having it, or any other kind of specialized memory, for that matter, are extremely unlikely. But that's okay. It's important to realize that we're using our memory all the time. We often think of memories as mental postcards, or movies, like Joan said, that we can call up when we want to. But most of the time, it's automatic. Memory is what teaches a child that a stove is hot and he shouldn't touch it. That said, there are exercises that a parent can do with his or her child to strengthen and improve memory.

MINDY

We've posted three of your exercises up here on our board and we'll also have them up on our website after the show. Thank you, Dr. Satcher. We'll be right back.

[Cheers and applause]

MINDY

Welcome back. Before we bring out our next child prodigy, we'd like to invite to the stage Joan's uncle, who says he has a big surprise for little Joan here. Please, have a seat and introduce yourself.

KEVIN

My name is Kevin. Kevin Deifendorf.

MINDY

Welcome, Kevin. Now, are you the one who records music or the one who works with Joan's grandfather?

KEVIN

Music.

MINDY

Got it. Now, before you reveal your surprise to Joan, tell us, what's it like to

have a niece with such a unique gift?
                    KEVIN
She's in a lot of trouble.
                    MINDY
Are you saying that HSAM is more like
a curse than a gift?
                    KEVIN
No, I'm not saying that at all. Look, I
really don't want to be on the show. I
just need to take Joan home.
                    MINDY
You seem very conflicted about this. Dr.
Satcher, let me ask you, what effect does
HSAM have on family members?
                    SATCHER
Well, I can't speak directly to HSAM.
But I can tell you that there is always a
ripple effect when it comes to these
extreme conditions. Feelings of neglect
and jealousy are not uncommon.
                    MINDY
Interesting. What do you do for work,
Kevin? Are you in the music business?
                    KEVIN
I really don't want to be interviewed.
                    MINDY
It's a simple question.
                    KEVIN
I'm not working right now. I'm on leave.

                    MINDY

From what?

                    KEVIN

Law enforcement.

                    MINDY

I see. Is there any particular reason why
you've taken leave?

                    KEVIN

Actually, I lost my partner.

                 [Murmurs]

                    MINDY

I'm sorry to hear that. Let me ask you,
why didn't Joan's parents bring her here
today? Why was it left to you, her uncle?

                    KEVIN

I'm not Joan's uncle.

                    JOAN

Me and Gavin — I mean, Kevin —
wrote a song together.

                    MINDY

You're not Joan's uncle?

                    KEVIN

No.

                    MINDY

I'm confused. How are you related to
her?

                    KEVIN

I'm not.

                    JOAN

The song is about memories.

                     375

MINDY

Is that right, Joan? You wrote a song
about your condition?

JOAN

Gavin wrote most of the lyrics.

MINDY

I'm confused. Is your name Kevin or
Gavin?

KEVIN

Kevin.

MINDY

And you wrote a song about Joan's
condition? But she's not your niece and
you're not related to her? What exactly
is your relationship?

JOAN

Gavin is a great person. He's a great actor and singer and songwriter and he's
my friend and my partner. I'm the
walrus and he's the blackbird. I don't
like that he doesn't think I should get
my hopes up about the song contest and
I don't like that he didn't want to come
on the show with me today and I don't
think it's good for him to wear that
bracelet and I don't like how his new
beard covers his dimple, but I like just
about everything else about him. I knew
Gavin was special from the very first
time I met him.

MINDY

Kevin, it's obvious that Joan is quite fond of you. It's clear to me that, with Dad not around, Joan is looking to bond with a male figure. Would you agree with that, Dr. Satcher?

SATCHER

I'm no psychologist, but it makes sense. I'd be curious to know more about Kevin's own upbringing.

KEVIN

It's none of your business. Look, we're done here. I'm taking Joan and we're leaving.

MINDY

Taking her? Hold on. If you're not her uncle, I don't think you should be *taking* her anywhere.

[Applause]

JOAN

I hate my HSAM! I want to play my song!

MINDY

Did you hear that, Dr. Satcher? Joan says she hates her HSAM. Is that normal, to reject oneself like that?

SATCHER

It's part of the process. We see this in cancer patients. No one wants to be defined by his or her disease.

MINDY

But you wouldn't call HSAM a *disease,*
right?

SATCHER

Correct, Mindy. I was just drawing a
parallel.

MINDY

Let's go to the audience. Yes, ma'am,
what's your question for our little genius
here?

WOMAN

Actually, my question is for him. Are you
Gavin Winters, the actor?

JOAN

I'm going to start playing my song now.
Hello, this is Joan Lennon on guitar.

MINDY

I thought you looked familiar.

JOAN

And Gavin will be singing. I mean,
Kevin.

MINDY

It *is* you. Oh my. This is quite amazing, ladies and gentlemen.

[Guitar strumming]

MINDY

Let's take a second and get everyone up
to speed here. Some of you will remember a story on the news a few weeks back
about an actor who set his house on fire

and then quickly vanished from the public eye. Well, he's just popped up on *our* stage — from TV's *The Long Arm,* Mr. Gavin Winters! [Applause] We'll get to our other whiz kids soon enough. But first, you're not going to want to miss the very first interview with this reclusive star, which'll be right after the break. Sit tight, everyone.

GAVIN

Let's go, Joan.

[Cheers and applause]

MINDY

We're back with Joan Sully and surprise guest Gavin Winters from the show *The Long Arm,* whose second season has been getting stellar reviews. Gavin, thanks for sticking around.

GAVIN

I didn't want to. Joan wouldn't leave.

MINDY

Gavin, let's start with the main question on everyone's mind: Where have you been?

GAVIN

[Expletive deleted]

MINDY

Please. This is a family show.

GAVIN

Look, I really shouldn't be here.

MINDY

But you are. Come on, tell us, where have you been hiding the last few weeks?

GAVIN

I haven't been hiding.

MINDY

You do understand, people have been wondering where you are.

GAVIN

Honestly, I haven't paid attention. I've been here the whole time, staying with Joan's family.

MINDY

Any particular reason why you left Los Angeles?

GAVIN

I felt like getting away for a while, that's all.

MINDY

Could it have anything to do with you setting your house on fire a few weeks ago?

GAVIN
[Inaudible]

MINDY

What was that?

GAVIN

Maybe.

MINDY

Some say the video was staged. That it

was just a ploy to boost ratings for *The Long Arm.* You're laughing. Why is that?

GAVIN

The fire was real. I don't care what at-KickingButtTakingDames says on Twitter. It had nothing to do with the show. If you want to know the truth, I was trying to burn all my boyfriend's belongings.

MINDY

From what I understand, he died quite suddenly.

GAVIN

Well, yeah. I woke up one morning and he was just lying there on the living-room floor.

MINDY

I'm sorry for your loss. That must have been devastating.

GAVIN

Yes.

MINDY

So you came all the way to the East Coast for what? To get away? To spend time with friends?

GAVIN

That's how it started, yeah. But then it turned into something different.

MINDY

What do you mean? What did it turn into?

GAVIN

Being home, in our house, was just impossible. I needed to get away from that. But then I got here and Joan had all these memories of him, memories I didn't have.

MINDY

This Joan?

GAVIN

Yes, this Joan.

JOAN

Gavin didn't want to hear the memories at first.

GAVIN

That's true. But then Joan and I started talking. It actually felt kind of good.

MINDY

What did?

GAVIN

Remembering.

MINDY

Fascinating. Dr. Satcher, you look like you want to say something.

SATCHER

Sharing stories can have tremendous healing powers. We see it all the time with war veterans.

MINDY

Very good, Dr. Satcher. But Gavin, take us back to the night of the fire. Those of us who have lost loved ones can certainly appreciate the pain you were in, but what made you take that next step and just all of sudden want to burn everything?

GAVIN

Who knows? It hits you when it hits you.

MINDY

What hits you?

GAVIN

I don't know, the unfairness of it all. Sydney shouldn't have died. But what can I do about it? I burned it all because I didn't know what else to do. It's not rational. I never said it was. God, I can't believe I'm spilling my guts to Mandy Love.

MINDY

It's Mindy.

GAVIN

Sorry. Look, Sydney wasn't a perfect man. Far from it. But he was good. He was good and he was positive and that's such a hard thing to be. He was the kind of person people gravitated to. He always made you feel better. And he chose *me* to have a future with. *Me.* He wanted us

383

to have a child. A baby. That's all he wanted. For us to share that experience. He was willing to travel far and wide to make that happen. Whatever it took. But I didn't believe. Not fully. I didn't trust. That's love, isn't it? Trusting. Believing. I wanted the same things he wanted but I was scared. And for that I'm sorry. It's something I'll regret for as long as I live. And it's hard, it's very hard to . . .

MINDY

Hey, it's okay. It's okay.

GAVIN

Really? Is this really happening? I'm crying on *The Mandy Love Show*?

MINDY

It's Mindy.

GAVIN

Sorry. I really am sorry.

32

I wouldn't necessarily recommend bursting into tears in front of a live studio audience during the taping of a network television show. But now that it's over, I don't regret that it happened. My whole body suddenly feels lighter, as if all the dense, unwanted energy stored up inside me has finally been forced out.

Joan sits next to me on the train back to Jersey. She's hugging her guitar the way another child might cuddle a boardwalk teddy bear.

I'm the adult here, theoretically, but I'm not sure how to handle this situation. Whether to be stern or compassionate. To teach or listen. All I know is that this little girl nearly made me lose my shit today. And frankly, I have very little shit left to lose.

I'm not the only one reeling. I called Paige before we boarded the train back and told her what had happened and that everything was all right, but she was so flustered she could hardly speak other than to ask when *exactly* we'd be arriving home.

"You really had us worried there, kid."

Joan mutters something in a faraway voice.

"Can you repeat that?" I say.

"Do you think they'll remember me?" Joan asks. "She wouldn't let me play my song and then you came onstage and she was more interested in talking to you."

I take the guitar from her and rest it on the bench. "Joan, listen to me. I've met a lot of people in my life, but never anyone like you. I mean it. And when I say that, I'm not talking about your memory. Fuck Mandy Love."

"Mindy."

"Right. I'm not talking about your songwriting either. I'm talking about you. All of you. The whole person. You're easy to admire, you know that? You're tenacious. It takes me forever to make a decision about something. But you know exactly what you want and you're not afraid to go after it. You're just like Sydney was."

They're really not so different, Joan and Sydney. Both maniacally driven and stubborn as can be.

"And you'll never forget Sydney, right?" Joan says.

It's the easiest question I've gotten all day. "Never."

The train screeches as it hugs a turn. Joan's head falls on my shoulder. I wiggle my arm free, pull her in. I'm clearly no parenting expert, but right now I'm pretty sure the thing to do is hold her.

"I wish you could live with us forever," Joan says.

And I was just now thinking it's time for me to leave. Paige and Ollie have been hosting me for weeks. They've been good friends and today, to repay them, I nearly lost their daughter. I think I've hung around long enough.

Plus, I have a little sister I promised I'd go visit. I think I'm done putting things off for another day.

Back in Jersey City, we turn up the street and immediately notice the hunched-over figure on the Sully stoop. Paige. She glances up from her phone, sees our approach, and rushes toward us until Joan is close enough to take in her arms. They embrace on the sidewalk, Paige unwilling to let go for what seems like minutes. She finally pulls away, keeping one hand firmly on Joan's shoulder, and she doesn't release her completely until we're through the front door and safely inside.

There's a moment of quiet in the living room, and then Paige's demeanor hardens. She sends Joan to her room and orders her to wait there until she comes to get her.

"I'm sorry," I say, once we're alone. "I should've watched her more closely."

"It's okay," Paige says, sitting down.

It doesn't feel okay. Not even close. "I don't know how you do it."

"Do what?"

"How you manage as a parent. It's terrifying."

"It is," Paige admits. "It really is." Her chest expands and then contracts, all the tension going out.

It makes me want to see my sister that much more, to hold tight to the family I still have left. "It's time for me to go."

"Not because of this, I hope."

"No. It's just time. I want to go see my sister in Florida. We need to talk."

"Are you going to tell me what happened yesterday?" Paige says. "I'm dying here."

I fill her in on the day I spent with Mara, doing my best to include all the details of the story. What sickens me most is the thought of Syd being driven to such extreme measures — flying across the country repeatedly to court a woman he'd just met — because of me and my indecision. It was all such a waste of time when deep down we both wanted the same thing.

"It's my fault," Paige says. "If I'd just said yes to Syd, you guys could've been parents."

"Don't do that."

"Ollie and I talk about having another kid. But I've waited so long to get to this point where my life is mine again. I can finally do what's right for *me.*" That last word echoes against adjacent buildings.

"You deserve it, Paige. Look, if anyone should be beating themselves up, it's me. If I had just asked my sister a year ago, when we first started talking about it, it would've been so simple. But I did what I always do. I waited and now it's too late."

She turns and stares at me. "Is it?"

"What do you mean?"

She stands up, making me even more anxious than I already am. "I've been thinking about this a lot, what Syd wanted and what he missed out on. What you *both* missed out on. And it suddenly dawned on me. Didn't you and Sydney freeze your sperm?"

It takes me a few seconds to sift through all the little moments and decisions of the last year. "The doctor told us it wasn't necessary," I say, "that it was mainly for people who were about to go through chemo or something like that. But Syd insisted on doing it anyway. Honestly, it seemed like a waste of money to me, but you know Syd."

"I do know Syd," she says, giving me a look that only confirms how little I actually know.

"Paige. I really don't understand what you're getting at here."

"Don't you see? The plan you and Sydney had from the very beginning — it doesn't have to change. You could still use your sister as the donor."

Now that she's finally arrived at her point, it seems obvious where she's been heading. Still, what she's suggesting sounds utterly absurd. "Are you crazy? If I wasn't ready to have a child *with* Syd, why would I go ahead and have a kid on my own?"

"Not just *a* kid. Sydney's kid. If you really wanted to, Gavin, you could totally do this. You're a natural. I've seen you with Joan."

"A natural? Are you kidding? I almost lost her."

She scoffs. "That can happen to anyone. Believe me, I've done worse."

"I don't get it," I say. "You just admitted to me how terrifying it is to be a parent and

390

now you're telling me to do it alone?"

She throws her arms out. "Yes, it's terrifying, but it's totally worth it."

"Really? You were also just saying how excited you were to finally have your life back."

"I say that, but I wouldn't change what I have for anything. Like I told you before, I wouldn't go back to college or high school or any other time. I have Joan now. If I go back, I don't get Joan. She's everything, Gavin. Her and Ollie, that's my whole life."

She stares at me with such heartfelt hope. I'd love to buy in, but I can't just ignore reality. "I've got an unpredictable career," I say. "I work long hours. I never know where my next paycheck is coming from. I'm going to need a new place to live. I mean, there's no way I can be a single parent."

"I get it," Paige says, nodding in agreement. "You've got plenty of good reasons not to do it. All I'm saying is, if it's something you really want, trust me, you'll figure it out."

33

By the time my bedroom door is pushed open, there's no sun coming through my windows. The ceiling light bursts on and Mom doesn't say anything at first. She sits on my bed and stares at a drawing on my wall. It's a cartoon version of me. The artist gave me circle glasses like John Lennon and made it so my fingers were doing the hand signal that means peace.

Mom takes a good look at me. "I like your hair."

"It's horrible."

"I think it looks nice."

The makeup people at *The Mindy Love Show* turned me into one of the cartoon models from my *Barbie* video game:

Normal hair  TV hair

The day didn't go anything like I'd planned because I didn't get the money to save the studio and no one paid attention when I played my guitar. Gavin finally cried, but not from my song, so it didn't count. Also, I didn't even get Mindy Love's autograph because Gavin squeezed my wrist and pulled me off the stage before I had a chance to ask her. When we got backstage, Gavin told Felicia she was unbelievable, which is what Dad says about the song "Across the Universe" but I know *unbelievable* also means "terrible."

I know what I'm supposed to say next, but I don't even get a chance because Mom says it first. "I'm sorry," she says. "I knew this change would be hard for all of us. Sometimes I just forget everything's a little harder for you."

This time I'm not mad at her for forgetting. I don't want to be mad anymore.

"I miss your father during the day too, you know."

"I know," I say, but actually I didn't *really* know until now. It wasn't always just me and Dad in the studio. I can remember one day when I was jamming on guitar and Dad was jamming on drums and we finished our song and the audience started clapping but really it was just Mom clapping because the rest of the audience was just stuffed animals that I lined up in a row on the couch. Mom has always been the loudest one in my audience.

I grab my Wally the Walrus stuffed animal because I want to put something between Mom and me before I tell her the truth.

"Okay," I say. "I was trying to get some money for the studio so Dad's music days wouldn't be over, because you said I could pay for it if I wanted to. I don't know how much money we need, but Felicia said she'll pay me in six to eight weeks."

Mom turns her whole body to me. "I understand you were trying to help, but you can't go to the city by yourself. You know that." Her forehead loosens and she pulls me in close. "You almost gave me a heart attack."

That makes me think of Sydney, which makes me realize that I still have a lot of questions. "Gavin said he and Sydney were supposed to have a baby."

She stops squishing me. "He told you that?"

"Yes. And he told Mindy Love and her whole audience too."

"Really?"

"He said it didn't happen because he was scared. Scared of what?"

Mom stares at the wall before she answers. "It's normal to feel scared when you're doing something you've never done before. It's like when you first learned how to swim. You wouldn't even get in the water. But there was one boy who jumped right in. Everyone's different."

August 2006: Dad holds his arms out wide and Mom points her phone at me, and my swimmies are pinching my arms. Dad promises he'll catch me, but I can't get my feet off the concrete, so Dad just lifts me up and dips me into the pool and everybody cheers like I did it on my own.

"Is that why you and Dad are taking so long to have a new baby?" I say. "Because you're scared?"

She gives a tiny nod and it's barely anything, but it's enough of an answer. I wonder if maybe that's why people say no all the time, because there are so many things to be scared of.

I want to talk to Gavin right now. I think maybe he's the only one who really understands me. "Can I go downstairs for a little while?"

"Not right now, honey."

"Why? Am I grounded?"

"I don't know. I have to discuss it with your father."

"Can I just go see Gavin?"

"No. Gavin needs some time to himself."

Now *my* heart is attacking. "Is he mad at me? I'm sorry he had to go all the way to New York City to get me. I already told him I was sorry. What else should I say to him?"

"Joan, listen to me. This has nothing to do with you."

"But why not?"

I fall onto my bed and pull the blanket over my legs. Mom hugs me through the blanket and tells me she loves me and strokes my hair. But none of it makes me feel any better because I've got a giant bruise on the inside of my body.

■ ■ ■ ■

The next morning, I go downstairs to see Gavin but he's not there. His room is cleared out and the dresser is empty and the closet is full of naked hangers. The blankets are pulled tight and it's a strange thing to see, because I don't think Gavin made his bed once the whole time he stayed here.

I hate going to sleep because adults do so many things when you're not around, like pack their bags and leave.

I press my head into his pillow and smell him. I look up at the Awake Asleep poster on the wall. It's weird because it hangs in our house, but it's really a memory from Gavin's life. I wonder if he liked looking at it every day or if it bothered him because memories come in different ways. Some make you feel warm all over and others jab a stick into your side.

I reach over to shut off the lamp but first I look in the garbage can and I open the drawer next to the bed and reach my hand in and feel around but everything is empty. I was hoping to find a note. He never said good-bye.

ACROSS THE UNIVERSE

34

There she is, waiting below: Veronica. It's been nearly three months since I saw her at the funeral. She spots me coming down the airport escalator, her shoulders scrunched up in giddiness. Sun-soaked hair, freckled doll face, and that stretched smile that reveals only her top teeth. Anticipating my touchdown, she lets out a puppylike yelp and then launches herself at me. I hug her for what feels like days.

Pulling away, she reaches for my face. "I love the beard."

"Mom hates it."

"Of course she does."

We exit the terminal and cross the street to the parking lot. Two beeps unlock the doors of a black BMW. "Is this your car?" I ask.

"Nope. I don't have a car."

We both get in. The leather seats are oven warm.

"Is it Tim's?" I ask.

"Tim and I broke up months ago," Veronica says casually. And then, seeing my confusion, "I told you that."

"When?"

She reaches her arm back and reverses the car. "When I was in L.A. You had bigger things on your mind, obviously."

"I had no idea. I'm sorry to hear it."

"It's fine. Just wasn't meant to be."

That overused phrase echoes in my brain as Veronica maneuvers out of the lot and merges onto a main road. With the windows down, her hair whips wildly, but it doesn't bother her one bit. Meanwhile, over in the passenger seat, I'm so lightheaded with possibilities I feel I might just blow away.

In less than ten minutes we've conquered the island, from New Town to Old. Veronica parks along the water. "It's about to rain," she says and then wanders into a building to return the keys to the car's owner. It belongs to someone named Larry, a man who Veronica swears is just a friend.

I walk to the edge of the pier and look across the Atlantic. Somewhere out there is Cuba. Closer than Miami, according to Veronica.

I feel a raindrop on my nose, then another.

In mere seconds, it comes down in clumps. I take cover under an awning and drop my luggage on dry ground.

A family rushes into the building behind me. I'm standing in front of an aquarium. My parents took me to zoos and aquariums as a kid. This was before Veronica was born. I always forget these neutral memories. I tend to remember only the great highs and deep lows.

I press my face to the window and watch the family at the ticket counter. It's a man and woman with two boys. The smaller boy reaches for his brother's hand, but the brother wriggles away. The smaller boy then grabs for his mother's hand and she takes it blindly.

My breath is fogging up the window. The storm has already passed. The sun is shining. Veronica returns. "You're soaked," she says, laughing. "I tried to warn you."

"It happened so fast."

"Yeah. It's the season."

We walk down Whitehead Street, a semi-busy thoroughfare with pedicabs, tourists, and street stands. Quaint homes slumber behind short white walls and tropical cover. Birds sing out from tree limbs as if paid by the town to set the mood. I wonder what it means that my sister has chosen to live in a place that feels like a permanent vacation. Then again, some people say the same thing about Los Angeles.

"What would you like to do?" Veronica says, playing with the charm at the end of her long necklace. "You hungry? You feel like going to the beach? Whatever you want."

"Whatever *you* want."

"Let's drop your stuff off. I'll show you my place and we'll take it from there."

Suddenly she's on my back. With my heavy bag in hand, I almost topple over. "I'm so happy you're here," she says, her legs dangling off me.

"Me too," I say, trying to stay on my feet.

I'm hunched over, but I've got her good enough. We don't have much farther to go.

Veronica shows me around her small apartment. The furniture seems like it came with the place, wicker chairs and matching glass end tables. She's always been a no-frills girl, a bit tomboyish, more about practicality than appearance.

But she's added a few personal touches. A potted snake plant by the window. A sign on the wall that reads it's only your life. Photos of people I know and don't know. In one photo, my father is holding Veronica in the crook of his arm, barely feeling the weight of her.

"The couch folds out," Veronica says. "I don't mind sleeping there if you'd rather have the bed."

"No, this is perfect."

I can't look away from my father, Alex Deifendorf, with the newborn baby pressed against him. He was about the same age I am now.

"Let me show you upstairs," Veronica says, guiding me up a tight spiral staircase to a loft. I immediately recognize the print on her bedroom wall.

"Thanks for sending that, by the way," she says. "I love her."

It's Mara's surfer girl. When I bought the print from Mara at the fair and sent it here to my sister, I didn't realize that it was going from one mother candidate to another. Sydney would recognize the magic in that. I think, for once, I have to do the same.

35

A whole week passes without Gavin, and just when I think I can't get any more depressed, which is something that Dad says all artists get, the weekend comes and Dad starts clearing out the studio.

First he takes all the posters and pictures and postcards off the walls and the corkboard. Then he takes all the mini-keyboards off the shelves and unplugs all the cords from his equipment and wraps the cords into neat loops. Then he takes his guitars off the rack and gathers all his microphones and puts everything into big boxes and tapes them all up. Pretty soon he'll carry everything out the door to the Sully and Sons van parked outside.

I look inside one box that hasn't been closed up yet and I find cassette tapes, CDs, ticket stubs, lyric sheets, set lists, backstage passes, and the spare key for Dad's old van. I pull out a broken drumstick and wave it in the air. Little pieces of wood fall to the ground. I wonder why Dad would keep a broken stick, but then I realize it's not a drumstick anymore, it's a reminder that leads back to a memory.

I love that Dad keeps all his old stuff, just like I keep my important art projects in the box under my bed. But Dad's things aren't staying in our house. Dad is going to bring them to his storage unit and once they're there, he won't be able to take his music stuff out whenever he wants.

At the bottom of the open box, I find magazines and newspapers. I flip through them and find a picture of Dad and Gavin in a black-and-white magazine called *Hub City*. Dad has long hair that he tucks behind his ears and his face doesn't have one hair on it. Gavin has jeans with big holes in the knees, and his eyes are like a raccoon's with dark shadows around them.

"That was a long time ago."

Dad is standing behind me and now we're both looking at the photo. "Is Gavin wearing makeup?" I ask.

He looks more closely. "Looks like it." He takes the magazine from me and starts to read the article. "This is the same day I met Mom. She came to the show that night."

I try to imagine being my mother in college and seeing my father play drums and then I remember that I don't have to imagine because I can go ask Mom to tell me about it right now.

I find her in the spare bedroom. The Awake Asleep poster is off the wall, and the blankets and sheets have been pulled from the bed. I fall face-first onto the naked mattress and press my nose against the pillowy top. I can barely smell Gavin anymore.

I turn over. "When you watched Dad's band play in college, did you think he was special right away?"

My memory movies load up quickly, but Mom has to wait for hers. She finds what she's looking for and her mouth makes a slanty smile. "I couldn't take my eyes off him. He had so much passion, like he was going to explode. I wanted to know what he was so worked up about."

I know exactly what she means, because Dad doesn't just *play* the drums, he slams on the skins like he wants to flatten them into pancakes. "So what was it? What made him like that?"

She squirts cleaner into the dresser drawers and she soaks up the wetness with a paper towel. "He loved it," she says, wiping with soft circles. She wipes in the same spot for a long time and it looks like she might have forgotten what she's even doing, which is what people do when they daydream.

"What's going to happen with that dresser?" I say.

Mom finally moves the paper towel to a new spot. "We'll see if the new tenants want it. The bed and the nightstand too."

I hope I never meet the new tenants because they're never going to be better than the guy who was just here. I stare up at the ceiling and I replay some of the memories Gavin and I had together: us on the train, on *The Mindy Love Show,* at the kitchen table earlier that morning when he was babysitting me. I keep going back, seeing everything again: eating pizza, walking through New York City, searching around Jersey City for clues about what Sydney was doing. I see him listening so closely while I tell my stories and I see his surprised look when I draw my picture of Sydney's face. I see his boxy stomach when he's wearing no shirt and his clear leg hair when he wears shorts and the way he used his right hand to write lyrics and his left hand to drink coffee or wine.

I watch him give me a plain bagel, hold my hand across the street, lift me onto his shoulders, do his blackbird signal, and run his fingers through his bouncy hair. I listen to him sing my melody and I remember his words: "A good song is a good song"; "It's just about relaxing and not overthinking things"; "It's too painful to remember"; "It's even more painful to forget"; "Fuck Mandy Love."

The memories are so clear and they make it hard to be here in this empty bedroom, but I don't know where else to go. The memories are with me wherever I am.

I go back to the studio and Dad is sitting in his roller chair with his arms crossed. He's staring at all the boxes like they're trying to talk to him but he can't understand what they're saying. Now Mom is standing next to me and she's watching Dad too and for once I think Mom is feeling what I'm feeling because she walks over to Dad and squeezes his shoulders. This room will never look the way it does in my memory and I hate when that happens, when the way things *are* and the way things *were* look totally different.

"I'm out of boxes," Dad says. "I have to take a trip to Home Depot."

I hear him say it and I know right away what I have to do. "I'm coming."

"Really? You hate that place."

Yes, but it might be the only choice I have left.

■ ■ ■ ■

The glass doors open for us and Dad and I walk through. It's not so scary until I see the orange shopping carts and I start smelling the wood or whatever that smell is. That's when I start to feel super-sleepy like I want to be home and hiding under my covers.

But instead of running away, I do the opposite. I bend down and touch the floor. It's hard and cold and it reminds me of when I used to lie on the kitchen tiles with Pepper because he liked it there and I liked him. I wish dogs could get wrinkles just like people so you'd know when they were getting old and it wasn't such a surprise when it was time to say good-bye.

I catch up with Dad. While he's looking for his boxes, I'm looking for a good jumping spot. The ceiling is so high that a giant could shop here without bumping his head, and the shelves are full of shiny packages that look a lot like toys. Toys for dads.

Dad stops to talk to a worker with an ugly orange apron. Now seems like the best time because there's a tall stepladder waiting in the aisle. I start climbing up before I can think about it too much, but it's really hard not to think about everything. I wonder what my memory is really good for, anyway, because the only people who seem to care about it are people like Dr. Robert and Mindy Love and they're not the nicest people.

I reach the top of the steps and I look down. I have to hold the rail because I'm so high up.

"Joan! What are you doing?"

Dad and the worker are staring up at me. Dad's eyes look like they're about to leap out of his face and I think the worker is saying something rude about me into his shirt microphone.

"Don't move," Dad says. "I'm coming up."

There's a little crowd now. An audience. Dad comes up the stairs and makes me sit down with him on the platform. He tries to get me to look at him, but I can't.

"Joanie, please. What's going on?"

"I'm tired and it's not the sleepy kind."

"What are you saying? I don't know what you're saying."

"I want everything to go back to the way it was."

"I know, honey."

"No, you don't, Dad. You've forgotten."

"No, I haven't. I swear I haven't."

I look up. I want to believe him.

"Come here," he says, and he hugs me hard.

■ ■ ■ ■

A DAY IN THE LIFE

■ ■ ■ ■

36

I tap his face. *Syd. Stop playing around. Wake up.* I listen for a breath, feel for a pulse. I blow into his mouth. Press his chest. Hold his nose, blow again. Press his chest, harder, harder. Try to lift his head, his body. So heavy. Find a phone. Call 911. Answer the dispatcher's questions, follow his orders, do everything he asks. Hang up. Go to the porch, listen for sirens. Come back inside. Shake him, scream —

I open my eyes, wake from the nightmare. But I can't turn it off fully, not when the nightmare really happened.

It takes a minute to remember that I'm in Veronica's house on her foldout couch.

I sit up, throw the afghan aside, wipe the sweat from my forehead. The window is open, but there's no air blowing in. My feet welcome the cool kiss of the tiled floor.

The last few nights, my dreams have been frighteningly vivid. Memories and images that I had evicted from my mind have been breaking back in. It's as if I'm living my life in delay. He died months ago but it's only hitting me now.

I find a note stuck to the coffeemaker: *It's Friday! We're going out tonight!*

The boyish handwriting reminds me of Joan, who I've missed rather intensely since leaving Jersey. Though she and Veronica are wildly different — the former quite serious, the latter rarely so — I've united them in my head as part of one family for which I feel responsible. I hope my littler sister is doing okay without me.

In the week I've spent here with Veronica, we've gone out every night but one. It would seem every day is Friday in her world. Unless this never-ending party is all for my benefit.

Incredibly, no matter how late we're out each night, it never hampers Veronica's productivity. Every new morning, she's up with her alarm and off to work on time. She heads up guest relations at a local resort. While she's away each day, I wander the island. I poke my head into galleries and antique stores, bird-watch on park benches, sip coffee at outdoor tables. Sometimes I just take a leisurely stroll to nowhere at all.

And when Veronica returns home in the

early evenings, we usually grab a bite and end up staying out way too late. These long nights have offered a welcome diversion from the turmoil in my head and heart. I've yet to ask my sister about the significant conversation she and Syd had without my knowledge. Turns out, fatherhood is, technically speaking, still a possibility for me. Part of me wishes Paige had never brought it to my attention. To learn that there's this one last convoluted way for me to resurrect a little piece of the person I lost is proving impossible to ignore.

And so, tonight, before the festivities begin, I've decided — just now, while standing sleepily in Veronica's narrow kitchenette — that I will make a trip to the market this afternoon for supplies. Tonight, my sister and I are going to stay home and have a proper meal together.

"I'm impressed," Veronica says. We're positioned at opposite ends of her glass coffee table, sitting cross-legged on the floor with couch pillows under our butts.

She's nodding in appreciation, her mouth full of mahi-mahi and black rice. "There's something sweet in here too," she says.

"Navel orange."

"Is that it? I never would've guessed."

"I'm glad it worked out," I say. "I found the recipe online."

I used to love to cook this way for Syd. It gave my days purpose when I wasn't working or auditioning. I'd scour the web for intriguing concoctions and venture out to Whole Foods in search of sumac or tamarind paste or whatever other ingredient I'd never heard of before. It's been several months since I've had the spirit to try out an untested meal.

"You can cook for me whenever you want," she says. "Seriously, this is the best home-cooked meal I've had in years."

"It looks like it's the only home-cooked meal you've had in years. Your spice rack consists of salt and pepper."

She shrugs, guilty as charged. "Turns out you're not a bad guy."

"What?"

"On *The Long Arm*. I knew you couldn't have murdered that man. You just don't have it in the eyes."

"Don't underestimate me," I say.

"I don't."

Veronica changes the subject yet again and starts describing how her bike tire was so flat she barely managed to ride it home. "That was Tim's job," she explains. "He made sure my tires were full of air. I always

420

forget to check."

"I'll fill them up for you."

She smiles in appreciation.

"What happened with him, anyway?" I ask, inching my way to the matter at hand. "You guys seemed pretty serious at first."

"We were. I met him right after I moved here. He introduced me to a lot of people who are still good friends of mine. Plus, he hooked me up with the job at the resort. He was sort of my whole world. But I just started to feel suffocated."

She relates the whole thing nonchalantly, more interested in her food than her story.

"So you're the one who broke it off?"

"Yeah," Veronica says. "And it's a really small town, so it's annoying. I'm surprised we haven't run into him yet."

"And you started dating him when?"

She calculates in her head. "It was about mid-December."

I pause for a drink. "And around New Year's was when Sydney asked you for your eggs, right?"

For the first time my sister looks thrown. It takes her several seconds to recover.

"He told me not to say anything," Veronica says. "He said you'd be mad."

"I'm not mad. I just wanted you to know that I know."

She stares at me, unsure what to say next. "He said you guys had someone else that you really liked. Someone through the agency. He said you weren't depending on me."

I wish it were true. "We never found anyone through the agency. He just didn't want you to feel bad." Judging from her crestfallen face, it's happened anyway.

She looks down at her food, the fork still in her hand but her attention elsewhere. "After he called me I didn't hear anything else about it. I asked Mom and she said you guys were putting the whole thing on hold."

"One of us was. That's true."

"He said you were going to call me, Gavin. I was waiting to hear from you. Why didn't you call?"

I try to find the words. All I can say is "I don't know."

She drops her fork onto her plate and crawls to my side. Her arms come over my shoulders and around my neck. "I'm sorry."

I am too. I should've called her, a year ago, seven months ago. I had so many chances, so much time. It seems so simple now. I would call, she would answer. We'd catch up for a bit, then I'd lay it all out. Tell her how scared I was to be a father. She'd tell me to get over it, that it was perfectly normal to have doubts, the same speech Syd and Paige gave me. She'd tell me she loved me, that she'd do whatever it took. Syd never would've had to resort to Mara.

Or maybe it wouldn't have happened that way. Maybe she would have said no. At least I would have had peace of mind. We tried, we asked, time to move on. Syd and I would have gone to the next candidate, together. We would have searched as a team, never stopping until we found our perfect match.

And if we had never found that perfect one, so be it. We would have been able to sleep knowing we tried. We were true of heart. We were honest. We were open. We believed. What a rare thing, to believe. We were lucky. We could've been.

"You okay?" Veronica asks. It's what everyone wants to know.

I ignore the question and say something that's one hundred percent true: "I'm ready to go out."

37

I'm all alone where the waves come onto the sand. The water rushes over my feet and it keeps my whole body cool in the hot sun.

If I move my eyes left or right, I'm not alone anymore because I can see all the sailboats. If I turn around I see my parents waiting just a couple of jump-rope lengths away. They're sitting in beach chairs and Mom is reading her book and Dad is sleeping with his earbuds in his ears. This isn't the vacation Mom wanted, that's not happening until next year, but it's a trip that Dad thought we should take right away after he pulled me off the stepladder in Home Depot.

It's nice of Dad to take us here to Cold Spring Harbor for the weekend and show me Cannon Hill, which is the mansion that John Lennon and his family lived in when they wanted to leave the city and feel like they were on vacation. But my brain is still working the same way it always does, which means that visiting a new John Lennon place only reminds me of the other John Lennon places I've visited and the other people I've visited those places with. That means I'm thinking of *him* again. I don't even like to say his name because he forgot all about me and that's not fair because I can never forget about him.

Mom startles me. "Want to swim?"

"Not really."

She stands with her arms crossed over her one-piece suit and stares out at the water, trying to see what I'm seeing. "It's beautiful here."

I'm having a hard time thinking about what's here because I'm mostly thinking about what's not here. I wish there was a way to know when you were seeing someone for the last time so you could pay extra-close attention to that person when it was happening.

Tuesday, July 30, 2013: We get off the train from New York City and Gavin carries me on his back the whole way up the hill. He lets me down and we turn onto our street and Mom is waiting on the steps. She runs to us and hugs me. She walks me into the house and then she sends me to my room and that part happens so fast that I never think to turn my head back once more and look at Gavin.

"Come on," Mom says. "Let's swim."

She holds my hand and we walk into the water. We go deep until my feet can't reach and I'm kicking. Mom tilts her head back and reaches her arms out and floats. I do the same and we both look up at the sky and I think back to when I first learned to float and the swim teacher had to hold my butt up because it kept sinking.

I think Mom is saying something but with my ears in the water I can't hear so well. I lift my head up and shake the water out of my ears and ask, "What did you say?"

She's not floating anymore. She's kicking her legs and now I'm kicking too. "I said, maybe we've been looking at this the wrong way."

I still don't know what she's talking about. "We?"

"Yeah," Mom says, looking at Dad back on the beach. "We get frustrated with each other, I know, but we each have our own strengths and weaknesses. Maybe it's best to just let people do what they're good at instead of forcing them to do something that doesn't come naturally to them."

I look back at the beach too and I see that Dad isn't reading his magazine anymore. He's playing his acoustic guitar, the Gibson, which is the only guitar he didn't stick inside a box.

"He's happiest when he's creating," Mom says. "That's what he does best."

Dad has that look on his face like his head is in the clouds. I don't love clouds because they sometimes get in the way of the sun, but I don't mind them when Dad has his head in them because that means he's getting lost in the music, which means he's forgetting where he is, and that's the only type of forgetting I really like.

"And what you do best, Joan, is remember." She's facing me now. "I know you get annoyed sometimes, but no one can remember like you and you shouldn't expect them to. That's not what they're good at. Remembering is *your* job. And it's an important one."

She winks and then dunks her head back. When she pulls it up again her hair is slicked down and she looks like the prettiest creature. I want to be a creature too, but a different kind. I hold my nose and dive under the water and I pretend I'm a walrus gliding around in the dark and quiet. When I run out of breath, I come up and open my eyes and I don't know how but it looks like the sun got a little bit brighter.

■ ■ ■ ■

The waitress takes our dinner plates away and she asks if we have room for dessert and Dad says yes. I'm glad we got a table next to the window because the sun is saying good night in a pretty way, making orange and purple swirls in the sky.

Cold Spring Harbor must be lucky because John Lennon wrote most of the songs for his *Double Fantasy* album here and he won his only Grammy award for that album. Also Billy Joel has an album named after this town and he's a very big artist even though I don't like his music. Dad tried to play some of Billy Joel's music in the car today but the only song of his I ever liked is "We Didn't Start the Fire" and I don't like that song anymore because now it reminds me of a person who actually did start a fire.

Dad orders coffee with his dessert but Mom is still drinking her wine. She's wearing her new white pants because Labor Day hasn't passed yet. I have no idea what happens after Labor Day but Mom loves to follow the rules. One of her hands is busy playing with her hair, or maybe she's just using her fingers as a comb. She didn't bring her brush with her to dinner because it was too big to fit inside her fancy purse:

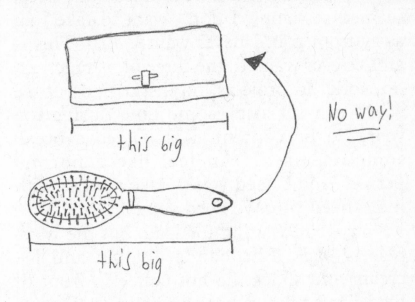

this big

No way!

this big

She's staring at Dad, turning her wineglass round and round, holding it by the stem, and she won't look away.

"What?" Dad says.

"I think we should keep the studio," Mom says.

That makes my ears open because that's all I've ever wanted to hear one of them say. Dad looks shocked, probably because he had to carry all those heavy boxes outside and now he'll have to carry all of them back inside again. "What are you saying?" Dad says.

"I saw you today," Mom says, "sitting on the beach, playing your guitar. I haven't seen you look that way in so long. You seemed so happy. I don't want to take that away from you. I never wanted that. This is all I've ever wanted, the three of us together, no work, no projects, no distractions. If we could just set aside some time during the year, I'd be content. I just need a break sometimes so I can feel like a normal person. And I need you to take a break with me. I need you. We need you."

Now we're waiting for Dad, but the waitress is back. She hands out pie and ice cream and slides the hot coffee in front of Dad. He smiles at her and when she's gone he says, "I'll make more of an effort. I promise. And we can take more weekend vacations like this. It's long overdue." He lifts the steaming mug to his lips. "But we're not keeping the studio."

"I'm okay with keeping it, Ollie, really. If it makes you happy."

"It doesn't," he says, sipping the coffee and setting the mug down carefully. "Today was the first time I can remember when I was playing guitar just because I felt like it. Not for work. Not to earn money. Nothing was on the line. It was just for fun. That's why I started playing in the first place. It was nice to feel that again. I don't have all that pressure anymore." He stares down at his coffee, which is so black you could show movie credits on it. "I'm okay with the way things are."

Dad smiles at Mom but I don't like what he's saying. For a second it seemed like one of my biggest wishes was going to come true. It's like being at the rescue shelter and you ask the person to take a dog out of his cage and he wags his tail when you pet him and he thinks he's coming home with you, but then you have to send him back to his cage because your mom says it's just too soon to get a new dog (Saturday, September 4, 2010).

And now there's some lady at another table staring at me and I'm wondering if it's because there's chocolate on my face or maybe I'm crying and I don't even know it. It's really spooking me out, the way her eyes are squinting but there's no sun in here. I'm trying to look away but for some reason I can't.

Now she's standing up and dropping her napkin on the table. She's coming to our table and I'm wiping my face just in case. Now she's standing next to Mom, but she's looking at me and she says, "I know you."

I point to myself nervously.

"I know!" she says again. "From *The Mindy Love Show*. You're the one with the memory." She reaches her hand out. "It's so nice to meet you."

I shake her hand but I don't know what to say. It doesn't seem to matter anyway because she's happy to do all the talking.

"Let me just say, you are an absolute delight. Just wonderful. It's Joan, right?"

"Yes." But I don't like how it comes out. It's way too quiet. I raise the volume on my voice so that my next words are very easy to hear. "My name is Joan Lennon."

I'm sitting at the desk in our hotel room, using Dad's laptop. I can smell his feet from here but I don't say anything because he looks so comfortable on the bed with Mom curled under his arm. Sometimes Mom seems so big and powerful but Dad can take all that away just by being near her.

I was in a very bad mood after Dad said we weren't keeping the studio but that was before I got recognized. Getting recognized reminded me of when my songwriting partner who I can't name took me to New York City and the two ladies spotted him and they wanted to take a picture with him. And now I'm thinking about *him* and our song and how he sang about starting over

432

and leaving the past behind. I never understood what he was talking about because I
can't leave the past behind no matter what I
do, but hearing Dad talk about music during dinner made me hear the words to our
song a little differently. Dad started a new
job and he said his music days were over,
but now he's going back to music in a new
way and he feels good about it. So now I'm
thinking that when my songwriting partner
who I can't name sings *Leave the past behind,* he really means *Leave the past behind
until it starts to feel good again and then go
back to it,* but that's too long to fit in a song
so he had to make it shorter.

And that gets me thinking about what
Mom told me when we were kicking our
legs in the lake or harbor or whatever it was
and that's why I've decided to take her
advice and do what I do best: remember.

I ask Dad for my songwriting partner's
e-mail address and I start typing. It seems
like my partner needs someone to help him
remember the right stuff because from what
Mom tells me and from what I've seen, he's
not very good at doing that by himself.

So I write it all out and now I'm clicking
the button that makes it go through the
wires and across the universe and into his
brain so that his brain can be full of all the

things my brain is full of. This way he'll know that it's okay to go back to the past now because there are a few things back there that are worth seeing a second time.

38

I'm dancing on a floor of sand while the band plays what I can only describe as island music. The singer performs barefoot on the low outdoor stage, but no one besides the chesty woman by the speaker is paying him any attention. The rest of us have our backs to the musicians, soaking up the sounds, receiving the vibrations, but indifferent to the source.

Veronica shimmies next to me, reaching for my hand every few minutes as if to verify that it's really happening, that I'm actually here with her in Florida. For now, there's nowhere else I'd rather be. That's not, however, an entirely organic determination. It's partly a choice. This music, both in lyric and atmosphere, is insisting that everything is going to be all right, all right, and for once I'm *choosing* not to dismiss the sentiment out of hand. I don't typically go for this don't-worry-be-happy thing. I've always preferred songs that are raw-hearted and honest. Songs with integrity and truth. A song like Joan and I tried to make. But tonight I want to be like my sister and Syd. I want to believe that this music isn't about willfully ignoring the tragedies of life but bravely choosing optimism despite them. Tonight, for once, I want to believe every-thing *will* be all right.

After retrieving two more beers from the tiki bar, I weave back through the crowd, hand Veronica her beverage, and semi-shout into her ear, "Paige says I should still do it."

"Do what?" Veronica yells back.

I sip from my glass, give her time to think. When that doesn't work, I stare into her eyes until they widen in acknowledgment.

She gets it now, she must, or else she wouldn't be pulling me by the arm to a quieter spot. We relocate to where the ocean waves produce more noise than the band. She faces me and says, "Yes. My answer is yes. Let's do it. I'm in."

This is exactly why I didn't ask Veronica back when I should've asked her. I knew she'd jump on board impulsively before she even knew where the boat was headed or how long the trip would be.

"Don't just say that," I tell her. "It's a huge commitment for you. It goes beyond just handing over your eggs."

"I know that," Veronica says, undeterred. "Whatever it takes."

But I'm still not sure she's understanding the full magnitude of what I'm suggesting. I'm not sure I understand. "I'm not saying I'd actually do it," I say. "I'm just putting it out there. I have no idea how it would work. I don't know how to take care of a kid."

"Come on. Yes, you do. You're great with children."

"Since when?"

She grabs my hand and forces me to sit down with her on a bench. "Since about as long as I can remember. When I was little you'd make these really detailed houses for my dolls out of cardboard boxes from Mom's store. And you always brought home those frozen-fruit bars for me when you were working at the day camp. And you'd let me sleep in your bed when I was scared even though I'd kick you the whole night. And I'd ask you to take me to the park after school and you'd always say no, because you had better things to do, but then you'd take me anyway. And when I was older and you were in L.A., you called my first boyfriend on the phone, and do you remember what you told him? You said he'd better act like a gentleman because you had people following him. He never wanted to kiss me in public."

She shakes her head, either because she can't believe I said that to her boyfriend or because he actually bought it. "Really, I can go on, Gavin. You were just a kid yourself but you were always so thoughtful and nurturing and protective and just *there,* even when you weren't."

I don't know how she emerged from her precarious beginnings with such positivity and perspective and gratitude. Maybe I did have something to do with that after all.

"And you even fill up my bike tires," she adds playfully. "Gavin, honestly, I can't think of anyone who'd make a better father than you. And the fact that you've hesitated this long just proves how seriously you'd take it when it finally does happen."

I look for my beer and find it resting on the ground next to me. "I appreciate what you're saying, but I can't do it all by myself."

"Why not?" Veronica says. "Mom raised us alone and she did a pretty good job."

I swallow it down, the beer and my sister's words. "Yeah, she did. But she didn't choose to do it that way."

"True," Veronica says, stretching her sandaled feet out in front of her.

We watch the band from a distance.

Strings of white lights dangle above the dance floor. I think of the man who made both of us, how after a long silence, he'd finally speak. Patience isn't just sitting back and waiting. It's enduring. Finishing the thing.

"This kid would really have it rough," I say. "His parents would be brother and sister."

"Yeah, one gay, one straight, and both unmarried. It would be a total shitshow. It would be great."

Above us, the black sky is crowded with stars. *I could sail into outer space. But even stars, they leave a trace.* The meaning of those lines has changed in the few weeks since I wrote them. At the time I was lamenting the fact that I'd never be free of Syd, the same way I had never really overcome the loss of my father. But there's no escaping the memories. And that doesn't have to be a bad thing. Actually, I'm thinking of Sydney right now, imagining what he would say about this crazy plan, the one he himself set in motion, and I have to say I feel just a tiny bit braver.

"Whatever you decide," Veronica says, "I'm here."

I can't wait forever. It's a mistake I've made before, thinking that the way things are at any given moment will be the way they are when I wake up in the morning. That's why I tell her. "I love you."

She turns to me, surprised.

"I just want you to know."

She leans her head on my shoulder and I gaze up at the stars. Millions of them, long gone but still here. Reminders, reminders, reminders.

The black sky flexes out until it becomes one with the ocean. A wave emerges from the vanishing horizon and crashes onto the sand. "Let's go swimming."

"Now?" she asks.

"Yes," I say. "Now."

Out of my sneakers and shirt, and into the water. I dive under a wave and feel the quick shock through my body. At once the world is black and empty and weightless.

I come back up and turn to shore. Veronica, dimly lit in bra and underwear, hesitates at the edge.

"Come on," I shout. "Just jump in."

She wades in until she's just a face and blond hair. I go under and swim blindly toward her. When I surface, she shrieks and splashes water in my face.

"Go under," I say.

"No. I'm freezing."

"Freezing? It's like a bathtub in here."

I come for her.

"Stop! Gavin, I swear!" She swims away. "I'm going back."

But I'm not ready yet. Not ready to walk on my own two feet. It feels good to be carried by the current.

"Be careful, Gavin." Her voice is already distant. "Do you hear me? Don't go too far out."

She swims to shore, nearly disappearing in the night. Meanwhile, I'm increasing the distance between me and land. Deeper. Deeper. It's peaceful out here, enveloped by nature's quiet. I wonder if it wouldn't be a fine way to go, while there's a brief sense of calm, all my cards on the table, all the words spoken. Fall off into the endless sea, reunite with him, my best friend ever since that first blind date, still today, always will be. The one who kept me afloat. I'm trying to do it alone. I'm really trying. But I get so tired. This bracelet is too heavy.

A graze against my leg just now, something bristly rushing by. It jolts me to attention. I look down. Can't see anything. The ocean is black. I hover in place, alert. Seconds pass. No sound but the rolling waves. No strange movements. My heart begins to settle. It was nothing, only my imagination.

I'm all alone.

But not really. I look up. My sister waits on land, small as a dot. Hard to tell from here, but it looks like she's waving. Just saying hello? Or is she calling me in?

Again, brushing my foot. This time it's unmistakable: there's something in the water.

I take off for shore, arms and legs knifing the surface. I lift my head, my sister so far away. I tempted fate just a moment ago, when everything was finally all right. How could I? I swim to her. I swim.

Again, clipping my foot, my toes. I turn, for some reason, I turn and there, breaching, a fin, a snout, a bump, and then gone, nothing. Back on shore, my sister waiting, but I can't move. Another nudge from underneath. I kick everywhere, claiming my space.

The water breaks, again, the thing surfacing, holy massive. Perforated nose, whiskers, brown, craggy. Beaming in the darkness, two long fangs, white sabers. Not fangs — tusks. Of course, tusks. A walrus. *The* walrus. It can't be.

It swoops down and under. I wait for it to resurface, scanning in every direction. All clear. Stillness. Then panic returns; I race to the shore.

I reach Veronica. She's hugging herself, shivering. "I told you not to go out so far. You scared me."

I struggle for breath. "Did you see that?"

"See what?"

"Out there."

"No," Veronica says, searching my face rather than the water. "Are you okay?"

I turn to the sea. I look. I look. I look some more.

And then I tell her, and whoever else can hear me, "Yes. I'm okay."

To: Gavin Winters
Subject: Top Ten Reasons

Dear Blackbird,

My mom told me you were scared to be a dad and I'm thinking that maybe it's because you aren't focusing on the right memories. Since you asked me to help you remember once before, I figured I could help you remember again. Also, I like to make lists.

Here are the Top Ten Reasons why you'd be a good father:

1. Because you remembered my name (Tuesday, July 9).

2. Because you said you liked my outfit (Wednesday, July 10).

3. Because you held my hand when we crossed the street and you helped me call my first taxi and you taught me how to do a change of scenery and you showed me that John Lennon didn't just write songs, he also drank coffee and went to the pharmacy (Tuesday, July 16).

4. Because you bought me a plain bagel (Wednesday, July 10) and a soft pretzel (Tuesday, July 16) and French fries (Monday, July 22) and you made me try pizza (Tuesday, July 16).

5. Because you liked my drawing (Wednesday, July 10).

6. Because you always did your hand signal even when you had a headache and you couldn't get out of bed (Tuesday, July 16).

7. Because you always told me the truth, like the time you said my song didn't make you cry (Wednesday, July 10) and my lyrics were dissing generous (Thursday, July 11), and I probably wouldn't win the contest (Thursday, July 25). You could be a little mean sometimes, but it felt okay because you treated me like a grown-up and you made my song better. And it's because you were always honest with me that I

could believe you when you told me that I was impressive and that you had never met anyone like me before (Tuesday, July 30).

8. Because you came to get me at The *Mindy Love Show* (Tuesday, July 30).

9. Because you taught me about the good kind of nervous (Tuesday, July 16) and I finally felt it (Tuesday, July 30).

10. Because you showed me that it's not just about waiting around for an idea to come but also about knowing when the idea has finally arrived (Thursday, July 18).

11. Because whenever I had good ideas for lyrics, you used them.

12. Because you listened so closely to my memories and you asked questions and you're pretty much the only person who's ever done that besides doctors and talk-show hosts.

13. Because you can speak with a British accent.

14. Because you know a lot about John Lennon *and* Paul McCartney.

15. Because you do the best rock-star look I've ever seen.

16. Because you have a great voice and not just for singing. I bet you'd be great at reading bedtime stories.

17. Because I love my dad more than anyone in the world. No matter what he does or says or where he goes, I love him. You have nothing to worry about.

18. Because you're my partner and I know that deep down you haven't forgotten me.

Sorry, I had more than ten.

Love,
The Walrus

■ ■ ■ ■

DON'T LET ME DOWN

■ ■ ■ ■

I fit the cassette into Dad's old Walkman. I rewind the tape and it squeals all the way to the beginning. I press down on the chunky Play button and through the hiss I hear Grandma Joan's piano and her voice. I shut my eyes and pretend she's here in my bedroom giving me a concert.

When Grandma lifts her hands off the keys and her foot off the pedal, you can hear her sigh and it's the kind of sigh you do after a tasty drink or a deep laugh or when you've just remembered a great memory.

The recording ends but the tape still plays. I let it hiss and it feels like she's still here.

"I wish you could hear my song."

The wheels spin through the plastic window.

"I wish it could go deep into your system."

Dad says I carry her memory and he's talking about my name when he says this, not my HSAM.

"I want to win because of you. I'm going to win."

I listen.

"Hello? Grandma?"

The wheels get slower and the cassette clicks and the hissing stops and the tape runs out.

My door opens. "Ready to go?"

Dad is wearing his lace-up boots and tight jeans and button-down shirt and a black jacket on top to fancy it up. It's the kind of outfit he used to wear for his meetings in New York before he shut down the studio and before the new lady moved in downstairs. Pam is her name and she's hardly ever home because she works part of the week in Toronto, which is in a separate country, and she says we can use the courtyard as much as we like. Also, she didn't make Dad tear down the Quiet Room because she says it's a good place to keep all her clothes. She swears my initials are still there above the socket.

Dad comes up behind me and sees the tape player. He lifts the ends of my hair and pretends to pull. "Are you going to be okay if you don't win, kiddo?"

"I don't want to think about it," I say.

"Just remember, art is subjective. People like different things."

"Like how some people like Paul McCartney and some like John Lennon?"

"And some like both."

"I like Paul McCartney too," I admit.

"So do I," Dad says. "I love all the Beatles."

He kisses the top of my head and walks to the door.

"No matter what happens," Dad says, "I just want you to know that I'm really proud of you. I hope you're proud too. You just have to keep making art that feels good to you. You can't control what happens after that. It seems like no one's paying attention, but then, when you least expect it, someone hears it. Just keep putting yourself out there. It's the hardest thing. But you never know. That's it. You just never know."

It resonates, which is something guitars do but also words. It resonates because one day this summer I was eating dinner with my family and I was worrying about my own stuff and out of nowhere a stranger asked to shake my hand because she saw me on TV (Saturday, August 17, 2013).

Dad taps his hand on the door, not like a drummer, more like a bee that's banging against a window, looking for a way out. "I'll go pull the car up," he says and leaves.

There are fewer than thirty people in the world with HSAM but right now there are only ten people in the world who can win the Next Great Songwriter Contest and I'm one of them. That means I'm even more special at music than I am at remembering. (Some of the finalists are more than one person, but there's only one award given out, so that's why my math works. Mom would be proud.)

Dad hates when a person says *to be honest* because it means that the person was just lying or is about to lie but I want to say it anyway. *To be honest,* I didn't think I'd actually make it to the finals because usually when I want something really badly it doesn't happen, like when I want to turn the TV off just by blinking my eyes or when I want a three-legged dog to grow back his missing leg.

"Come on, boy. You can do it!"

To be even more honest, I thought *my* music days might be over too because wanting something so badly is tiring and it makes me do things I shouldn't do, like sneak off to the city by myself. And to be really, really honest, I haven't been thinking too much about the contest over the last two and a half months. I've been busy with other stuff like Dad taking us to Six Flags and Grandpa taking me to the music store to buy a new guitar and Mom taking me to the dentist and also to swim at Harper's house and also to shop for school supplies. And then I started school and I wrote new songs that are even better than my old ones and I watched the walrus swim up and down the coast until they finally caught him all the way up in Nova Scotia, Canada.

That's why when Dad got the e-mail inviting me to the ceremony in New York City on Friday, October 25, which is today, I was surprised. Now that the contest is on my mind again, I know I have to win, no matter what Dad tries to tell me. He's been so great to me these last few weeks but I still worry about my memory not being safe with him or Mom or anyone else. I can be the busiest girl in the world but I'll never forget my dream to one day be important enough to be remembered. Not just today but always.

I get up off the floor and straighten out my dress and take a look at myself in my long mirror: navy and red dress, sparkle Converse, glitter barrette. That stuff is there, but not really, because my mind is somewhere else. My mind is always somewhere else but I finally found the look to match how I feel.

Or maybe I always knew how to do the rock-star look. Maybe it's the kind of thing you can't watch yourself do in a mirror, just like you can never see what you really look like in sunglasses, because it's something only other people can see for you.

Dad says we're here, but this can't be the right place because there's no red carpet or reporters or cameras and there's no sign outside announcing the contest. It's just a fat doorman with a clipboard.

Dad gives the doorman outside the club our names and he angrily checks his list. The doorman draws a big *X* on my hand and I hurry through just in case he tries to eat me.

We push past the crowded front bar. I can hardly hear Dad tell his story about performing in this same venue with one of his bands because the room is so loud. Also I'm thinking about how long it took to get here, how I first had to meet my partner, write our song, make the finals, sit in traffic through the Holland Tunnel, walk through what Dad called the East Village, and finally step into this tiny back room which does not look like a giant theater with stadium seats and a red curtain but more like a dark cave with folding chairs and a ceiling that comes down on you and makes you want to bend over so you don't get crushed. There's no one else here except the long-haired man sitting behind the sound booth and he's too busy looking at his phone to say hello to us.

"We're in the wrong place," I say.

"Nope." Dad points to a piece of paper taped to the first row of chairs that says *Reserved for Finalists.* He sits with me so I'm not alone and Mom takes a seat in the area behind us.

Cold air blows down from a spot in the ceiling and I hug myself to stay warm. This may be the loneliest place I've ever been to except maybe the Turtle Back Zoo where each of the reptiles is kept all alone in its own glowing hole in the wall.

The doors to the front room open and finally the people start coming in. They sit in chairs and stand up in the back of the room. The front row starts to fill up, but the other finalists don't look anything like me. Maybe I should feel happy that I'm the youngest one here but I don't like it because I'm always the youngest, even with HSAM, and this time I just want to be like all the others. I want everyone to know how serious and important I am.

Dad is chatting my ear off. "Remember what I told you. Some of these people have been doing this a long time. There are plenty of other contests you can enter. You have your whole life ahead of you. I love you. You know that, right?"

"Yes, Dad."

I look around some more and stretch my neck high. It looks like all the people are here now. No one else is coming through the back door.

So far this contest is nothing like I pictured. My metal chair is ice-cold and the soundman is playing the worst music and I don't even see programs anywhere. When you go to a play or a wedding they normally give you a program so you know exactly what's going to happen and when it's going to happen, but there's nothing under my chair except dust and a flattened cigarette. I don't understand why they'd want to announce the next great songwriter in a place like this. I'm worried that I made a big mistake thinking this contest could help spread my song around the world. I'm learning that it's a mistake to trust just about anyone because they'll say things to get you excited and then they'll forget what they said and just do something else. I want to slide onto the dirty floor and crawl on my knees under all the chairs and go past the hungry doorman and call a taxi, maybe even Adisa's taxi, and have him drive me home to Jersey City because this isn't how it was supposed to happen.

"Pardon me, love."

I sit up straight, and it's the only fake British person I know. His face is smooth and his hair is longer and his dimple is bumpy and his palms are flapping like wings.

I do my hand signal back to him.

"Thanks for saving my seat," Gavin says to Dad. Dad says something back but I'm too busy staring at Gavin. If this ends up being the last time I ever see him, I want to make sure I notice all of him, like how the cuffs of his jacket are unbuttoned and the bottoms of his jeans are rolled high and the buckle on his belt looks rusty and his beer bottle is curled in his left hand and it says BROOKLYN on the label and his right arm is hanging down and his right wrist is naked where Sydney's bracelet used to be.

Before I ever met Gavin Winters, I heard a lot about him from my parents and from Sydney and from TV and then I got to know him in my own way. Then he disappeared but I was still hearing about him from my parents and from TV and so he was never really gone, even when he was. It's hard to know if he's really here right now or if it's just a memory or something else. I touch his hand and he looks down while he's listening to Dad and he squeezes my hand and I'm not even mad anymore because he promised he'd be here and here he is and I know it's true because I can feel him.

Dad looks at his watch. "It's almost time." He bends over and chokes me with a strong hug. He pats Gavin on the shoulder and walks back to where Mom is sitting.

Gavin takes Dad's seat. "How are you feeling?"

"Fine."

"You don't look fine," he says, ruffling up my hair.

"Stop."

"Relax, the messier the better. It shows you don't care."

"But I do care."

His dimple fades a little as he sips his beer. I'd feel a lot less nervous if I had my guitar with me, but Dad says it's not that kind of event. Not all the finalists are performers, they're writers, so instead of a guitar, he told me to bring a speech just in case I win.

I reach into my dress pocket and feel the folded piece of paper inside my palm. Mom helped me with the words. I take it out and read it again for practice. Behind me, Mom smiles big and I smile back at her but my smile is only small.

When I face forward again there are two women onstage. The one woman looks like a grown-up Orphan Annie and the other has long white hair that's folded on top of her head in layers, like a wedding cake. My chair starts vibrating like it did when we had an earthquake in Jersey City on Tuesday, August 23, 2011, and I grip my chair because I'm afraid the floor will open up and the ceiling will collapse and I'll be crushed and I'll never know who won the contest. But it's not an earthquake. It's just my knees.

Annie lifts her chin up to reach the tall microphone. "Hello." She waits for the room to quiet down. "Welcome to the award ceremony for the first-ever Next Great Songwriter Contest."

Annie pauses so people can cheer and clap, and most of us do.

"As some of you know, Coral and I have a blog and the gist of the blog is that we disagree about pretty much everything and that leads to what we hope are interesting discussions about music and art and culture and whatever. But one thing we actually agree on is that there is far too much attention paid today to the singers of the world and hardly any consideration goes to the songwriters. We're big fans of stories and storytellers. And we're also big fans of our respective home states, New York and New Jersey. We've always known that there was a lot of talent hiding right here in our backyards. We wanted to see if we could find some of you and help get your names out there."

I look over at Gavin and he looks at me. His face says *We got this* but I'm not sure. We both turn back to the stage.

The woman with the wedding-cake hair takes over the microphone. "We were shocked by the amount of entries that came in. We had a really difficult time narrowing it down to just ten, but we did our best and here we are. In the front row are our ten finalists. Let's hear it for them."

I'm ready to take a bow, but no one else is standing up, so I stay in my seat.

"Each of our finalists will receive a prize pack from our generous sponsors that includes gift certificates, music distribution, and a magazine subscription. So that kicks ass."

I didn't realize there'd be prizes for the losers. That does kick ass.

"And our first-place winner will get his or her song featured on our blog and it will also stream on some of our partner sites. Plus, he or she will get a check for five thousand dollars, thanks to Zeem Music."

It's too late to use the prize money to save Dad's studio but I wonder if five thousand dollars is enough to take a trip to Los Angeles because Gavin said it's the capital of entertainment and that sounds like the perfect kind of place for me.

Annie bends the mike back to her. "I know we're here to find out who will take home the grand prize. But before we get to that, we have a few things to get out of the way first."

A pointy man in a suit walks onstage and he thanks a long list of people and then Annie comes back. She invites someone else onto the stage, someone she calls a great artist who's been "featured a ton" on their website, but this guy does not look great to me. He's bald and he's got a big belly that pushes his acoustic guitar far away from his body. He has to reach his arms out to play it and his voice sounds like a sick bird. I'm not impressed. This is not a rock star.

The worst part is that I don't know his song. If he's so great and his music was on the contest website, then I should know it and everyone else should too.

The man finally finishes his boring song and Annie helps him off the stage. I'm not sure why he can't get down on his own.

"Let's hear it one more time for the great Bisk Weatherby."

I'm clapping, which scares me because I don't mean to be clapping. I'm just trying to be nice. What if that's all clapping is? A big lie to be nice? Gavin is clapping too.

Annie calls another musician to the stage and this guy looks much cooler. He's a singer-songwriter that everyone seems to know, but I barely hear him because there's already too much happening in my brain and also my body. I really have to pee.

The singer-songwriter finishes his song and the women come back to the microphone. "So we're going to move things along now," Annie says. "When I announce our third-place winner and runner-up, please stand up and take a bow."

So we *are* bowing. That's more like it. I just hope my legs work.

Annie looks down at an index card and I grab Gavin's hand.

"Without further ado," Annie says. "Third place goes to Olsen T. DeLawrence for his song 'Quiver.'"

Olsen is a goofy guy with glasses and when

he stands up he almost hits his head on the low ceiling. My heart is pecking like a woodpecker. I tell Gavin, "I really have to pee."

"I think it's a little late for that."

"I have to go."

"You're going to miss it," Gavin says.

"I don't care."

"Just hold it."

"I can't."

"You can."

And then Annie calls out the second-place winner. She says two names.

"Gibson and Ren," Annie says. "They wrote a heartbreaking song called 'Third Chance' that I swear I cannot listen to without bursting into tears. I've tried. It's impossible."

A crying song. I told Gavin we needed a crying song but he wouldn't listen to me. He told me to forget about the crying song, which was bad advice because crying is all about remembering and that's what girls like to do and sometimes dads too, like when they're driving home from seeing their moms.

But it's not over yet. We're so close. Just one more winner left. It can happen. It can really happen. *Come on, Annie, just say my name.*

Annie clears her throat and I drop my head down to my knees. "And now, the moment we've all been waiting for."

Dad holds my hand past the hostess and past the people talking loudly at tables and past the waiters balancing trays, all the way to a glass door that I can't see through because of the white curtain.

"I'm not hungry," I say.

"You don't have to eat," Dad says.

"Where is everybody?"

For the first time in my life, I don't remember a single thing that happened. Actually, I remember exactly two things, and the first thing is the name of the girl who won because a name like Victory is so strange and unfair. The second thing I remember is that Annie and the wedding-cake-hair woman took a picture with all the finalists and then everybody wanted to take separate pictures with just Gavin and they couldn't believe he was a part of their stupid contest. I can't remember if Victory was pretty or ugly but she was probably very pretty, and I can't remember if the check for five thousand dollars was one of those giant checks or the kind that fits into your pocket, and I can't remember what Gavin said into my ear when we lost, and I can't remember how we walked out of that back room, or how we got outside, or what Dad was trying to tell me as he carried me down the street and into this crappy restaurant. So this is what it's like to have a normal brain. I think I hate it.

"You'll see," Dad says.

I'll see what? I don't even remember what we were just talking about.

The door opens and there's Mom and Grandpa and my uncle and my two aunts and Gavin. I don't know the rest of the people: an older woman with short boy hair and big hoop earrings, a serious-looking man with a button-down shirt and sweater, and a lady with blond hair and a nice tan.

Gavin grabs a big plastic bag that's leaning against the wall. He reaches for me with his other hand and tells the group, "We'll be right back."

We walk outside into the busy night and stand against the building.

"What place do you think we came in?" I ask.

"It doesn't matter."

"Yes, it does. There's a big difference between tenth and fourth."

"It's just an opinion."

"But tenth is last place," I say.

"Who cares?" Gavin says. "Think about

the thousands of people who entered. Look how far you got."

The city people walk around us with smelly cigarettes in their hands and interesting clothes on their bodies and wires sticking out of their ears.

"I only got here because you helped me," I say.

"So what? Everyone gets help somehow."

"It doesn't matter, does it? No one cares. No one even remembers his name."

"Whose name?" Gavin says.

"The guy who came onto the stage and played his song. They said he was so great but no one knew his name or his music and no one knows Dad or me, and no one will remember us, and it's just so sad and I can't even think about it anymore."

I heard on the news that when there's an avalanche the snow gets as hard as concrete and that's how it feels right now, like there's concrete all around me, because there's nowhere else to go. I'm out of ideas.

"Let me show you something."

Gavin reaches into his big plastic bag with both hands and slides out one of those foldable wooden TV trays. He shakes the plastic off the tray and turns it over and it's not a TV tray after all.

"This is for you," Gavin says.

"My friend is a painter," Gavin says. "Actually, she was Sydney's friend. I visited her yesterday and told her exactly what I wanted."

"What's on the bird's wing?" I ask.

"A bandage."

468

"He's hurt?"

"Yes. But he's getting better. And see here in the corner?"

He holds the painting up to the street lamp. I push my face close and see a word in all capital letters: IMAGINE.

I feel a chill. The night isn't cold, but I feel a chill.

"You and Sydney have that in common," Gavin says. "You believe."

He's glowing under the street lamp and I wish I had a camera so I could take a picture of him. I'd have Dad turn the picture into a poster and I'd put the poster on my wall and I'd stare at it every night before falling asleep. But it's okay that I don't because I have my own built-in camera.

"Thank you," I say.

"No. Thank *you.*"

He scratches his forehead and makes small shapes with his mouth. When I'm nervous, I bite the insides of my cheeks. "You know, I've always wondered," he says. "Do you really like John Lennon's music that much? Or is it just because your dad loves him?"

I think about it. It's hard to figure out. "I like that we have our own special thing."

Gavin smiles. "I like it too."

It looks like he's ready to go back inside

the restaurant but I'm not in a party mood and I don't want to share Gavin with all those people because he's my partner and it took me so long to get him back.

"We should write more songs together," I say.

"We should."

"We can call ourselves the Reminders."

"I like that," Gavin says. "It's a good name."

"We just need one song. That's all it takes. One song that the whole world never forgets."

He looks at me for what feels like a very long time and then he says, "I heard 'God' the other day. We were talking about that song the first day I heard your music. We were talking about magic."

I love when people remember.

"Do you know what John is saying in that song?" Gavin says.

I don't.

"He's saying he *was* the walrus, but not anymore. Now he's John. Now he's himself. Everybody builds these people up to be bigger than they are. Elvis, the Beatles, Zimmerman. Do you know who Zimmerman is? That's Bob Dylan. It's a myth. I named myself Winters, but I'm a Deifendorf. That's my family. And that's what John is saying.

He's talking about family. He's saying that all that really matters is him and Yoko." He points at the restaurant. "Those people waiting in there, they're the ones that matter. No one else."

He won't stop staring and I try to smile but it won't stop the tears. "I don't want to say good-bye to you."

He pulls me in and into my ear he makes a promise and everything is upside down but it feels right this way because it's kind of like a dance song and a crying song wrapped into one.

In the middle of dinner, Gavin taps his knife against a water glass. This happens after Grandpa lifts me into the air with his strong hands and tells me he's going to throw me across the room unless I give him my autograph. The problem is that getting thrown across the room actually sounds like fun, so it's a hard choice to make.

It's after Gavin brings me over to the serious-looking man who Gavin calls his agent and says, "Carl, I'd like to introduce you to your newest client." Carl tells me that he's heard all about me and he says I'm very photogenic, which sounds like a disease but it's the opposite.

And it's after Gavin takes me to meet the

lady with the boy hair who's actually his mom. She hands me a bouquet of flowers from her garden and she explains in a very excited way that these flowers are "completely chemical-free" and she also tells me that when she looks at me she feels the same way she did about Gavin when he was little. I ask her what that means and she says, "You have that star quality," and Gavin rolls his eyes but I think it's a very nice thing to say.

And it's after Gavin walks me over to the last stranger in the room, the one with the same light blue eyes he has, and I go to shake her hand but she gives me a high five instead and tells me she adores my outfit. Her name is Veronica and she's a daughter and a sister and she's also going to be a mother soon, but in a way that doesn't make your belly get fat. Gavin already knows that the baby will be named after the father because it's a name that works for a boy *and* a girl and I hope even though we'll be ten years apart that baby Sydney and I can still be friends.

And it's after Mom and Dad stare at each other with anniversary looks on their faces, and Dad, who will always be my favorite musician, lays his head on Mom's shoulder in a way that looks familiar, something about how moms make us feel, because Mom makes me feel the same way at the table when she puts her arms around me and tells me how proud she is of me.

It's after all this that Gavin starts tapping his water glass and everyone stops talking. Dad reaches under the table and opens a case. He takes out his Gibson guitar and hands it to me. I'm not sure what to do with it.

"Play it," Gavin says.

I'm not in the mood but I want to make a good impression in front of Gavin's agent so I hang the strap over my shoulder and I play the first thing that comes to my mind, which is "Look at Me" by John Lennon.

"Not that," Dad says. "Your song."

I stop for a drink of water and take a deep breath and make a G chord. I don't have Sydney's guitar picks with me so I use my fingers, just like Dad taught me. I look down at the strings and I feel them shake beneath my hand.

Someone in the audience is squeaking his chair and it's Grandpa. He taps Gavin's mom on the shoulder and takes her by the hand. They move into the corner of the little room and he twirls her and dips her and she laughs.

I try to hold on until Gavin starts singing,

and he does, his voice making my heart beat even faster. We're really going now and everyone is here, so many eyes, the ones that matter, singing and smiling and dancing and crying. I'm not sure about tomorrow, tomorrow never knows, says John, but they're looking at me now, all of them, like they really see who I am. I want to stay with them forever and I guess there is a way. I'll save them in my box. I'll keep them safe always. It's what I do. I remember.

ACKNOWLEDGMENTS

It took me a long time to get here and I wouldn't have made it without the help of a number of golden humans.

Thank you to my dedicated team of wise and graceful editors, Judith Clain, Francesca Main, and Amanda Brower, for trusting and nurturing me and this book with unwavering faith, uncanny sophistication, and a whole lot of love; I adore you all. Thank you to Nicole Dewey and Lucy Kim at Little, Brown and to Tracy Roe for making this novel what it is. And deep thanks to all the foreign publishers for championing this book and jumping on board so early.

Thank you to my meticulous agent, Jeff Kleinman, for believing in me way before I was ready, for molding me into a real writer, and for always pushing me harder and further than what seemed possible. Thank you to the other exceptional souls who represented this novel with gusto: Molly

Jaffa, Lorella Belli, and Sylvie Rabineau.

Thank you to Brent Monahan, Jen Doktorski, and Jenn Northington for providing astute critiques of this book in its earliest stages. And thank you to those who encouraged my previous writing attempts: Mike Emmich, Matt Schuman, Jason Cupp, Kate Rockland, Michael Rockland, Jon McGarry, Melissa Niglio Gelade, Eileen DeNobile, Chris Maltese, Joey Arbagey, and Karen Haney.

Thank you to Arielle Eckstut, David Henry Sterry, Chris Goldberg, and the Huevos Rancheros Book Club. Thank you to Ed Paparo and Harris Katz for legal guidance as well as creative feedback.

I took many liberties with my portrayal of highly superior autobiographical memory, but Jill Price's *The Woman Who Can't Forget* and Marilu Henner's *Total Memory Makeover* aided my understanding of how HSAM works in the real world. *The Kid,* by Dan Savage, and *Mommy Man,* by Jerry Mahoney, provided insight into what same-sex couples face when trying to become parents. For helping me add authenticity in other key areas, thank you to Amanda and Arianna Mondelli, Kara Franklin, Michelle Chapman, Olivia Gelade, Dan Coughlin, Ralph Hanan, Daniel Baker for "hibachi pancakes," and Sydney Gelade for supplying Joan's handwriting.

Thank you to all my loyal music listeners who were my first ever readers and who continue to *remind* me that I have a voice. And thank you to those I've made music with for helping me refine another type of storytelling.

Thank you to my family, who support anything and everything I do: Erica, Marie, Mike; the Emmichs, Bakers, Caterinas, and Gelades; Mel and Lois, for always treating me like your own; and especially Valentine and Joan, for never once questioning my unusual path.

Thank you to Harper and Lennon for existing and inspiring me every single long day. Extra thanks to H for tolerating my fictionalization of what was a harrowing day. And most of all, thank you to Jill, for her patience and intelligence and willingness to dream — you are the reason for me doing or being or having anything in this world.

ABOUT THE AUTHOR

Dubbed a Renaissance man by the *New York Post*, **Val Emmich** is a writer, singer-songwriter, and actor. He's had recurring roles on *Vinyl* and *Ugly Betty* as well as a memorable guest role as Tina Fey's coffee-boy fling, Jamie, on *30 Rock*. Emmich lives in Jersey City, New Jersey, with his wife and their two children. *The Reminders* is his first novel.

The employees of Thorndike Press hope you have enjoyed this Large Print book. All our Thorndike, Wheeler, and Kennebec Large Print titles are designed for easy reading, and all our books are made to last. Other Thorndike Press Large Print books are available at your library, through selected bookstores, or directly from us.

For information about titles, please call:
  (800) 223-1244

or visit our website at:
  gale.com/thorndike

To share your comments, please write:
  Publisher
  Thorndike Press
  10 Water St., Suite 310
  Waterville, ME 04901